EASY MELODY

BOOK THREE IN THE
BOUDREAUX SERIES

KRISTEN PROBY

EASY MELODY
Book Three in The Boudreaux Series
Kristen Proby

Cover Art: **60923786**
Photography by: K
Models: John Kirtc
Cover Design: Oka

ISBN 978-1-63350-009-9

OTHER BOOKS BY KRISTEN PROBY:

The Boudreaux Series:
Easy Love
Easy Charm

The With Me In Seattle Series:

Come Away With Me and on audio
Under the Mistletoe With Me and on audio
Fight With Me and on audio
Play With Me and on audio
Rock With Me and on audio
Safe With Me and on audio
Tied With Me and on audio
Breathe With Me and on audio
Forever With Me and on audio
Easy With You

The Love Under the Big Sky Series, available
through Pocket Books:
Loving Cara
Seducing Lauren
Falling for Jillian

Baby, It's Cold Outside
An Anthology with Jennifer Probst, Emma Chase,
Kristen Proby, Melody Anne and Kate Meader

PROLOGUE

~Callie~

"What do you mean, he left it to me?" I ask, leaning forward and pounding my fist on Bernie's desk. "He knew I didn't want it!"

Bernie shrugs and sits back in his creaky chair, folds his hands over his round belly and sucks on a peppermint from the jar on his old oak desk. "Doesn't change that he left the bar and all of its contents to you, Callie."

"And all of its debt, no doubt," I mutter and rub my fingertips on my forehead. "I have a life in Colorado, Bernie. What am I supposed to do?" I sit up straight as a brilliant thought occurs to me. "I'll sell it!"

"Well, here's the thing."

"Don't tell me that there's a clause in the will that says that I have to marry a virgin and live in a haunted castle for a year in order to inherit," I reply dryly. "That's cliché, even for my dad."

Bernie grins. "No, nothing that dramatic."

"Good."

"Your dad tried to sell it a few times over the

years, but it never sold. It needs some work, Callie."

I stare at him, confused. "He never told me he tried to sell."

Not that I spoke to him often.

"He never even got a nibble."

"But, it's located in the heart of the French Quarter. Surely, someone would want to buy it, fix it up and either flip it or run it."

Bernie's face transforms into a smug smile. "Perhaps someone would."

My eyes narrow. "I'm not buying it."

"No, you're inheriting it." He leans forward again, and his brown eyes soften. Eyes just like my dad's. "I loved your father, despite all of his faults. He loved three things in his life: your mother, The Odyssey, and you."

I refuse to cry in front of my uncle.

"He was awfully fond of whiskey too," I reply, but he just narrows his eyes at me. "Uncle Bernie—"

"You've been spending all these years up in Denver, running that club and flipping houses, and your dad was real proud of you. But maybe it's time to come home, darlin'."

Denver is home.

"I'll flip it," I reply and stand to leave his office. "I have savings."

"Call me if you need me," he calls as I saunter out of his office and down to my rental car, then swear like a sailor when I see the parking ticket on the windshield.

This isn't my fucking day.

I pull my phone out of my purse as I pull into traffic and call my long time boyfriend, Keith, who owns *Boom*, a popular nightclub in Denver that I also happen to manage.

"Babe," he answers, making me smile.

"Hey."

"Are you coming back yet?" he asks. I can hear voices in the background and check the time. Mid-afternoon. They're getting ready for tonight at the club, I'm sure.

"So, there might be a snag in that," I reply and change lanes, headed downtown to the bar. "Turns out that I have some work to do here regarding my dad's bar."

"How long will that take?" he asks, his voice calm but hard.

How long will it take to flip a bar and make a profit? Too long.

"Honestly, I might be here a couple of months." I cringe. "But I can commute back and forth."

"Actually, Cal, I've been wanting to talk to you anyway, and this is as good of a time as any. Remember when I asked you to come in for a meeting last week?"

"The morning my dad died," I reply, not at all wanting to hear the next words to come out of Keith's mouth. Because I'm pretty sure it's not good.

"I think it's time for you to move on, Callie. You're a great manager, but I feel like the club has stalled."

I pull into a parking space, throw the car in park, and stare straight ahead. "Bullshit. You've never made a secret that you can be a dick, Keith. That's something we have in common, and over the two years we've been together, we've never lied to each other."

"You're right." He sighs and I can picture him loosening his tie. "It's time for us to move on, Cal."

"You're firing me *and* breaking up with me?" This day just keeps getting better and better.

"I'm going to offer you a very generous severance, Callie."

I want to tell him to shove the money, but I'm not that stupid. "Why?"

"It's time," he replies simply.

"Because you don't do forever," I add, remembering all the times he's warned me of that very fact in the past.

"I'm sorry, Callie. I'll give you an excellent letter of recommendation. And if you ever need anything, all you have to do is call. In fact, if you decide to relocate to New Orleans, I'll have your things moved for you."

"For someone breaking up with me, you're being very nice."

"There's no reason not to be," he replies and then sighs. "I care about you, Cal. We had a great time together, and you did a good job in my club, but you're just not my forever girl, and it's time to move on."

I nod, swallowing hard.

"Thank you."

I end the call and stare at my phone for a long few minutes. My dad is dead, and I just lost a job I love and a man that I tried to talk myself into loving all in one fell swoop.

I guess I'm staying after all.

I climb out of the car and stand on the sidewalk, staring at the outside of The Odyssey. If the inside is as bad as the outside, this is going to be one very expensive project.

I open the door, surprised to find it unlocked, and a million memories come washing over me. The floor hasn't been refinished since I was a kid. The wood is original, but needs to be repaired and resurfaced. My heels click and echo through the dark, empty room. The tables and chairs are the same from my childhood as well, most looking much more wobbly. The windows are wide but dingy, making the space feel even darker.

The bar is huge, spanning one long wall. It was an antique when Dad bought it thirty years ago, and I'm pleased to see that it's been well taken care of.

Suddenly, the door to the back room swings open and in walks Adam Spencer. He halts when he sees me, his sexy eyes traveling up and down as he takes me in. He sets the case of wine on the bar and hurries to me, lifts me in his arms and turns a circle, making me catch my breath.

"Finally decided to stop by, eh?" he asks as he sets me down.

"I figured I'd see what Dad left me." I meet his eyes and shrug. "Thank you."

"For?"

"Taking care of Dad. Taking care of this place." I pace away, cross my arms, then turn back to him. "For loving me."

"You're my best friend," he replies. "And your dad was good to me. Always has been."

"He should have left this to you."

Adam shakes his head, his brown eyes kind and calm and maybe sad. "It belongs to you. And I'm here to help you in any way you need me."

"You're a good friend."

"I'm a kick-ass friend," he replies. "Just don't expect me to call you Boss Lady or Your Highness."

"What about She Who Is Always Right?"

"Not a chance."

I laugh for the first time in a week and feel my chest loosen, just a bit. "I'm staying."

"What about Keith?" he asks.

I shake my head, not ready to talk about it, and sigh. "I'm going to overhaul this place. Maybe flip it."

"Why not keep it? You'll make a killing." Adam winks. "With your expertise at fixing stuff up, and my charm, you can't lose."

"Maybe. I'll think about it."

I run my hand over the smooth wood of the bar

and feel the sadness settle in. "Dad's gone, Adam."

"I know." He rubs wide circles over my back.

"I can't stay upstairs." My dad lived over the bar in an apartment, and I just don't have it in me to live there. Too many bad memories.

"You'll stay with me until you get stuff figured out."

I cock a brow.

"I have a guest room," he says defensively.

"I'll take it." I sigh and lay my forehead on my arm. "Who would have thought I'd be back here fifteen years after I left?"

"Not me, that's for sure. But here you are."

"Here I am."

CHAPTER ONE

~Declan~

I'm performing at The Odyssey for the first time in three months tonight. It's been closed for renovations, and I admit, I miss it.

Fuck it, I miss *her*.

And I barely know her.

What that's all about, I have no idea. I don't get hung up. There are too many women out there, in all shapes and sizes, to enjoy. I've never been the type to think about monogamy.

Not that I'm a prick. I just make sure women know the score before *I* score.

But I admit, I'm looking forward to seeing the feisty owner of The Odyssey, almost as much as I'm looking forward to seeing what she's done with the place.

According to her bar manager, and my friend, Adam, the transformation has been incredible.

I carry my guitar through the front door, noticing the new sign and paint job on the outside of the building, and then take a deep breath as my eyes adjust to the dimmer light inside.

Holy fuck, Adam wasn't kidding.

"Hey!" the man himself calls from behind the bar, tossing me a smile. "I'm glad you're early. I want to show you around."

"This is amazing," I say, meaning every word. The floor has been refinished and polished to a honey blond, gleaming where sunlight streams through. New tables and chairs are sprinkled around the room, and new stools sit in front of the bar, which has also been polished.

"You haven't seen anything yet," Adam replies with a smile. "Wait until I show you the roof."

"The roof?" I grin and set my guitar on the stage, then turn and almost swallow my tongue as Callie herself comes down the new staircase on the far side of the room. She's in her signature killer heels, pink today. Her arms and cleavage are showcased in a simple black tank top and those mile-long legs are mostly bare, thanks to a ripped pair of cut-off denim shorts.

All I have to do is take one look at Callie and know that there's a God.

And I hope to make her call out his name in thanks in the very near future.

"Declan," she says.

"Callie," I reply and feel my lips twitch into a smile as she crosses to the bar and sets a clipboard down. "Nice place you have here."

Her blue eyes flare in happiness. "Thank you."

"I was just telling Declan that I'll take him up and show him the roof," Adam says just as his phone rings. "Crap. I have to take this. Cal, will you show him?"

"She'll show me," I reply, still smiling.

Callie simply shrugs. "As you can see, we have new tables and chairs. I also replaced the stage area. It was so old, I'm surprised you never fell through it before."

"It held up," I say and follow her as she leads me

toward the stairs. I'm eye-level with her ass, and I'm fucking salivating. "I didn't know there was anything up here. I figured it was storage or something."

"It was my dad's apartment," she says simply. "I tore it out, made most of it open so it's now outside seating, and kept some of it covered for the bar."

We walk out to the best rooftop bar I've ever seen, and I'm no stranger to bars. She found an antique bar to match the one downstairs, and it's indeed covered, with maybe half a dozen tables and chairs nearby. But the outdoor space is just plain kick ass.

"Wow," I breathe and stop, hands on hips, glancing around. Couches are grouped together around gas fireplaces and covered with red, blue and yellow umbrellas to block the hot sun. But my eyes are drawn back to the woman responsible for all of it. I'd thought it was all in my head, that she couldn't possibly be as beautiful as I thought she was.

But nope. She's hot.

"This is the best part," Callie says with a smile that I've rarely seen and leads me to the railing to look out over the Quarter. We can see right into Jackson Square. People are bustling about, munching on beignets, wandering through shops. Music from street performers drift up, tickling my ears.

The saxophonist near Café du Monde is damn good.

We lean here, side by side, and take in the Quarter.

"This is the part I missed." Callie's voice is soft, softer than I've ever heard it.

"What's that, sugar?" I ask, not looking over at her, but she's stiffened up, as if she didn't mean to say that out loud.

"The Quarter," she replies and takes a deep breath. "All of the people."

"There are a lot of them," I agree. "This is

beautiful, Callie. You're going to pack people in here."

"I hope so," she says with a laugh. "This sucked up most of my savings."

"It'll pay off."

"You'll help," she replies and turns to walk away, but I catch her elbow and turn her back to me.

"Wait. Are you being *nice* to me?"

"I've never been mean to you," she says, her voice cool and eyes even colder, making them so fucking blue I'd swear they came from the ocean. Her skin is soft in my hand, making me think of long, sweaty nights.

"Let's be honest. I don't think you like me much, and I'd love to know why. I'm a likeable guy."

"I don't dislike you," she insists and pulls her arm out of my touch, making me want to just touch her somewhere else. "I'm just not typically drawn to men who drink whiskey. Daddy liked it too much. I don't like it at all."

I knew when I ordered the whiskey, the last time I saw her more than three months ago, that it struck a nerve.

"I don't always drink whiskey. Frankly, I'm happy with tap water."

She cocks a brow and then chuckles. "You'll be good for business, Declan. And I'm thankful for it."

"I will be," I agree, not at all afraid to admit that I'm popular around here. It pays my bills nicely, and does the same for the business owners I play for. "I've missed playing here."

"You have?" she asks, seemingly surprised.

"I have."

"Well, good." She clears her throat and leads me back to the stairs. "Maybe I can talk you into giving me Fridays *and* Saturdays."

You could probably talk me into just about anything,

darlin'.

And that just won't do. Women are a great distraction, but that's all they are.

"I'm booked on Saturdays," I reply.

"We'll see," she says with a smile as her heels click down the stairs back to the main bar where Adam has finished with his call and is stocking bottled beer in the cooler.

"What do you think?" he asks.

"I think you'd better stock more beer. This place is going to be hopping in about two hours."

***

God, I love to perform. I love every part of it: singing, playing all of the instruments, watching the crowd as they dance or sing along. Music is as necessary to me as breathing and it's always come naturally to me. They call me a prodigy, but I don't know about that. All I know is, it's a part of me that I'll never let go of.

I'm toward the end of my last set, and I was right. The place is packed, wall-to-wall, standing room only. Adam and another bartender I haven't seen before are working the bar, and two waitresses are working the room.

Callie has been mingling, helping wherever she's needed, and working her ass off in general.

How she can do all of that in the shoes she wears is a mystery to me, and my sister Charly owns a shoe store. I've come to realize that I'll never solve that particular mystery.

As long as women continue to wear them, I'm good.

Speaking of Charly, my eyes meet hers in the crowd. It didn't surprise me that she showed up with our brother, Eli, and his girlfriend, Kate. It *did* surprise me, however, to see that she brought a date along.

I wonder who the fuck this one is.

Not that he'll be around for long. Charly doesn't keep men in her life. Odd, how our parents were married for the better part of five decades, faithfully and in love for every day of those years, yet most of their six children are commitment-phobes.

"Are y'all havin' a good night?" I ask the crowd as I tickle the keys on the piano and smile when the room erupts into applause and cheers. "I am too. Let's give the owner, Callie, and the staff of The Odyssey a big round of applause for making this place so beautiful."

My eyes link with Callie's as the crowd cheers loudly. She smiles and waves, then simply lifts a perfect eyebrow in my direction.

God, I love how sassy she is.

"I'd also like to send out a little hello to some of my family in the audience this evening." I smile down at Eli, Kate and Charly. If any of my family takes the time to come to a show, I take a minute to thank them. "And this here's gonna be the last song this evening. It's one of my favorites. Thanks for listening tonight, friends."

I move easily into a slower rendition of Adele's *Set Fire to the Rain*, loving the lyrics, losing myself in the melody. And when it's done, I stand and wave, give one bow, then climb off the stage and head straight to my family.

"Hey," I say and kiss Kate's cheek, then Charly's, and give my brother a man-hug. "Thanks for coming." Then I turn to Charly's date. "Who are you?"

Charly rolls her eyes. "God, you're such a man."

"I'm a brother," I correct her, still holding the stranger's gaze with mine. He's not as tall as me or Eli, but then few are. At roughly six-foot-four, we're taller than most. He's dressed smartly, like an accountant or a lawyer, in a dark button-down and khaki pants.

And, because she's Charly, and this is her type, he has dark blond hair and light eyes. "I'm Declan."

"This is Harrison," Charly says.

"Can I call you Harry?" I ask with a smile, but Harrison doesn't smile. He simply says, "No."

I glance over at Eli, whose eyes are narrowed, and he gives a small shake of his head.

Harrison won't be around long.

"Okay then. I hope you enjoyed the show."

"Not my usual type of music, but you're very talented," the rude and stuffy Harrison replies.

My eyes meet Eli's again, and a whole conversation takes place in the matter of two seconds.

Can I deck him?

Not worth it, man.

"We need to go soon," Kate says with a smile. Her green eyes look happy as she tosses her red hair over her shoulder and gazes up at Eli. "We fly out early tomorrow morning."

"Where are you headed?" I ask.

"Aruba," Eli replies with a satisfied smile. "Kate and I have earned a vacation."

"I'm going to sit on the beach and read a book."

"Under an umbrella," Eli adds and drags his hand down her hair. "And after I've had my way with you."

"Ew," Charly says, scrunching up her nose. Harrison simply clears his throat and shuffles his feet.

He's wearing Chucks. With khakis.

We won't have to run him off. Charly won't be okay with that.

"I'd like to make it an early night, too," Charly adds. "I'm working tomorrow."

I lean down and hug my sister tight, then whisper in her ear, "I don't like him."

"Me either," she whispers back, and smiles up at me as I pull away.

Good.

Goodnights are said, and I make my way over to the bar. The crowd has thinned significantly, and now just a few people are left, from the sounds of it most of them are on the roof enjoying the cool fall evening and the view.

Callie's manning the bar alone. She's still in her killer pink heels, but she changed out of the cutoffs and tank into a killer little black dress that hugs her in all the right places.

She has great tits and ass, but she's more slender than I usually like. There is nothing soft about her, which suits Callie because she's not a soft woman. I don't know her well, *yet*, but I know that she's strong, in charge, and she'll kick ass when needed.

God, she's adorable.

I get comfortable on a stool and grin when she makes her way down to me.

"Whiskey?" she asks with cool eyes, and no hint of a smile. I ordered a whiskey not long after she took over, before renovations started, and I could tell then that it irritated her.

"How about a shot of tequila tonight? If you'll do one with me."

Without missing a beat, she reaches for two shot glasses and pours the clear liquid—the good stuff—and hands me one, then clinks her glass to mine. "To one hell of a night."

"I'll drink to that."

We shoot our drinks, and then she holds the bottle up. "Another?"

"Sure."

She pours me more, but not herself. "You're not joining me?"

"I'm driving," she replies with a smile.

"Where do you live?" I ask.

"Not close enough to walk," she replies and washes out her glass, then puts it away.

"You have beautiful eyes." I lean my chin on my hand and watch her bustle about. I'm the only one at the bar now, and I admit I like having all of her attention.

She bats her eyes. "Thanks."

"The rest of you isn't so bad, either."

"Back at you," she says and laughs. "You're ridiculously attractive."

This gets my attention. Not that she didn't already have my attention.

"You think I'm hot?"

"I said attractive," she replies and rolls her eyes.

"Okay, what do you find attractive about me?" I take the shot she poured me and set the glass down, shaking my head when she offers me more.

"I seriously doubt you need me to feed your ego," she says and chuckles.

It's been entirely too long since anyone fed my ego because every time I consider taking someone home, a certain blond bar owner pops in my head.

It's ridiculous.

"Humor me."

She sighs and leans on the bar, then rakes her killer eyes up and down me. "You have nice hands. I like that you're tall. And your teeth are straight."

I stare at her for a long minute, then bust up laughing. "You like my hands, my height and my teeth." I shake my head and then laugh some more. "My ego is safe, sweetheart."

She's smiling now, and that just about knocks me off my stool. Jesus, she should smile all of the time.

"You have a killer smile." I scratch my nose and lean my chin on my hand again, watching her. "I want to bury my hands in your hair and feel how soft it is.

And your legs have to be the sexiest I've ever seen."

"You're charming," she says cautiously, but her cheeks are pink and her smile is back.

"I'm honest."

"Can't fault a man for being honest, given how rare it is these days."

"I'm taking you to dinner, Callie."

Her smile doesn't slip as she cocks a brow again. She takes a long minute to reply, holding my gaze, and finally, as if she mentally thought *why the hell not*, she says, "You can pick me up at six on Monday."

"I'm gonna need to know where you live to do that."

"I'm staying with Adam for a while."

I tilt my head and consider her. Adam is more of a player than I am.

"He's my best friend." She doesn't look away or blink, doesn't explain herself further, almost daring me to accuse her of sleeping with him, and I simply nod.

"I'll pick you up at six on Monday."

"Don't be late." And with that she saunters down to the other end of the bar to pour a beer for a customer.

I won't be late.

***

What am I doing? I'm being an idiot, that's what I'm doing. I'm waiting outside The Odyssey for Callie to finish closing up so I can escort her to her car.

What is this, 1945?

I sigh and lean against the building. No, it's the French Quarter, and it's dangerous at night, and I'll be damned if Callie walks to her car alone this late.

A few moments later, the woman herself steps outside and sets the alarm, then locks the door and jumps about three feet into the air when she turns and finds me standing here.

"Sorry. Didn't mean to startle you."

"I almost maced you," she says and covers her chest with her hand, panting.

God, I want to make her pant like that for entirely different reasons. Just the thought of it has my cock on high alert.

"Sorry," I say again and try to think of dead puppies and spaghetti to calm my dick down.

"Why are you here?"

"To walk you to your car," I reply and fall into step beside her.

"That's very chivalrous of you, but I'm fine walking a block by myself."

"Yes, you carry mace." I smirk, and then laugh when she bites her lip guiltily. "Let me guess. You don't really have any mace."

"I could stab someone with my heel," she suggests and I can't stand it. I have to touch her, so I take her hand in mine and kiss her knuckles.

"You're adorable."

"No. I'm not."

She is.

"Okay."

"My car is right there," she says and speeds up, trying to pull her hand away, but I don't let her go. Not yet.

"I like it." She drives a '68 Camaro. Jesus, I might have to marry her.

"So do I."

She unlocks the driver's door, but before she can open it, I turn her and lean in, her back against the door, my body inches from hers. I feel the heat coming off of her, I can smell the fruity shampoo she uses, and it's a big boost to my ego when she takes a long, deep breath, then braces her hands on my hips.

She's not pushing me away, so I take that as a

good sign.

"You're a beautiful woman, Calliope."

"How did you know my name?" she whispers, those ice blue eyes pinned to my mouth.

"Adam," I reply.

"He'll pay for that. I hate that name."

"I like it." I lean in closer and drag my nose down her cheek, breathing her in. God, she's more potent than the tequila. "It's pretty and unusual, just like you."

"Is that a compliment?"

I grin. "Yes, ma'am."

Her hands travel up my sides, over my shirt, and fist over my ribs, gathering the cotton tightly as my left hand glides down her side to her ass.

"I like your height too, you know," I murmur. "When you're in heels like this, I don't have to practically bend in half to reach you."

"Happy to oblige," she whispers. She's still gripping onto me, but she's not leaning in to me, as if she's waiting to see where I take this.

And if we weren't in the middle of the street, I'd fuck her brainless. Right here.

But instead, I let my lips drag up her neck and then hover over mouth, barely touching her. "If you're going to push me away, do it now."

She doesn't push me away. Instead, she pulls me in, and our mouths take over, nibbling, exploring, enjoying.

I could kiss her all damn night.

And I will.

But not tonight.

Before I boost her up and bury myself inside her for all of God and the whole French Quarter to see, I pull back just a bit and turn the kiss from hot to sweet. She purrs.

She mother-fucking purrs.

And then, she lets go of my shirt, drags her hands down my sides, and with a cocky smile on those full red lips, she grabs my ass, her nails digging in just enough to bite, and tugs on my lower lip with her teeth.

Without moving away, I leave my lips on hers and say, "Monday."

Then I pull back and stand on the sidewalk as I watch her lower herself into her car, cool as a damn cucumber, and drive away.

Jesus, she's going to be fun in bed.

CHAPTER TWO

~Callie~

"Up or down?" I ask Adam as I rush out of my bedroom to where he's cooking something that smells just nasty in the kitchen.

Adam never could cook worth a damn.

"What you do with your pants is none of my business," he replies, not looking at me at all.

"You're a riot. My hair, Adam. Up or down?"

"I don't care."

"Look at me!" I'm still in my cami and yoga shorts and Declan is going to be here in fifteen minutes. Adam turns from the stove, his eyebrows raised. His light brown hair is a mess, he's shirtless and barefoot, wearing only old ripped jeans. I tug my hair up into a messy knot, then let it fall around my shoulders. "Up or down?"

"Umm, down?"

"Okay, good. I don't have time to pin it anyway." I turn and run back to my bedroom and stare at the six outfits I have spread over my bed. "Do you think it's gonna be a casual dinner?" I yell out at Adam.

"How in the hell should I know? I'm not dating

Declan."

"But he's your friend," I yell back. I suppose I could go middle of the road with a pair of black capris and a blue peasant blouse. I pull them on, then walk out to the kitchen. "Does this shirt show too much cleavage?"

"Cal, we really need to find you some girlfriends. I'm not qualified to answer these questions."

I spin and head back for the bedroom after throwing Adam the bird and quickly change out of the blouse and into a red, sleeveless button down, then return to the kitchen.

"Better?"

"Callie, they're both fine."

"I don't want *fine*," I reply with a scowl. "I want sexy."

"I'm really the wrong person to ask. You're practically my sister. I don't want to have sex with you."

"I'm relieved to hear it," I quip and turn a circle, showing off the open back. "I can't wear a bra with this one."

"Jesus, Callie," he says, a pained look on his face. "It's the first date. At least start it out with most of your clothes on."

I cock a brow. "Are you preaching to me about keeping my clothes on, Mr. I Walk Around The Apartment Mostly Naked?"

"I'm not on a date."

"You don't date."

"Exactly."

"I don't even know what we're talking about anymore!" I groan and stomp back to my bedroom, changing into a baby blue cami with a pretty chiffon see-through blouse over the top and return to the kitchen. "This is pretty and not slutty."

"I didn't say you were slutty before," he replies, but stops chopping and looks me up and down. "That works."

"Okay." I smile, dance a little jig, and run back to my room for my black heels and handbag, then return to the kitchen to put on my jewelry.

"You're excited about tonight," Adam says casually while completely destroying an innocent stalk of celery. "What changed your mind about Declan?"

"What do you mean?"

"Didn't seem like you liked him, and now you're going out with him."

"It's been a while since I went out on a date with a reasonably attractive man," I reply, not giving away that there's something about Declan that pulls at me. "A girl's entitled to want to look pretty."

"Well, you do," he says and sighs. "Look, it's none of my business who you date. I like Declan, and we go back a ways. But he's also a bit of a player. Not as bad as me, because well, I'm me, but he goes through his share of women."

I cross my arms and grin at my friend. "I love you too. I'm not marrying him, I'm letting him buy me food."

"And letting him talk you out of that blouse."

"Maybe." My grin spreads as I slip my favorite Alex and Ani bracelets on my arm. "We'll see."

The doorbell rings, and I plaster on my completely calm face as I cross to the door and answer it. As soon as I see him, my stomach is full of butterflies on speed and I'm quite sure my upper lip is sweating.

Not sexy, Callie.

"Hi," I say lamely and grin as I let my eyes wander up and down his long, lean body. I wasn't kidding when I told him that I love his height. I love that no matter what shoes I wear, he's taller than me. At five foot nine, that's rare for me.

His dark hair is just long enough to touch the collar of his T-shirt, and his clear hazel eyes are soft and sexy as they travel up and down my body. He always looks at me just like this, and it makes me crazy.

It makes me want to climb him, and that's probably not appropriate for a first date.

Damn it.

"You are gorgeous, darlin'," he says as he takes my hand and kisses my fingers, sending warm currents up my arm. "You'll be the sexiest woman in the stadium."

"Stadium?" I ask.

"The Superdome," he says with a shrug. "The Saints are playing tonight, and my family has season tickets."

I simply blink at him for several seconds before my heart skips into overdrive.

"You're taking me to a *football game*?"

"Do you hate football?" he asks and cringes. "I'm sorry, we can just go to dinner or anything else you might want to do."

"I *love* football," I reply honestly. "I had season tickets to all of the Denver games when I lived there."

"Perfect." He looks over my shoulder at Adam and frowns. "Dude, you're naked."

"I'm wearing pants." Adam looks down and shrugs. "What's wrong with how I'm dressed?"

"Nothing at all, if you're Christian Grey," I reply and roll my eyes. "Bye."

"Are you going to wear those shoes?" Adam asks. "You're going to a football game."

"Yes. I am." I wave and walk out ahead of Declan, who closes the door behind us and escorts me down to his car. "I expected you to drive something a little more… posh." I watch him as he starts the car and pulls out into traffic.

"Why?" he asks and takes my hand as he maneuvers his way through the after-work rush. I stare down at our hands and briefly think about pulling away, but his hand feels so good around mine, I leave it.

What's the harm?

"I know who your family is, Declan."

"It's a big family. Hard to miss."

I roll my eyes and then chuckle. "So, Declan Boudreaux, the youngest son of a billionaire, drives a Jeep?"

"And a fancy bar owner drives a '68 Camaro." He laughs and squeezes my hand. "Aren't we both just full of surprises."

"I didn't mean that to sound insulting," I reply. "I was just surprised."

"I leave the Bentleys and Maseratis to Beau and Eli."

"They drive Bentleys?" I ask and then shake my head when he laughs.

"No. Mama and Daddy always had sensible cars. I like my Jeep. It's fun."

"I like it too," I reply, feeling a little embarrassed for the whole conversation.

"How did you come to own your car?" he asks with genuine interest. "She's a beauty."

"It was a gift." *From Keith.* Declan glances over, but doesn't press me, and rather than shut up, I keep going. "My ex bought it for me for my last birthday. I was raised by my dad, and I was an only child, so I have a thing for cars and football."

"Those aren't bad things to enjoy at all, darlin'," Declan says with a smile. Rather than rolling his eyes, or accusing me of not being feminine enough the way Keith used to, Declan just smiles at me, accepting me for me.

I haven't felt that from a man in a very long time. I can feel my guard lowering more and more with Declan and it's exciting and scary all at the same time. He's so laid back, easy going, easy to talk to.

When's the other shoe going to drop?

Stop worrying!

"So your daddy raised you?" he asks as he takes the exit for the Superdome.

"Yes. It was just the two of us. My mom passed away when I was about eight." I shrug, the way I always do to make it seem like it's no big deal.

"I'm sorry."

"It was a long time ago."

"Doesn't make it hurt less," he murmurs and kisses my hand. He finds parking, but before I can climb out, he turns toward me and cups my cheek. "I'm also sorry that you lost your daddy a few months ago. I didn't have a chance to say that before."

I blink at him, willing myself not to cry. Who is this guy?

"Thank you."

"Losing a parent is hard, but I can't imagine losing both of them."

"I'm doing okay."

"You're doing better than okay, Callie. And you should be proud of that." He leans in and places a soft, gentle kiss on my lips, then leans back with a wide smile. "Okay, let's go watch some ball."

***

"What are you, *blind*?" I yell at the ref hands cupped around my mouth. "He was off-sides!"

"Why are you cheering for the Lions?" Declan asks with a laugh.

"I always cheer for the underdog," I reply and sip my beer as he passes me a plastic bowl of nachos. "Yum."

"See? I promised you dinner and I delivered."

"You did." I nod as I chew the cheesy goodness, not even trying to worry about all of the preservatives in what I'm throwing down my throat. "I love game food."

"Me too. Who is your favorite team?"

"The Seahawks." I grin and steal a bite of Declan's hotdog, then hold a cheesy chip up to his lips, which he takes and licks my thumb at the same time.

My nipples are rock hard at a football game. That's a first.

"I thought you always cheer for the underdog."

"They've done well the past few years," I concede, "but they were the underdogs for a long time."

"Have you seen them play?"

"In Denver, but never in Seattle. I've never been to Seattle, now that I think of it."

We sit in companionable silence for a while, watching the game, eating our food. Suddenly, Declan leans down and kisses me, hard and deep, right here in the middle of the stadium.

"What was that for?"

"Kiss cam," he replies simply and steals my last chip. I glance up, but there is no kiss cam being displayed. "There's no kiss cam."

"I could have sworn there was. My mistake." He grins, in that way he has that says that he knows he's sexy and charming and doesn't give a fuck what anyone else thinks.

God, I love that look.

"I really do love what you've done with the bar," Declan says, serious now.

"Thank you. It took all of my savings, and what I couldn't afford to hire out, I did myself."

"Really?" He turns to me, very interested now.

"Yep. I had a good side business in Denver of

buying and flipping houses. You make more money if you're able to do some of the work yourself." The Lions make a touchdown and I turn to Dec for a high five, but he just leans in and kisses me again. "What was that for?"

"We're having a good time, and I enjoy the fact that you know football, but you're not my buddy, Callie. You're my date."

I blink twice, then lean in and kiss him back. "Point made."

"Good." He rubs his nose over mine, then pulls back and dives back into the conversation. "You should see the house I'm renovating."

"Wait, what?" I shake my head to clear the kissing cobwebs out of the way. "You're renovating?"

"Yes, ma'am. I bought a big ol' house in the Garden District last year, and I've been slowly fixin' it up."

"How old?"

"Built in 1884," he replies easily. "Hasn't had much work done in the past fifty years to speak of, so it's been quite the project."

"I want to see it." Did I just blurt that out? Jesus, Callie, show a little bit of decorum for Godsake.

But Declan just smiles and leans back in to me. I love the way this man leans. He can lean all damn day. "I'd like to show it to you."

The buzzer pierces the air, signaling the end of the game. The mass of people around us stands and moves toward the exits, but Declan and I just stay where we are, pressed against each other.

Because of all the people. We're pressed together because of all of the people around us.

Yeah, right, and New Orleans is in the desert.

I drag my fingers down his cheek and watch his eyes go almost gold with heat. He isn't the first man

I've dated since moving back to New Orleans, but he's the first that I've felt any kind of chemistry with. He's the first who's actually turned my head, made me smile.

Made my body come to life.

"Will you please show me your house tonight?"

"Whatever the lady wants," he murmurs.

***

"I'm warning you now, some of it's done, but most of it has a long way to go," Declan says as he unlocks the door and leads me inside the enormous plantation-style home in the heart of the Garden District. I love this old neighborhood. When I was a teenager, I'd walk up and down the streets here, admiring the homes.

"Perfect," I reply honestly. "I can't wait to see it."

We walk into a wide foyer with a double staircase on either side. The floors are dark walnut and polished.

He's already redone the floors down here, and he's done them perfectly.

"I sanded and varnished the floors myself," he says proudly.

"Original?" I ask as I follow him through to a beautiful living area with a fireplace almost as tall as I am.

"Yes, or most of it. Some boards here and there had to be replaced, but I had them matched to the original."

"This mantle is gorgeous," I breathe, running my hand over the smooth marble.

"It's original. I was shocked that it wasn't cracked or broken."

I nod and follow behind as he leads me into a library, turning on lights as we go. As with the other rooms, the ceilings are high and bookcases rise from floor to ceiling, all covered with white sheets.

"I haven't done anything in here yet," he admits.

"Are there books on those shelves?"

"Yes." He turns to me and grins. "Also original."

I gasp. "Are you kidding me?"

"No, the bookcases were full when I bought the place. It had stood empty for about ten years, the former owners had died, and no one wanted them, so they were left here."

God, I want to get my hands on this place. I can picture the furniture, the molding, the rugs I'd place in here.

Next, he leads me through an empty formal living room with horrid, peeling wallpaper, to a brand new state of the art kitchen.

"You didn't go crazy in here," I sigh in relief.

"No. I wanted all of the modern comforts, but I wanted it to blend with the style."

I can't help it. I grip his shirt in my fists and pull him in for a long, deep, thorough kiss. My lips explore every inch of his, biting, licking, and when I pull away, his eyes are glassy. He licks his lips, still tasting me on them I'm sure, and grins.

"What was that for?"

"This is all very sexy," I reply truthfully.

"Wait till you see me in a tool belt, darlin'."

I. Can't. Even.

I take a deep breath and have to turn away from him, wander around the kitchen, exploring the double ovens and hidden pantry. The cabinets are white, the countertops light grey granite, and the walls are painted one shade darker than the counters.

I could cook some amazing meals in here.

"This space used to be much smaller," he says as he watches me wander around. "I knocked out the wall that led to the butler's pantry and made the kitchen bigger."

"No butler?" I ask with a smirk.

He simply shakes his head slowly no, his arms folded over his chest, his legs spread, standing tall and sturdy.

I'm not leaving here tonight. And I don't care if it's a first date. I want him.

God, I want him. But he doesn't need to know that quite yet.

"What else is down here?"

"A guest room and bathroom that I haven't touched yet," he says as he leads me to them, and I can just picture the room in my head when it's finished. Widen the window, add a stand-up shower where a broken claw foot tub was.

It's simply amazing.

Next, he leads me upstairs.

"How many bedrooms are up here?" I ask as I watch his ass, not two feet away from my face, and it suddenly occurs to me that this was his view the other night when I led him up to the roof at the bar.

Thank God I was wearing the shorts that show off my ass nicely.

"Six," he replies. "Four bathrooms. But I'm going to make it four bedrooms. The master is small, with no closet to speak of, so I'm going to open it up to the bedrooms on either side of it, add a closet and make the bathroom bigger."

I'm moving ahead of him now, opening doors, exploring the second floor like a kid on Christmas morning.

"Is there a third floor?"

"It's attic space, or was."

"What are you going to do with it?"

"I was thinking theater room and game room."

I grin, nodding. "That would be so great."

"You approve?"

"I do. Not that it's mine to approve of, but yes, I

love it. What's in the room behind you?"

"My room," he says simply, then cradles my face in his hands and looks me dead in the eyes. "And if we go in there, we're not coming out until morning."

Thank God.

"What if I get thirsty?" I whisper, watching his lips as they quirk up into a half smile.

"Unless you're thirsty," he amends. "Callie, I want you in my bed, naked and moaning beneath me, but I'm not one for rushing things."

Hearing those words, in that growly sexy voice of his, has my panties soaked.

If I wore panties. Which I don't.

"I don't feel rushed," I reply and push my hands under his shirt. His skin is smooth and warm under my fingers, and all I can think is, *give me more.*

"I didn't bring condoms," I whisper.

"I have that covered," he whispers back.

He brushes his fingertips down my face, then he pushes his fingers into my hair at the back of my head and tips his forehead against mine. "I'm going to fuck you like no one else ever has."

I simply smile, reach behind him and open the door, and walk in with him, our bodies *almost* touching, our lips only millimeters apart. We're already panting. His eyes are blazing, and I couldn't look away from them if I tried.

"Wanna look around?" he asks.

"Later." I guide his shirt up over his head and drop it to the floor, then take my sweet time letting my hands graze over his muscled torso. "I'd rather check you out for now."

"Not complaining here, darlin'," he drawls. So, when he's turned on, his accent is about twenty times stronger.

So noted.

His hands are balled into fists at his side and he simply watches me as I explore him, tracing a tattoo on his shoulder with my fingertip, then dipping into the crevices of his biceps.

God, he's ripped.

"How does a musician stay in such good shape?" I whisper.

"Martial arts," he replies. "I'm having a hard time not touching you right now, sugar."

"I never said you couldn't touch me," I reply and place an open-mouthed kiss over his left pec and down to his stomach. "Your abs should be illegal."

"I'll call the cops."

I grin, then lick a circle around his navel and down the faintest trail of hair that disappears into his jeans.

"I thought these were a myth," I say as I trace the V in his hips with my fingers, and suddenly, I'm lifted into the air and being carried to the bed. "Didn't like that?"

"I want a turn," he replies. All humor is gone from his voice, but the heat hasn't left his eyes. "I need to get you naked."

He sits me on the bed and lifts my blouse over my head. Since I'm eye-level with his cock, and I can see that it's straining against his jeans, I reach up and unfasten them, then guide them down his hips.

"You don't wear underwear either?"

"Either?"

I look up at him through my lashes and send him a coy grin. "Either."

"That's it." We're a tangle of fabric and limbs as we strip each other down, throwing clothes haphazardly around the room. Finally, we're facing each other, completely naked, and I can't take my eyes off of him.

"You know that movie with Emma Stone and

Ryan Gossling, where he takes her home and she makes him take off his shirt, and she says he looks like he's photoshopped?" Why am I talking so damn fast?

"I don't know," he replies, his eyes roaming over me, as if he doesn't know what he should look at first.

"Well, you look like you're photoshopped. Seriously, Declan, your body is…" I can't finish the statement. I can only swallow and blink, and when my gaze finds his again, he's advancing toward me. But rather than the mutual attack and scramble to make it go fast that I'm expecting, he guides me back on the bed, climbing over me, and rests his cock against my center as he covers me and brushes stray hairs from my face.

"You're stunning." His lips nibble mine while his eyes watch me. "I want to make you moan." He kisses his way down my neck, to my collarbone. "Call out my name." Takes my nipple into his mouth and tugs with his teeth. "Come so hard you don't know what day it is."

"I don't know what day it is," I reply and plunge my hands in his hair, reveling in how soft it is. He licks down to my navel, then farther down still and I can't help but fist my hands, tugging on his hair, but not wanting him to stop. "I like the little bit of hair you keep here," he murmurs, brushing his nose over it, then sinks even farther and licks me from labia to clit, and back down again, making my back arch right up off the bed.

"Holy fuck!"

"Mmmm," he agrees as he latches onto my lips and sucks, while simultaneously plunging his tongue inside me. Dear sweet God, he's good with his mouth.

"Declan!"

"That's right, Calliope, what's my name?"

"Declan."

My head is thrashing back and forth as he resumes fucking me with his mouth and plants the pad of his thumb against my clit, and I see stars. I'm pretty sure that's my voice crying out as I fall apart, coming harder than I can remember coming before. I can barely feel Declan kissing his way up my body, pausing here and there to bite me gently, which only sends more shivers through me, until he's finally braced over me.

"How was that first one?"

"First one what?" I mumble. His lips twitch as he lowers himself to rest his lips on mine, and I can smell and taste myself.

"Orgasm," he whispers.

"One for the record books," I reply and circle my hips, rubbing my sopping wet pussy against his hard, throbbing cock. His eyes cross.

"Fuck, you're so damn sexy," he growls.

"I don't know if you can tell by what I'm doing down there, but you're invited to slip inside me now." I smile and grip his ass in my hands, digging my nails in. He tips his forehead against mine and does exactly that: slips inside me, but stops when he's halfway there. "Don't stop."

"You're tight, Callie."

I tilt my hips and take him the rest of the way, and that's it. He doesn't hold back any more. He's pounding me now, hips moving fast and steady, and God, he just fits me. His pubis hits my clit with every thrust, and before long, I'm seeing stars again.

"So good," I moan. "Declan, you feel so good."

He grins and kisses me, devouring me, until I can't stop the orgasm that moves through me. I'm clutching at him, holding him close.

"Shit, I'm going with you," he groans, just before his whole body tightens and he moans as he lets go of his own release.

After a long moment of panting and bodies slowly relaxing, Declan rolls off me, then pulls me against him.

"We're messy."

"I don't care," he replies and kisses me softly. His fingertips are lazily dragging up and down my back, making me sleepy.

"I didn't see a music room," I murmur against his neck.

"I didn't show it to you," he replies softly.

"Why?"

I feel him shrug beneath me. "It felt personal."

"And this isn't?" I ask with a chuckle as I lean my head back so I can see his eyes.

"I wasn't sure I was going to get you in here," he replies and kisses my forehead. "It's not done yet. I'll show you when it's finished. You should sleep."

"You really want me to stay?"

"Yes." His arms tighten around me. I've never felt this at home with a man. Not even with Keith, and I'd been with him for years.

This is all so different. Better different.

"Did you lose a parent, Declan?" I ask, remembering what he said earlier before the game.

"My father passed away almost three years ago." He doesn't stiffen up, or turn away. But his voice sounds sad.

"I'm sorry."

"Me too."

"Did you get along well with him?"

He nods. "Ours is a close family. We had our moments, but I don't know if there's anyone in the world I've ever admired more."

"That's nice." I close my eyes against the tears that want to form. "I didn't admire my father. I loved him, but I didn't admire him."

"No?"

I shake my head and appreciate that he's not pressing me to continue. He just waits.

Declan might be the most patient man I've ever met.

"He fell apart after Mama died. Most men would have recovered, but he never did. So I took care of him."

"Who took care of you?" Declan asks softly. I simply shake my head and continue.

"Dad was an alcoholic, and owning a bar didn't help that at all. He wasn't a mean drunk, Dec. He was a sweet man. But he would get sad. As an adult, it's easy to look back and see that he was just trying to be numb. He loved her so much.

"We lived in that apartment above the bar, and I'd wait for it to close every night, and for him to come upstairs. I learned to have a bucket near the door so he could be sick, and then I'd help him to bed, then go to bed myself."

"And get yourself off to school the next morning," Declan guesses correctly.

"After I graduated, I just couldn't do it anymore. I felt so much guilt, but I knew the best thing for me was to go. So I did. I went to college, majored in restaurant management, and thought I'd come back here and help Dad, but I just couldn't do it." I'm surprised that there are no tears. I'm just telling him the story as if it belongs to someone else.

Sometimes it feels like it did happen to someone else.

"No one would blame you for that, sugar. I'm sure your daddy didn't."

"No, he didn't. But I can't help but feel guilty that I never came home to see him. Not once."

"You never saw him after you graduated from

high school?" he asks incredulously.

"He visited me a couple of times," I reply and sigh deeply. "I should have come home. But I didn't. Maybe that makes me weak."

"I wouldn't call you weak."

"I couldn't keep the apartment upstairs. It had too many bad memories."

"So you made it into a kick ass, amazing space that others can enjoy."

"Thank you," I reply happily.

"Just speaking the truth again."

My hand glides down his chest, his stomach, and finally finds his semi-hard cock. I stroke it a few times, fully waking it up, and climb on top of him.

"The truth turns you on?" he asks with a smile as his hands grip my ass and he guides me up and down.

"You turn me on," I reply and lean back to brace myself on his legs, and then begin to ride him in earnest.

"Jesus, Callie, you make me crazy."

CHAPTER THREE

~Declan~

"Thanks for the ride home," she says with a smile as I pull up to the curb just outside of Adam's condo.

"I couldn't have you walking home," I reply and shove the car in park, then lean over and kiss her thoroughly. I had her in several positions through the night, and yet I'm ready to take her again, right here.

She sends my dick into overdrive.

"The walk of shame," she replies with a smirk.

"Nothin' we did was shameful, darlin'," I whisper and kiss her once more before I hop out and walk to the other side of the Jeep and open the door for her.

"I had fun," she says with a flirty smile. Her hair is disheveled from my fingers, her classy clothes rumpled from spending the night on the floor, and she looks even better than she did when I picked her up last night.

She looks thoroughly fucked.

And damn if it doesn't look good on her.

"Me too." It's the truth. I don't remember the last time I had such a good time with a woman. Not to mention, I let her stay the night.

That's rare.

She kisses me one more time, then turns and waves before she enters her building and disappears.

I'm gonna count last night as a success. Nothing much better in this world than sharing some laughs, conversation, and amazing sex with a beautiful woman.

I drive into the city to the head offices of Boudreaux Enterprises. I'm meeting my oldest brother Beau, along with our good friend Ben, for an hour or so of Krav Maga training and some good-natured ribbing.

What are brothers for, if you can't give each other shit? I'm pretty sure it's in the job description, and we all have an excellent work ethic.

When I reach the executive level, I toss a smile over at the receptionist and walk back to the gym with a spring in my step, humming a Keith Urban song. The others are already here, which is typical, given that I'm usually late.

"You're chipper," Ben says.

"And late," Beau adds as he ties his shoes.

"I'm here," I say simply and shrug. I snatch a bottle of water out of the mini fridge and take a long gulp. I always arrive dressed to work out. These idiots stop working in the middle of the day, change out of their monkey suits, then have to shower and change back.

Just one more reason that I wouldn't be a good fit for a desk job. Suits make me twitchy.

"Has anyone heard from Eli or Kate?" I ask as I wipe water off my chin. "They should be in Aruba by now."

"We won't hear from them. They've gone radio silent," Beau says with a smirk.

"I wouldn't call you ugly assholes if I had a hot woman on a warm island all to myself," Ben says then looks over at me and frowns. "Something's up with you."

"Nothing's up with me," I deny.

"Yeah there is," Beau agrees. "You're humming."

"I'm a singer." I roll my eyes and drink more water.

"You got laid," Ben says with a wide smile. We've known Ben since we were small kids, and he's really more of a brother to us. He's not quite as tall as the three of us, but as a Krav Maga master, he's much stronger.

Ben is badass. No one fucks with him. I'm just happy he likes me.

"The fact that you say that with surprise in your voice tells me that I haven't gotten laid often enough lately."

"Who was it this time?" Beau asks as we take to the mat. "Some chick you picked up at the bar?"

Close.

"What do you care?" I duck as Ben comes at me, but he's a slippery fuck, and he switches tactics and has me on my back in about two seconds.

"Hey, I'm engaging you in conversation," Beau replies with a grin, standing over me.

"Her name's Callie," I say and sit up.

"The owner of The Odyssey?" Ben asks.

"That's the one."

"The one you were telling us about a couple months ago, when we gave Rhys the what-for?" Beau asks, making me grin. That was a fun day. Our youngest sister, Gabby, fell in love with Kate's cousin, Rhys, and we had to scare him a bit.

Because that's what brothers do.

Except I don't think we scared him much. Either way, Rhys stuck, and he and Gabby are disgustingly happy, which makes *me* happy.

All of my sisters should be happy.

"Yes, that's her," I reply.

"I didn't think she wanted to have anything to do with you," Ben says before he wraps an arm around Beau's neck and tries to take him to the mat, but Beau twirls and slips out of the hold, pulls Ben's arm behind his back and plants him in the mat face-down.

"Good one." I clap once and rub my hands together. Today is going to be fun. "And I told Callie I was going to take her to dinner, and she didn't argue."

"You told her?" Beau says.

"I did."

"Huh." Beau scratches his cheek and scowls. "I thought you were supposed to *ask*."

"If you ask, they can say no," I reply with a smile.

"True. So, what did you do?" Ben asks.

"I took her to the football game, then back to my place." Ben and Beau exchange a glance, then both scowl at me.

"Of all of us, you're the romantic one," Beau says and takes a swig of his own water. "You took her to a game and then fucked her?"

"I didn't fuck her," I reply immediately, then regret it when they both just stare at me speculatively. "I mean, I did fuck her—"

I break off and sigh, and these two yahoos just grin. Damn it.

"So, which was it?" Ben asks.

"And I thought you said you *told* her you were taking her to dinner?" Beau adds.

"I did. I bought her stadium food." I walk over and punch the punching bag. "She likes football."

God, why do I sound so defensive?

"Okay." Ben nods. "And she was so impressed by your season tickets and popcorn that she begged you to fuck her?"

"It wasn't that stupid. Or disgusting." My voice is hard now, and I'm starting to get pissed. I know that in the past I would have laughed with them, and we would have moved on to another topic, but this time it grates. And I'm not sure why. I mean, Callie is a beautiful woman. I set my sights on her, took her out and tumbled her around in my bed.

No harm, no foul. Pretty much the standard operating procedure for me.

"You like her," Ben says quietly while Beau busts up laughing.

"Of course I like her. I wouldn't have slept with her if I didn't like her," I reply.

"No, you *really like her.*"

"You sound like a sixteen-year-old girl," I reply and punch the bag again.

"So, she really was just a quick lay." Beau nods, wiping his arm over his sweaty forehead.

"I didn't say that," I reply, again cursing myself for my fucking mouth. Why can't I just shut up? Or change the subject?

Ben and Beau simply stand, arms crossed and watch me.

"Shouldn't you be beating each other up?" I ask.

"This is more interesting," Beau says.

"Why?"

"Because you're not the one to get a crush. You enjoy women, you're good to them, then you move on."

"Who says I'm not moving on?" As soon as the words are out of my mouth, my stomach rolls. I don't want to move on. I don't have Callie out of my system yet. Not by a long shot.

"Have you already told her you'll be taking her to the zoo?" Ben asks with a smirk.

"No, asshole. We didn't make plans."

"So what is the score?" Beau asks. "Are you going to actually pursue a woman?"

I frown. "Why do I have to decide this right now? I had a good time last night. I dropped her off thirty minutes ago. It's a little soon to go shopping for china patterns."

"You didn't even say 'I'll call you'?" Ben asks.

"No. We both said we had fun and she went inside and I came here."

"Maybe she doesn't want to see him again," Beau says to Ben, who nods while rubbing his chin thoughtfully.

"Could be."

"I'm standing right here," I remind them through clenched teeth. "Maybe it's still really early, and we're just enjoying each other and you all are over-thinking it."

"I think you're under-thinking it," Beau replies. "She's a woman and she had sex with you. She's going to want some attention from you."

"I'll give her attention." Jesus, what does he think I am, an asshole?

On second thought, yeah, he probably does.

"Doesn't mean I have to text or call her every five minutes all day."

"Look, if she's what you want, good luck with her." Ben claps his hand on my shoulder. "It's going to be fun to watch you navigate this, especially since you don't know what the fuck you're doing."

"I've had girlfriends," I protest, but they just laugh. "I have."

"A fuck buddy is not a girlfriend," Ben says. "But if you want Callie to be a regular booty call, nothing wrong with that either."

I definitely want her to be a booty call. I'd like to spend as much time between her long, slender legs as I possibly can.

But I don't think that's all I want, and it's confusing the fuck out of me. I don't do strings. And then it occurs to me: I didn't have the *you know this is just a fun time* conversation with her so she knew the score beforehand, the way I always do. Why didn't I do that?

"I'll figure it out."

"Gonna be fun to watch," Ben says again, right before he surprises Beau with a body slam to the ground.

I have a feeling I'm in way over my head.

***

After my night with Callie, the week took a serious nose-dive into the pit of hell. I've been down with food poisoning—I'm pretty sure it wasn't the flu—and still had to perform every night this week. So I basically spent every minute not performing wishing I was dead in bed. Now that the weather is starting to cool down from Satan's neighborhood to just normal warm, tourist season is ramping up again, and with that comes gigs. I am fortunate to not *have* to play every night to make ends meet, but I love it. The music, the audience, all of it. And I refuse to cancel a gig with only a few hours' notice.

I'm finally beginning to feel human again as I walk into The Odyssey Friday night for my gig. There is a decent crowd already enjoying drinks and the small but delicious bar menu offered. My eyes skim the room, looking for a certain tall blonde. I haven't seen or spoken to her since Tuesday morning, and I need to get an eyeful.

Maybe even a handful.

Adam waves from behind the bar as I make my way through the tables.

"How's it going?" I ask.

"It's busy, so it's good," he says with a grin. "You look like shit."

"And here I thought I covered it up before I left the house." I scrub my hand over my face and sigh. "It's been a hell of a week."

"I don't think it's going to get better in the very near future," he warns me then gestures for me to turn around. Callie, draped in a killer red dress with matching red lips and black heels is marching across the room. She's stunning.

And her amazing blue eyes are... *cold*.

"Adam, can you help me get some cases of Corona in the elevator so I can stock the bar upstairs?"

"Sure."

"Hey," I say and slip my hand on her waist, but she backs away and cocks a brow.

"Declan."

"How are you, Callie?"

"Busy." The fun, sweet woman from Monday night is nowhere to be found, and I'm smart enough to know that it's my own fault.

"I think we need to talk."

"I'm working." Her tone is calm and nothing but professional, her face passive, and yet I get the distinct feeling she's telepathically telling me to go fuck myself.

Callie marches back across the room and up the stairs just as Adam returns from the elevator.

"I think I screwed up," I mutter with a sigh.

"Probably a safe bet," Adam says, with way too much joy in his voice.

"Fuck." I stalk toward the stairs and climb them, eyes scanning the rooftop for Callie. They haven't opened the roof yet, so it's deserted. Her blond head pops up behind the bar where she's currently stocking beer. "Can I help with that?"

"This isn't in your job description," she says

without looking over at me. She's pissed.

Really pissed.

"We need to talk," I say again.

"I'm. Working."

"Look, let's do this now, while we're alone."

"Fine. Let's do this." She stands and props her hands on her hips, and my eyes immediately zero in on her tits, and the lust is a million times worse than it was before. Now I know what they look like under that dress. I know how she gasps when I tease the tips with my teeth. "My eyes are up here, Declan."

"I'm aware," I reply lazily without looking up.

"You're an ass."

My eyes find hers now, and I see that she's not just pissed. She's hurt.

"Talk to me, sugar."

"You don't get to call me sugar, or baby, or *darlin'*," she says, mimicking my accent.

"Okay. What's wrong, Callie?"

"Look." She sighs deeply and rubs her forehead with her fingertips. "I get that I probably misunderstood the signals on Monday. I'm a big girl, and I can take responsibility for my own actions. I enjoyed myself."

"I did too. I'm glad we're on the same page—"

"I just wish," she continues, interrupting me, "that you had made it clear from the beginning exactly what the score was, because I wouldn't have been as open with you about my family as I was. I dropped my guard with you, and since then you made it clear exactly what I am to you. At first, when I didn't hear from you *at all*, I felt a little cheap, a little used, but then I just felt... *stupid*. And I'm not a stupid woman."

"I never said you—"

"So I appreciate that you find me attractive, and the chemistry is pretty great, but I'm not looking for a fuck buddy. And you know what?"

God, I wish she'd slow down for two seconds so I can get a word in edgewise.

"What?"

"I also realized that I'm not looking for *anything* from you, Declan Boudreaux."

"Callie, I admit, in the past I've not been great at understanding women, or even taking the time to try to. There are reasons for why I didn't call this week—"

"I don't want your reasons," she interrupts, still calm. "I don't want anything from you, except for you to do your job when you're in my place."

She turns to walk away, and it feels like I'm burning from the inside out.

"Callie, I didn't mean to hurt your feelings. It was a shitty week."

She glances over her shoulder at me and smirks. "That's one way to describe it."

And without another word, she goes back to stocking the beer, making it clear that I'm no longer welcome here, so I walk back downstairs to the bar where Adam is flirting with a group of women, mid-twenties, obviously out on the town for a bachelorette party, due to the sash and tiara on one of the girls.

When he sees me, he winces. "Doesn't look like it went well."

"I couldn't get a word in edgewise," I reply, feeling shell-shocked.

Adam just shrugs and shakes his head, looking at me like I'm the biggest idiot on the planet.

The worst part is, he's right.

CHAPTER FOUR

~Callie~

He has his reasons for not calling. I just bet he does. Probably a woman. Or work. Or family. But nothing, *nothing* makes a person too busy to just send a simple text to say hi, or hope you're well, or kiss my ass.

Anything.

Instead, I've spent the past four days with my phone permanently attached to my body in the hopes that Declan would call, only making me feel like a complete, embarrassed idiot as each day passed.

Beer bottles clink against each other as I slam the cooler door closed, making me wince.

I like him. The second I saw him downstairs, my nipples puckered and the sound of his voice as he groaned while coming the other night were front-row, center in my brain, which only pissed me off more.

I'm reliving some of the best sex I've ever had, and he couldn't even be bothered to send me a simple text this week.

The thing is, he was nice, and apologetic, and he *should* be, but if I just smile and say it's okay, he'll think that the behavior is okay.

And it's not.

I wipe down the bar one last time, satisfied that the rooftop is clean and ready for business tonight, then walk back downstairs to help Adam man the bar. Our third bartender will arrive in about an hour, and I'll send her upstairs.

I may not want to date him, but I'm not going to pass up the chance to watch Declan play. Masochistic? Probably, but I can't help it.

"Did you tell him to fuck off?" Adam asks as he pours a beer and I join him.

"I'm not talking about this here."

"He looked like you told him to fuck off," he continues, completely ignoring my statement. "But, in my defense, I warned you, Cal."

"Shut up," I reply and walk to the other end of the bar, smile at a customer, and focus on what I do best, work. "What can I get you?"

"Gin and tonic," the girl replies and flashes me her ID. I turn to fill her order, my eyes skimming the room, looking for Declan. He should be on stage in a few minutes. I find him standing at a table, laughing. I don't recognize the two women he's talking to, but his hand is resting on the small of the slender brunette's back, and the other brunette, more petite than the first, is laughing and gazing at Declan like he's the best thing since the invention of the cosmopolitan she's sipping.

Tramps.

I shake my head and continue to serve drinks. The thing is, those girls don't look like tramps. They look like people I would like.

And maybe that's what pisses me off the most.

"What'll you have?" I ask a tall, light brown-haired guy standing with his head turned the other way. When he looks at me, my eyes widen and I feel myself smile. "Pete?"

"Callie? Holy shit, I didn't realize you were home!"

I run around the bar and hug Pete tight, then walk back around and grin. "What'll it be? On the house."

"A hurricane," he replies, his familiar brown eyes shining. "How are you, Cal? I was sure sorry to hear about your daddy."

"Thanks." I settle in, building Pete's drink, thankful to have a friendly person to talk to. "I'm doing okay. Renovating this place has helped a lot."

"It's fantastic," Pete says and sits on a stool, as if he's going to stay and chat. "And so is this drink."

"Just one of my many talents."

"I remember," he says, his eyes wandering up and down my body. I've changed a lot since we were sixteen and I lost my virginity to him in his childhood bedroom. Of course, so has he. Pete and I dated until we graduated from high school, and then it just felt right to break it off and go our separate ways.

Long gone is the tall and lanky boy that charmed me back then. He's filled out, not super muscular, but not big. He's a man now. Unfortunately, there isn't the chemistry here that I feel every time Declan enters a room, but it's great to see Pete.

"What are you up to these days?" I ask.

"Real estate," he says and pulls a business card out of his back pocket, passing it to me.

"Really? Hold on." I hold my finger up, signaling for him to wait, just as Declan takes the stage and the crowd cheers. I fill several more orders, and when I'm satisfied that all the customers are taken care of, I turn back to Pete. "I may be in the market for a real estate agent."

Pete's eyes narrow just a bit and he leans forward. "Is that so?"

"It is. I like to flip houses, I'm pretty good at it, and I've been thinking about finding something down here to sink my teeth into."

"I'm pretty sure I can help you out with that. You have my number. Just call any time."

"I will." I smile and tuck his card in my bra. I don't have any pockets in this dress. "Thanks."

Pete takes a sip of his drink. "I don't see a ring on your finger."

I laugh and shake my head. "No. You don't."

"Good to know." He winks and then takes his drink and stands. "I'll talk to you soon."

"Sounds good." I watch Pete walk into the crowd and sigh.

"What are you doing?" Adam asks as he comes to stand next to me, arms crossed.

"This is called working," I reply, enunciating each word in case he's slow.

"No, it's called flirting with men."

"Oh please. Like you don't spend every evening you work flirting with the young girls you pour drinks for." I roll my eyes and wipe the bar with a wet rag.

"I'm not you," he says simply and then nods toward the stage. "And I don't put on a show for the person I was with just days ago. And the thing is, that's not you either." He gives me a pointed look and walks away.

I glance up at the stage with a frown, surprised to find Declan's eyes on me, but he blinks and looks away without missing a beat of the bluesy song he's playing.

I was *not* trying to make Declan jealous. I was talking to an old friend. I didn't do anything wrong. Declan was flirting with a table of women—touching them!—not thirty minutes ago!

Not to mention, he's not my boyfriend.

But there's a small part of me that feels just a tiny bit bad. So, I do what I do best. I raise my chin, fasten a smirk on my face and do my damn job.

***

It was a long night. The Odyssey was busier than ever, and Declan even played for an extra fifteen minutes when the crowd yelled for more. He looks so comfortable on a stage, an instrument in his hand. He makes the singing sound easy, when I know that it's anything but.

He's at home there.

The stage is empty now, along with the rest of the place, and I sigh, enjoying the quiet and the solitude. How an introvert fell into a career that involves so many people, I have no idea.

But I love it. Almost as much as the quiet. I glance around, then flip off the lights and slip through the front door and lock it behind me.

"You're later tonight."

"Jesus, Mary and Joseph!" I screech, jumping about five feet in the air, then clutch at my chest and scowl at Declan. "Stop doing that!"

"I'm sorry," he says with a lazy grin. He looks tired. Actually, as I take a closer look, he looks worse than tired.

Do not ask him what's wrong.

"Why are you here?" I ask and walk briskly down the sidewalk toward my car.

"Walking you," he replies simply and easily keeps up with my stride. His legs are so long, it's nothing more than a leisurely walk for him.

"Why?"

"Are we going to do this again?" he asks with a sigh. "Because it's dangerous here at night. Why isn't Adam walking you out? You guys could just ride together."

"That would cramp Adam's sex life up," I reply with a laugh. "I don't want any part of that."

"Where are you parked?"

"About four blocks up," I admit and bite my lip. I will never admit this out loud, but I'm glad he's here to walk me. He's right, it is dangerous in the Quarter at night.

"Why in the hell did you park so far away?" He reaches down to take my hand, but I pull it away.

"It's all I could find."

"Isn't there parking in the alley?"

"It was full when I got here." I scowl up at him. "I didn't ask you to walk me."

"No, you'd be too stubborn for that," he mutters and sighs. "Since your car is so far away, let's talk about this week."

"I already told you—"

"I know what you told me, sugar, but you didn't give me a chance to tell you *anything*, and I'm going to have my say." He takes my hand again, holding tightly so I can't pull away, and rather than be a baby about it, I let him keep it.

"Fine. Say whatever you want."

"I was sick this week, and I had to work every night. So, I was either in bed, wishing I was dead, or I was singing, still wishing I was dead."

Do not offer to make him soup, Calliope Marie. "I'm sorry you were sick."

"So that's why I didn't call."

"Let me ask you something." I stop us on the sidewalk and face him, looking up into his eyes, which are almost gold in the streetlights. "If you hadn't have been sick, would you have called? Not that it matters now, but I'm curious."

He swallows and frowns and I already know the answer. Probably not.

"I figured." I nod and keep walking.

"Look, Callie, it's not that I didn't have fun."

"I get it." I shrug and almost do a happy jig when I

see my car in the next block over. "This is all on me, Declan. You didn't make me any promises. You never said you'd call. I just thought the chemistry was on point and that we had a great time, in and out of bed."

"I agree," he says, that frown still in place. "Like I said earlier, I've never claimed to understand women. I do enjoy you, and I like you, a lot."

I nod. "Okay. Thanks for the walk. I'm fine, Declan."

"Hey." He grips my elbow and stops me beside my car. "Are we okay? Friends?" He smiles softly. His hair is disheveled and sexy, and I can smell him. I want to climb him and have my way with him, but that is a definite bad idea, especially knowing that that's not what he wants.

"Friends."

And then, to my utter bewilderment, he leans in, his eyes pinned to my lips, and I barely have time to duck out of the way before he could lay those lips on mine.

"Not that kind of *friends*, Declan." Without looking back, I get in the car and drive away.

What in the hell was that?

Why do I pick men who are emotionally unavailable and commitment-phobes? Keith made it pretty clear from the beginning that the sex was great, and he enjoyed my company, but that's all it would ever be. We didn't see other people, it was exclusive, but it was never going to be forever.

And I settled for that. Looking back on it, I'm irritated with myself. Even if I was content with the arrangements, I should have known that I deserved better. And I don't even think I was content with the arrangements; I just went along with it because that's what *he* wanted.

And I wanted him.

And now I find another guy who is interested in my body and a few laughs, but that's it. And he just made it clear that we could go on that way if I want to, but we would always just be *friends*.

I'm not just a friends with benefits girl.

Yes, the sex with Declan was fantastic. On a scale of one to ten, it was about a thirteen and a half, and I'm being conservative on that number. But what I enjoyed the most that night was the *fun*. The banter at the game, when he showed me his amazing house.

Talking about my family and his and how we feel about the loss of our fathers.

That's what I didn't even realize I'd been craving in my life. Yes, I work hard to keep the packaging looking good, but damn it, I want someone to be interested in what's happening in my head and my heart too, and for one evening, I thought that might be Declan.

But, just like always, I was dead wrong.

***

It's time to focus on *me* for a while.

I spent the weekend cleaning Adam's condo, steering clear of his bedroom and bathroom, because only God knows what happens in there, although I have a pretty good idea from the noises coming through the wall that connects his bedroom to mine.

I need to invest in earplugs.

The result of all of the scrubbing and sweating was the realization that I need to focus on me and what I enjoy. Make myself happy.

I can do that. I don't need a man for that.

Now that the bar renovations are finished and business is running smoothly, I'm ready to find a house to fix up and flip.

So I'm meeting Pete at his office, and he's going to take me to see a couple of homes that might be perfect for me.

"Hey," I say as Pete lowers himself into my car. "Thanks for doing this."

"My pleasure," he says, his eyes surveying the inside of my car. "Nice ride."

"Thanks. Where to?" He pulls up the first location on his phone and shows it to me. "I know where that is."

"It was so great to run into you the other night," Pete says.

"It really was. It's been a long time. Are you married?"

"Divorced," he replies with a shrug.

"Kids?"

"Three," he confirms and flips through his phone, then turns it so I can see a photo. "Mike is six, Emma is eight and Dina is ten."

"Wow. That's a handful. Congratulations." Pete, the boy who couldn't keep his mouth off of me just fifteen years ago, has three kids.

Crazy!

"How about you? Kids?"

"No." I shake my head and pull up in front of the first house we'll see today, already thinking it's a no. That entire roof needs to be replaced, and on a house this size, that's a large chunk of a reno budget. But it doesn't hurt to look.

"Ever married?" he asks as he joins me on the porch.

"Nope." I flash him a smile. "Too busy with work and other things to get there."

He simply nods and unlocks the door, pushes it open, and gestures for me to go first.

"It's empty," I say as I enter a small foyer and look left into a formal dining room.

"It's been empty for about three years," he says,

consulting the information on the papers he printed out on the property.

"Not good," I murmur and continue through. There's obvious water damage along the ceiling in the living room, and the brick fireplace is crumbling.

But there is a gorgeous staircase with a solid oak banister that, with some wax and elbow grease, would be magnificent.

The kitchen is small and sorely outdated, as are the two small bathrooms upstairs. The bedrooms just need new flooring and paint.

"What do you think?" Pete asks as he locks the door on our way out.

"I think this is a no," I reply, inspecting the porch, and not happy to see evidence of termites. "This place is going to have to be gutted, and I think that's outside my budget."

"I understand. I have one more to show you today."

This house is only a few streets over from the first one.

"This is better," I say. "The roof is in better shape." The house is larger, too, and definitely needs work.

"This is empty too, but only for about a month, so there shouldn't be extensive damage inside."

"Let's have a look."

He unlocks the door and when I walk in, I stop in my tracks and cover my mouth and nose with my hand. "I think you were wrong, Pete."

"Holy shit," he mutters. "This just went on the market yesterday, and it's obviously not been cleaned."

"They'll have to tear it down," I reply, stupefied by the sight before me. There is a hole—a *hole*—in the ceiling, all the way through to the second floor, and a bed, the object that obviously caused the hole, is in the middle of the living room. There is garbage everywhere, and it smells like a sewer.

"Do you want to see the rest?" he asks.

"Is it safe?" I turn wide eyes to him and then shrug. "Meh, I'm always up for an adventure, and I've never seen anything like this."

We move carefully through the living room, stepping over garbage and God knows what, to the kitchen, where I have to will myself not to throw up.

The fridge is standing wide open, and no one bothered to empty the contents, so rotten food permeates the room.

"They tore off all of the cabinet doors," I say in surprise. "And how in the bloody hell did they manage to crack this granite?"

"I have no idea," he says, obviously as taken aback as I am. "I'll call the other realtor as soon as we leave and tell him that he needs to take care of this before he shows it again."

"I've never seen anything like it," I reply in awe and open the French doors leading out to a back yard with a pool. "Pete?"

"Yeah?" he says from inside.

"You'll want to see this."

He comes out behind me and gasps. "Callie, there's a car in the pool."

"Yep."

"I've officially seen it all."

I giggle and shake my head, my eyes surveying the back yard. "I wonder where that toilet is supposed to go?"

"I'm assuming that the rose garden isn't the right answer," he says and leads me back inside and upstairs, where we find the home of the toilet now living with the roses, along with a dead squirrel. "Someone had a campfire going in here." I follow Pete into one of the bedrooms and stare at the perfect circle of rocks and burned wood in the center of the room. "They left the sticks they used to roast marshmallows."

"Or, you know, body parts, because this place has the vibe of a serial killer's house." I laugh, but I'm not really kidding.

This place gives me a serious case of the willies.

By the time we reach the master bedroom, I can't take any more. "Are those shackles on the wall?" I ask quietly, on the verge of tears. This isn't fun anymore. It's scary.

"They are."

"I think you should call the police before you call the realtor." There's another toilet, just sitting against the wall, not actually hooked up to anything. The carpet was ripped out, exposing just the sub-floor. There is no hardwood.

"Let's go." He wraps an arm around me and leads me down and out of the house and to my car, but I'm not ready to drive. We both stand outside as Pete dials the cops and tells them what we discovered, then calls the other realtor and gives him the same report, along with a tongue lashing for not inspecting the property before listing it.

When he hangs up, my nerves have calmed enough for me to drive, but we're quiet on the way back to Pete's office.

"I'm so sorry about that," he says softly and wipes his hand over his mouth. "That's not only unprofessional, but so disturbing. I never would have taken you there if I'd known, Cal."

"I know." I nod and then shiver when I think of those shackles on the wall. "I wonder what happened there?"

"It's probably best if you don't think about it."

"Right." I pull up to his office and turn to face

him. "Thanks for your time today, Pete."

"Anytime. We've just started looking. We'll find you something."

"I know."

"Can I take you to dinner sometime?"

The question is blurted out and I have to blink at him for several seconds, trying to catch up. "Dinner?"

"I'd really like to take you out, Callie."

"Well, I—" All I can think is, *you have three kids*, and I'm so not ready to date a guy who comes as a boxed set.

"Just dinner." He holds his hands up as if he's surrendering. "We'll just catch up a bit. No pressure."

Well, it *is* nice to see an old friend, and really, what could a simple dinner hurt?

"Okay. Sure."

"Great." He grins and opens his door. "I'll call you tonight and we'll make plans."

"Talk to you later." I wave and smile, then pull away and shake my head. This has been the weirdest day I've had in a very long time.

CHAPTER FIVE

~Callie~

"He's sure here a lot over the past few weeks," Adam says as he pours a beer next to me. "Even on his days off."

I simply shrug and finish cutting a lime, then grab another. It's been two weeks since my night with Declan, and in that time, he's shown up before closing to walk me to my car almost every night. We've slipped into an easy camaraderie with each other, and rather than wait outside to scare the shit out of me, he just comes inside to wait.

And the fact that my pulse speeds up and an army of butterflies takes up residence in my belly when I see him is irrelevant.

"He's just walking me to my car," I reply and lift my gaze to survey the bar., Sure enough, Declan just walked in and is sitting at a table on the other side of the room. He's in his usual dark, plain T-shirt and jeans, showing off a bit of ink on his arm. He pushes his hair off his forehead, and I have to swallow hard. I know how it feels to have his fingers in my hair, and it feels damn good.

"Why?" Adam asks.

"Why what?"

"Well, two whys, actually. Why does he walk you to your car, and why are you looking at him like he's a plate full of hot wings?"

"Awww, you remember my favorite food." I pat Adam's shoulder and move on to stocking napkins. The place is almost empty, and closing time is almost here.

Thank God.

I like my place, but I'm ready to get off my feet.

"Answer the questions."

"Well, I'm assuming he's walking me to my car because the Quarter is dangerous at night and *you* usually go home with some unsuspecting victim at closing time. And two, I wasn't looking at him like he's delicious, but now I want wings, thank you very much."

"So you're not seeing each other?"

"We're friends," I reply, making sure Adam knows that the subject is closed.

I didn't lie. Declan has been nothing but a complete gentleman in the past few weeks, just chatting with me about our days as he walks me to my car.

The fact that I keep parking just a little farther away each day is something that I'll deny until I take my last breath.

I walk around the bar to where Declan's sitting.

"Hey, friend, can I get you anything?" I smile, but I'm cringing on the inside. *Friend*. Even though it's true, why does it feel wrong?

"I'm fine." He shakes his head and offers me a smile, but his eyes look tired. "I'll just wait here."

"I can bring you a water if you like," I offer, but he simply shakes his head again, so I nudge his shoulder with mine playfully. "Hey, you okay?"

"Of course." He nods again, so I return to the bar

and help Adam with the last of the clean up and shoo out the few remaining patrons.

Finally, I slip into the back office to grab my handbag and check my hair in the mirror, then join Declan. "I'm ready."

He waits for me to lock the door, and then we set off down the sidewalk.

"How was your day?" I ask, as I always do.

"I can't complain," he says, but doesn't elaborate. Silence falls between us, and I frown up at him, confused. Something's wrong.

"Well, my day was just dandy, thanks for asking." He smirks, but still won't look me in the eye. "I had to have a plumber come in to look at a toilet in the men's room because some idiot tried to flush his pants last night. My wine order didn't come in; it was routed to freaking Delaware for some reason that only God knows."

"Sounds like a busy day," Declan says. I don't know what else to say, so we walk a couple blocks in silence. It's getting cooler at night now, thankfully giving us a break from the blistering heat of summer. There's a breeze blowing through the trees. Any other night, I would say that it was lovely.

If I said words like lovely.

But tonight I'm just irritated. Finally, I pull Declan to a stop, grip his arm, and turn him toward me so I can look him in the eye. "Fuck this. Spill it. What in the hell is eating at you?"

"I'm fine," he repeats, but I shake my head vigorously no.

"No, you're not. You're sad or angry or *something*. If you don't want to walk me to my car, it's okay. It won't hurt my feelings if you tell me you don't want to do it anymore."

Except it might hurt my feelings a little.

"It's not that at all. I'm usually working near here anyway, so this isn't out of my way." He sighs and wipes his hand down his handsome face, and then he pins me in that whiskey-gold gaze of his. "Okay, I've been wanting to ask you to come to the house and give me some help. I want to spend the day with you tomorrow, if you're up for it."

"Okay." I frown up at him, completely confused. "Why does that make you mad?"

"Because I'm fucking nervous as hell, and I don't get nervous, Callie." He chuckles and paces away two steps and then back again. "Because I don't know how you'll take it when I ask, and I really just want to enjoy your company in my house tomorrow. That simple."

"Sounds good," I reply with a smile. "Is ten in the morning okay? Given how late it is now, I'd like to get a little sleep."

"That works," he replies and sighs, and then breaks out into a laugh. "That was way easier than I thought it was going to be. I thought I'd have to really do some fast talking."

"I've wanted to get my hands on your house since I first saw it," I remind him. *I've wanted to get my hands on you since I first saw you too.*

Damn Declan for being so damn hot.

"Well, there are two rooms that I don't know what to do with, and I figure you'll have some ideas." He opens my door as we approach my car, and I lower myself inside before I do something stupid like lean in and kiss him.

We're friends.

"I'll come up with something awesome," I assure him. "See you tomorrow morning."

***

Declan opens the door at exactly ten o'clock sharp and my mouth goes dry. Why, for the love of the baby

Jesus, is he *shirtless?*

"Are you early?" he asks, eyeing the coffees in my hands and the bag full of bagels and cream cheese. "And is that food?"

"No and yes," I reply and shove past him before I start to drool. "I'm right on time. And this is breakfast." He follows me into the kitchen and reaches out to help me, but I wave him away. "Shouldn't you go put a shirt on?"

Please, God, go put a fucking shirt on.

"You don't like me like this?" he asks with a teasing smile. When I simply stare at him, he shrugs. "Fine. I'll be right back."

As he jogs up the stairs, two at a time, I divvy up the bagels and coffees, and lean against the island counter as I nibble my plain bagel with jalapeño cream cheese and give myself a pep talk to forget Declan's almost nakedness.

He's a friend. Just a friend. You've seen him shirtless before. Get over it.

"It smells great," he says as he rejoins me, in a flannel button-down this time, and digs in to his bagel. "Sorry, I overslept."

"It's okay." I can't help but watch his jaw work as he chews, the muscles flexing in his neck, and I wish with all my heart that I'd worn underwear.

So much for that pep talk.

"So, what rooms do you want to work on?" I ask to distract myself.

"I'll show you," he replies as we both finish our food. We grab our coffees and walk into a series of small, awkward rooms on the first floor. They've been closed up, so they smell a little musty. There's carpet—yellow shag—that needs to come up. "I have no idea what to do with these three rooms."

"What's on the other side of this wall?" I ask,

turning a circle.

"The kitchen."

I turn my back to the wall facing the kitchen and survey the windows to the back and side yards. "These were probably butlers' quarters back in the day," I mutter and chew my lip as I think. "Do you have much of a pantry in the kitchen?"

"Just a small closet," he replies.

"Okay, here's what I would do. I would take this third room and wall it up, put in a door with access from the kitchen and make it a nice, big pantry. Then I'd open these other two rooms up to each other and the kitchen, making this long wall a half-wall of windows. Then—" I turn around and point at the windows. "—I would make these windows much larger, turning this space into a sun room." I can even picture how I would decorate it in my head, and oh my God, it's so pretty.

"That's a lot of work," Declan replies, rubbing his chin in thought.

"It's mostly demo," I reply. "We'll have two walls to take out, but it'll open the space up and make the whole floor feel really open."

"Okay," he says and claps his hands together. "Let's do it."

"Right now?"

"Right now."

"Don't you have a contractor?" I ask and prop my hands on my hips.

"I do, yes, but we can do the demo ourselves. This carpet has to go too."

"Without a doubt," I agree and cringe at what could be living in this carpet. "I'm betting there's original hardwood under here."

"There was in the other rooms that I've already done." He nods, still looking around. "This is a great idea. I have a couple of sledgehammers. In the mood to knock down a couple walls?"

"Hell yes I am! Demo is my favorite part of the job."

"Helps you release some built-up aggression?"

"That, and it's just a great workout." I pull a box cutter out of my back pocket as Declan leaves to find the hammers and crouch in a corner, cut the carpet and peel it back, revealing exactly what I thought: gorgeous wood floors. They need to be sanded and refinished, but they're beautiful.

"You came prepared," Declan murmurs behind me. I stand and turn in time to catch him looking at my ass and cock a brow, but he's not embarrassed in the slightest.

I'm wearing my usual outfit for this kind of work: a fitted black T-shirt and jeans with work boots.

"I love my girlie girl clothes," I tell him and sheath the cutter in my back pocket. "But there's a time and place for them, and this isn't it."

"You're right." He grins and hands me a hammer, along with some safety goggles.

"Ready?" I move over to the smaller wall and smile at Declan, and when he nods, we both start taking swings at the walls, making giant holes in the drywall and sending dust into the air. I make the mistake of glancing over at Declan in time to watch his biceps flex as he hits the wall, so to pull myself together, I focus on my wall until I have all of the drywall off the studs.

When I turn, Declan is done as well, his arms crossed over his dusty chest, watching me with humor-filled eyes.

"You're hot when you're beating the shit out of a wall."

I bark out a laugh, scoop up a piece of drywall, and

throw it, hitting him square in the shoulder, leaving a white mark. He simply looks down at his shoulders and then back at me, his eyebrows hiked up near his hairline.

"No. You. Didn't."

I snort with laughter and clap, delighted with myself. "I did."

"You'll pay."

"How?"

He takes two steps toward me, his face determined, just as my phone pings with an incoming text.

"Saved by the bell!" I cry and pull my phone out of my pocket, then frown when I see Pete's name. *Busy for dinner tonight?*

Ugh. Pete. He's nice, and we do have a history, but it's ancient history, and the chemistry just wasn't there.

Plus, he has three children, and I'm not in the market to be anyone's mom, step or otherwise.

Rather than reply, I just shove my phone back in my pocket.

"Something wrong?" Declan asks.

"No, it's nothing." I glance around, surveying our handiwork. "Do you see the brick I exposed near the outside wall?" I ask, pointing. Declan nods and we walk over to inspect it. "I didn't see any brick on the outside of the house."

"It's not brick," he confirms with a frown. "Back up."

I comply, and he continues to punch out the dry wall on the adjoining wall, exposing more brick.

"I bet it was a fireplace," I say, excited that we found it. "Someone decided they didn't want it anymore and just hid it."

"You're right," he says as he uncovers the actual fireplace part and smiles. "Let's take this drywall out too and expose the brick. Even if it's no longer functioning, the brick is beautiful."

We spend another hour carefully uncovering the fragile brick. We don't want to take out too much. It's going to be a challenge for the carpentry crew as it is.

When we're finished, Declan offers a fist for me to bump.

"We kicked ass today," he says.

"And made a mess." I wince and survey the dusty mess around us. "Let's haul it all out to the dumpster, then rip out this carpet."

"Then I'll order in pizza."

I check the time on my phone. "How did it get to be four in the afternoon already?"

"Knocking down walls takes time," he says as he picks up an armful of drywall and heads out back to the dumpster. Hauling it all away takes almost as much time as it did to tear it down.

Finally, we rip the carpet out, roll it into manageable strips, and take it out to the dumpster together. After the last of the carpet is in the garbage, I brush the dust and dirt off my clothes then Declan's back, and he returns the favor.

"We are dirty." As soon as the words leave my mouth, I know it was the wrong thing to say.

"Not in a couple weeks," Declan says, right on cue, making me laugh.

"Har har," I reply. "Okay. I'm starving. You promised me pizza."

"Coming right up."

***

"It's so nice out here," I say between bites of loaded pizza. We're sitting on the front porch now, me on the top of the steps with my back leaning against the top of the railing, and Dec sitting opposite me, in the same position. The box of pizza is open between us.

It's early evening now. Traffic, both motor and foot, has slowed. The trees are moving a bit in the breeze.

"Mmm," he agrees, his mouth full.

"How old do you think these oaks are?" I ask, looking up into their branches.

"A few hundred years," he replies lazily.

This. This right here is what I want with someone someday. I want the comfort. I want to be able to laugh and work hard together. Share a pizza and soak up a nice evening.

It's a good start, anyway.

I reach for a third slice and sigh in happiness with the first bite, then swig the beer Declan opened for us.

A piece of my hair slips out of the bun on the back of my head, so I set my pizza down and fix it, then glance at Declan, who's stopped eating and is just watching me quietly with sober eyes.

"What?"

He shakes his head and turns his attention back to his pizza. I feel like I just missed something, but I have no idea what it is.

Finally, after a long ten minutes of silence, I wipe my hands on a napkin and then throw it at Declan, hitting him in his hard head.

"You have a habit of throwing things at me, sugar."

"What are you thinking?" I ask with a smile.

"That you throw things at me."

"Before that."

"Why do women always ask what men are thinking when they don't speak for a while?"

"Because we want to know," I reply and sip my beer. "Come on. Spill it."

He laughs and shakes his head, takes a sip of his

own beer, then leans in like he's going to tell me something really good. "Do you want to know that big secret? The answer to the question every time a woman asks a man what he's thinking?"

I nod.

"Nothing. He's not thinking anything, except maybe *damn, this pizza is good*."

"You were that quiet because the pizza tastes good?" I tilt my head to the side, not buying it, but he just shrugs good-naturedly and sips his beer.

"Tell me about your tats," he says, looking at my arm. "They're amazing."

"Thanks." I glance down and look at the ink, thinking of the dozens of hours I sat in Brock's chair while he worked his magic. "I found a great artist in Denver."

"Do they mean anything?"

"They all mean something," I reply and bite my lip. "I'll tell you about them sometime."

"But not now."

"Not now." I shrug and lean my head back against the post, watching Declan through my lowered lashes. "Are you going to tell me what you were really thinking?"

"Are you going to tell me about your ink?"

I shake my head slowly, and he joins me, moving his head slowly back and forth while watching me with a soft smile on his full lips. The electricity between us is a living entity, crackling and popping. Can't he feel it too? How could he miss it?

Finally, I stand and gather the empty pizza box and beer bottles and carry them into the house to the garbage. Dec follows me, but he's a man of few words tonight.

He has something on his mind, but doesn't trust me enough yet to talk it out. That hurts, just a little, but

I understand it too. There's still plenty I don't want to talk about with him.

I turn to go back outside, and bump right into a solid six foot four inch wall of muscle.

"Sorry. I didn't see you there." I brace my hands on his arms to catch my balance and before I can back away, he reaches out and brushes his thumb over my lower lip.

"You have some pizza sauce here," he says softly. But he doesn't just wipe it away. Oh no, that would be too friend-like. Instead, he tucks his fingers under my chin, lifting my gaze a little higher, tilting my lips toward his. He's leaning into me, and I'd bet all of the tea in China that he's going to kiss me.

Please, God, kiss the fuck out of me.

His warm fingers are burning my skin, his hazel eyes holding on to mine. I couldn't look away if I wanted to. When his lips are mere inches from mine, he pulls in a long, deep breath full of regret, and backs away with the exhale.

"You'd better go," he says softly. I lick my lips and blink rapidly, as if I'm coming out of a trance.

Without a word, I walk past him, but before I can get out of the kitchen, he says, "Callie."

I glance over my shoulder, cocking a brow.

"Thanks for today." He smiles softly. His body is still tight with lust, and I want nothing more than to run back to him and fuck him, right there on the kitchen counter. Even if it is just a one-night stand.

Except, that's *not* what I want. And that's all he'd offer me.

Not good enough.

Instead, I nod once and walk out of the room, scoop up my handbag and beeline it to my car.

I don't take a breath until I'm three blocks away.

"What in the hell just happened?"

CHAPTER SIX

~Declan~

The door closes behind her, and it feels as if all the air in the room went with her. I lean my palms on the counter and drop my head. God, I'm such a fucking idiot. I should have kissed her. I should have boosted her up on the counter, sunk to my knees, and ate her out for about an hour, and then I should have fucked her for the rest of the night.

But what am I doing instead?

I'm missing her.

I sigh deeply as my phone rings in my pocket. I don't want to talk to anybody. I should go in the music room and close up in there for the night. Playing soothes me.

But when I glance at the phone, it's my baby sister Gabby.

"Hey, Gabs."

"Hi Dec. I'm calling to invite you out for dinner on Sunday. We're inviting the whole family. Y'all haven't been out in a while, and Ailish is getting so big, and she misses you."

"She's an infant," I reply, but can't help but smile.

"As long as she's fed and dry, she doesn't miss anyone."

"Not true," she says. "Say you'll come."

"I'll come."

"Good. Now tell me what's wrong."

I shake my head and pace the kitchen. "Nothing's wrong."

"Don't lie to me, Declan Francis."

"You sound like Mom." I chuckle as I rinse a glass out and load it into the dishwasher.

"I'm *a* mom," she reminds me. She's the best fucking mother there is. Her son, Sam, is smart and funny, and has had me wrapped around his little finger since the day he was born nine years ago.

And little Ailish is the sweetest baby ever born. Gabby and Rhys did a good job there.

"Talk to me. Is this about Callie?"

"How do you know about Callie?" I ask and resume pacing the kitchen.

"Beau told me," she says cheerfully. "He says you're deeply in love and that we can expect you to elope any day now."

"Beau is delusional, and we should get him medical help as soon as possible."

Damn brother.

"I figure the truth is somewhere in the middle," she says. She always was a smart girl.

"I like her," I confess softly. "I want her."

"So what's the problem?"

"I'm an idiot."

"Duh." I roll my eyes and try to figure out how much I want to tell her. But before I know it, I've told her everything, from the moment I told Callie I was taking her out to dinner, to the moment she walked out of my house not half an hour ago. Gabby is quiet the whole time, letting me tell the story.

"That's it?" she asks.

"That's it."

"I really think you need to talk to her. Tell her how you're feeling."

"She's decided that we're friends, Gabs. And the thing is, she's an awesome friend. I enjoy her. She's smart, we laugh, we have a good time together."

"But you want more."

I take a deep breath. "I want more. I don't know where it will lead, but I want more." There's a pause on the other end of the line. "Are you sniffling?"

"It's just so great," she says with tears in her voice. "I was beginning to wonder if you'd ever find anyone, and you have."

"I'm not proposing."

"No, but this is the first time I've ever heard you this smitten with anyone."

"Men don't get smitten."

"Yes they do."

"No. They don't."

"Hold on." She doesn't even bother to take the phone away from her mouth when she calls out to Rhys, her husband. "Babe! Declan says men don't get smitten, but they do, right? That's what I thought. Rhys is smitten with me," she informs me.

"Of course he is. He wants to get laid tonight." I laugh, only slightly uncomfortable at the thought of my baby sister having sex.

"My point is, just talk to her. Tell her how you feel. Maybe she feels the same way, but doesn't want to tell you."

"I'm scared," I admit. "If I tell her I want more now, she could pull the rug out from under the whole thing, and then I lose her altogether."

"You could lose her anyway," she says softly. "But you never know if you don't try."

"Thanks, baby girl. I'll see you on Sunday."

"Bring Callie!"

"Too soon. Bye."

I hang up before she can argue further and march into the music room.

I need to play.

***

Here goes nothing.

It's still early in the evening, but it's not a typical busy night, and I'm hoping I'll be able to get Callie alone, even if it's just for a few moments so I can talk to her. I don't want to wait until later tonight to walk her to her car.

I walk in and sigh in relief. It's slow in The Odyssey, with just a few tables occupied, and a couple of guys at the bar. The roof is closed, which tells me it's been mellow all day.

Perfect.

As I walk toward the bar, I see Callie at the far end talking to a tall suit-type who's handing her *flowers.*

"Oh, Pete, you didn't have to do that." She's smiling as she buries her nose in the blooms.

"Well, dinner out just hasn't worked out, so I decided to come to you."

Who the fuck is this?

"We've both been busy," Callie says as she shifts her gaze and finds me standing not far behind Flower Boy. Her eyes widen and her cheeks pinken. I stand firm, cross my arms over my chest, and watch unapologetically.

Mine.

"I know things ended between us a long time ago," the dude continues, "but I've never forgotten you, Cal. Let me take you out, like old times."

Fuck that.

"Callie," I say, my voice calm but firm. "Can I talk

to you for a minute?"

"Adam can get you a drink. We're having a conversation," Pete says, obviously pissed at being interrupted.

I bet he's been practicing his speech for a week.

"Now," I say simply.

"I'll be back," she says to Pete, then walks around the bar and motions for me to follow her. As soon as we're in her office, I close the door and move her against it, caging her in.

"Is he who you want, Callie?" I'm panting, adrenaline taking over. Callie's blue eyes are wide and pinned to mine. She's gripped on to my shirt over my ribs, holding on tightly. "Say he is, and I'll leave right now."

She blinks once, then again.

"That's what I thought." I plunge one hand into her soft hair, fist my hand in it and tilt her head back, and kiss her. Hard. She moans, long and deep, pulling me to her with those hands, and I'm lost in her. Our tongues explore each other, and then I nibble the corner of her mouth and kiss her softly. "I'm tired of trying to keep my hands off of you," I murmur, my lips still against hers. She's hitched one mile-long leg up around my hip, and my cock is hard and pulsing against her. "I know you just want the friend thing, but damn it, Calliope, I don't."

Her eyes widen, and when she would speak, I cut her off. "No, this is my turn to talk. If you want to waste your time with the douche with the flowers, fine, it's none of my business, but I can't watch it. I'm sorry, I can't just hang back and be your *friend* when I want you so badly I can't breathe. Yesterday was the best day and the worst, all at the same time because I had you with me, but I couldn't touch you."

"Declan—"

"I want to talk with you, learn you, lose myself in you. All of those things. And I don't have any experience in that shit, but damn it, I want it with you. Because those little things, Callie? The talking as I walk you to your car, or laughing with you as we demo my house? Eating pizza on the porch? They aren't little things to me. I've never done that with any other woman that I'm not related to by blood. I never wanted to.

"Until you, and it's confused the hell out of me. All I want is a chance to start this over with you. We did it all backwards, and that's on me. I get it. But damn it, let me try it again, because if you don't, it'll be the biggest regret of my life."

Her mouth opens and closes, as though she doesn't know what to say first. But finally she says, "Pete's waiting."

Well.

I guess I know where she stands.

I back away, untangle my hand from her hair and walk away, not looking back, through the bar and out into the dark evening.

I poured my heart out and she chose someone else.

Fuck.

***

The music is loud, but not loud enough to drown out my thoughts. Boy, did I blow it. I'm a grade-A asshole. I had the chance to have something really great with Callie, and I messed up so bad that all she sees when she looks at me is a friend, and she's sweet on the moron with the flowers.

Probably because he's nicer to her than I ever was. Although he looked pretty smarmy to me.

Not my problem.

I sigh and rub my hands over my face. It'll be fine.

It's not like I don't have plenty of women in my life that are more than willing to have a good time.

But I don't have the need to confide in any of them. To listen to them talk about their day, or watch football with them.

No, they're pretty much only around for one reason, and until a sassy blonde walked into my life, that was fine with me.

But now, it just doesn't seem like enough.

The doorbell rings. I scowl and stay where I am, hoping they'll go away. I'm definitely not in the mood for company.

But it rings again, and then again, and I can't stand it anymore. I stomp through the foyer and yank the door open, shocked as fuck to see Callie standing on the other side.

"Hi," she says softly.

"You're working," I reply, hating the cold in my voice.

"I left."

I nod and watch her, not inviting her in. "What do you need?"

She winces and I immediately feel like an asshole. "I don't *need* anything." She shakes her head and frowns and I let my eyes rake up and down her. She's in a ripped Metallica T-shirt and a denim skirt with the same black heels she wore to the football game.

I shouldn't have looked.

"Can I come in?" she asks.

I push the door back and step aside, gesture for her to come in, then lead the way back to the sitting room I'd been crashed in when she arrived.

I turn the music off, bathing the room abruptly in silence.

"I'm sorry," she says.

"For what?"

"Earlier. Can I tell you what you saw?"

"I'm not slow, Callie. I know what I saw."

"Look." She squares her shoulders now and lifts her chin. There's the girl I know. She's determined, and I have a feeling I'm in for quite a show. "I know what you saw, but you don't know how I feel about it."

"How do you feel, Calliope?"

"Bulldozed," she says and paces around the room. "I feel fucking bulldozed."

God, she's magnificent. The way her legs move as she walks, the strength in her arms, the determination on her face.

"Pete is an old boyfriend from high school. Until two weeks ago, I hadn't seen him since I was eighteen. Now he suddenly thinks that we should get back together."

My jaw tightens at the thought, but I don't interrupt.

"He showed me two houses, and that was it. And I'm pretty sure one was involved in the slave trade."

"Excuse me?" My voice is deceptively calm.

"He sells real estate," she says, waving that aside as if it doesn't matter. "He asked me out twice, and I didn't go. And I don't even know why I feel like I need to defend myself or explain myself to you, but damn it, I do. So I am."

She turns to me now, her blue eyes on fire, and she's never looked sexier.

"He shows up tonight and hands me flowers, and before I could say *anything* to him, there you were, in all your sexiness, and I was just... thrown."

"What happened after I left?"

She bites her lip and looks down at her hands, but I catch her chin in my fingers and tilt her head up to look at me. "What happened, Callie?"

"I gave him back his flowers and said thank you,

but I'm not interested in dating him."

"Why?" I'm whispering now as hope surges through me. Her eyes drop to my mouth. "Why, baby?"

"Because the little things aren't little to me, either. And I didn't know—"

"Don't stop now." I smile and cup her cheek in my hand, while the other brushes through her soft hair.

"I didn't know that the little things were so big until you."

I take a deep breath, so fucking relieved. I tip my forehead down to hers and close my eyes, reveling in the feel of her against me.

"I don't know where this is going—" My voice is a hoarse whisper. "—but I want to find out."

"Me too."

My hands glide down her back to her ass, and I grip the globes and lift her easily. "Wrap your legs around me."

I head for the stairs, moving fast, making her giggle. "What was wrong with the parlor?"

"Nothing, and I'll have you there eventually, but once we get started, we're not going to stop for quite some time and I want you to be comfortable." With my eyes locked on hers, I push inside my bedroom. But instead of taking her to the bed, I brace her up against the back of the closed door and hike her skirt up over her hips.

"It's so convenient that I don't wear underwear," she pants as her hands gather my shirt and urge it over my head.

"Thank you," I say with a smile and I just can't stand it anymore. It's as though my lips haven't touched hers in years as I take her mouth with mine, kissing, licking, biting. My cock is ready to burst through my jeans, but I don't want to move from this spot. She's grinding against me, with her legs locked around me like a vice, her hands are in my hair, gripping at my shoulders, scratching down my back, as if she doesn't know where she should touch first, and I love every bit of it.

"In me," she says, her voice heavy with urgency.

"I'll get there."

"Declan." She frowns, but I smile and nibble my way down her neck.

"Yes, sugar, that's my name, and I'm the one in control here. I'm going to fuck you blind, but I'm going to do it in my own way on my own timeline." I bite her collarbone, and then growl in frustration because she still has too many clothes on, so I spin and carry her to the bed and strip her down as she manages to help me out of my jeans and makes my eyes cross as she jacks my cock.

"Put your hands on the headboard." She's on her back now in the middle of the bed, and if she keeps touching me, this will be over way too fast.

"I want to touch you."

I cock a brow. "I didn't ask."

She cocks a brow right back at me, which makes me want to bark out a laugh, but I keep my face sober, watching her until she complies, holding on to the headboard.

"Keep them there."

"Yes, sir," she says primly.

"I'll spank you for that," I mutter and let the smile show when she replies with "I hope so."

I take a minute to just take her all in. She's spread before me like a feast, and I'm going to fucking devour every inch of her.

I start with kissing down her chest and over to each nipple, making them hard and wet, then blow on them. Callie squirms under me and sighs in delight.

"So responsive," I whisper before placing wet kisses down her belly, gently tugging on the navel piercing with my teeth. I spread her legs wide and grin in satisfaction at the sight of her perfect, glistening pussy. "You're already wet."

"Are you sure?" she asks. "Maybe you should double check."

"I *am* a thorough man," I reply and settle in to taste her. I lick her from anus to clit, and back down again. Her hips buck and she grabs my hair in her fist. I back away and glare up at her. "I said keep your hands above your head."

"Right, like I can do that when you're doing *that*."

"You can do it." I wait until she complies and then I dive back in. I pull her lips into my mouth and fuck her with my tongue, then lick my way up to her clit and sink two fingers inside her.

"Fucking hell!" she cries out, thrashing on the bed. Her body is flushed and tight, her belly moving up and down as she chases her release.

Suddenly, I flip her over and slap her ass, and with her up in the air, I bury my face in her again, licking, biting, sucking, until I feel the muscles inside her convulse around my fingers. She cries out, the words incoherent, and rides the wave as far as it'll take her, until she collapses, ass in the air, panting and purring in my sheets.

As she calms, I reach for protection and drag my fingertips up and down her legs, and then just to stir her up again, I lick her from clit to anus and rise up on my knees, guide myself inside her and cover her with my body, bracing myself on the headboard above her, pounding her in earnest.

"Holy shit," I growl when she tightens around me. "That's right, baby, come for me again."

Her back bows, her hands fist in the sheets, and

she comes so fucking hard she almost pushes me out. I plant my hand on the small of her back and push against her, letting her milk my cock with her strong muscles, and I'm completely lost to her.

I come hard, shivering, sweating, my mouth pressed to her shoulder. As I breathe through the orgasm and come back to my senses, I wrap my arms around her and lay us on our sides, tangled up in each other.

Mine.

CHAPTER SEVEN

~Callie~

Mine.

He said it last night, whispered it actually, as he wrapped himself around me and settled us both in to catch our breath. I'm not sure if he intended to say it out loud.

Not that it matters.

Except, I'm not sure how I feel about it. And frankly, after a night of some of the best sex I've had in... *ever*, I guess it means I'm okay with it.

Because I definitely feel pretty possessive when it comes to him too.

But now it's the morning after, and historically speaking, we're not good at this part. Is it going to be awkward? Is he not going to call for a week again, and then act affronted when I'm mad?

Ugh, this part sucks.

He's not wrapped around me anymore. Thankfully, he's the same as me in that the snuggles are nice for about three minutes, and then it's time to roll away and sleep in a position that isn't as hot as the devil's house. But the sweet thing is, even in sleep, he keeps tabs on me. His hand on my arm, his foot on my calf. He's always touching me in some way.

And I like it. It makes me feel safe. I don't remember the last time someone else made me feel safe. Even my own father loved me, but I didn't ever dare let my guard down with him.

With Declan, I sleep like a baby. Of course, that could simply be exhaustion.

The man knows his way around the bedroom. And the bathroom and the stairs, if memory serves correctly.

I grin and stretch, look over my shoulder at the man himself, then slip from the bed and hunt up my clothes, scattered about the room. The sun is up, but just barely, bathing Declan's bedroom in that early morning glow.

I pull my bra on, and am just slipping my shirt over my head when I hear, "Where are you going?"

"Home." I grin at him as push my hands through my hair, shaking it out. "Sorry I woke you."

"I'm not," he replies and sits up. His hazel eyes, heavy with sleep, narrow on me as I wince. "What's wrong?"

I'm sore from you fucking the living hell out of me all night long. Not that I can tell him that. "Just stepped wrong," I reply, hearing the lameness with my own ears.

"Thanks for—"

"Maybe you should—"

We both speak at the same time, then smile. "You go," I say.

"Stay," he simply says and slowly crawls out of bed, gloriously naked, and walks to me. I can't stop my eyes from roaming up and down his lean, tall body. His tanned skin is smooth over lean muscles, his arms tattooed.

"I can go home," I murmur, but Declan reaches

for me and pulls me against him. His hand slides from my neck to my ass, where he grips onto me firmly.

"I've never asked anyone to stay before," he whispers, then kisses my forehead. "I'm asking you, Calliope, to spend the day with me."

"I really should—"

"Let me put it this way," he interrupts and kisses, then bites my lower lip. A moan escapes my lips, damn him. "I'm telling you to stay."

"You're bossy," I whisper.

He simply grins and waits for me to reply, pulling my shirt over my head.

"Since you're undressing me again, I guess I'll stay."

"Good." He kisses me hard and deep, and I'm suddenly naked again and being led to the bathroom. "You have a shower, I'll bring up breakfast."

"Breakfast in bed?" I ask with a laugh.

"The best way to eat breakfast," he confirms, kisses my nose and then he's gone and I'm left standing, naked as the day I was born, in the middle of his old bathroom. I turn a circle, taking in the vintage—another word for old—fixtures and tile. This space was probably last renovated in the fifties. I can picture it in my head, the way it should be, with updated double sinks and countertops, subway tile in the shower.

Let's face it, I'm itching to get my hands on Declan's house. And it has nothing to do with the man himself, and everything to do with the magnificence of this space.

Okay, it has a *little* to do with Declan.

My shower is quick. I don't have to wash my hair, thank God, because that's a project. I examine my skin, and grin when I see fingerprint bruises on my thighs, where he held my legs up so he could feast on me for what felt like an hour.

The man has mad oral skills.

Then again, so do I, and he hasn't given me much of an opportunity to show those off yet. That's going on today's agenda.

I smile as I finish drying off, hang the towel, and walk out of the bathroom to find Declan sitting on the bed, a tray before him, and the remote to the television in his hand.

"You look all soft and pink and... *happy*," he says, tilting his head to the side as he takes me in.

"I'm all of those things," I reply and climb on the bed to sit next to him, my back against the headboard. "What's for breakfast?"

"Cereal," he says proudly, gesturing to the Fruity Pebbles and a carafe of milk on the tray. "And coffee."

"Yum." Is it possible that we both love kids' cereal for breakfast? Because if so, I'm marrying him right now.

If I planned to get married, that is. Which I don't.

"Are you just humoring me?" he asks as he engages Netflix on the TV.

"Nope, I love this stuff." I pour myself a heaping bowl and settle back to munch. "Is this your favorite?"

"One of them." He takes a bite and flips through movies. "My very favorite is Cap'n Crunch."

"That stuff will tear the roof of your mouth up."

"And yet it's so delicious, we eat it anyway."

I nod. "Oh! That one!"

"It's a chick flick," he says, moaning in agony. "Are you going to make me watch it? What about Pulp Fiction?"

"Never seen it," I reply. "I want the romance."

He blinks, sizing me up. "If you watch Pulp Fiction, I'll watch your girlie movie."

"Deal. Mine first." I pour more cereal and settle in

next to Declan as the opening credits begin. "This is nice."

"Cereal and Netflix?"

"Yeah."

He smiles and nods, kisses my forehead and opens his mouth, waiting for a bite of mine. I spoon some into his mouth. "Yours is better than mine."

"It's the same as yours."

"Better," he says with a shake of his head.

***

"Are you sure about this?" I ask him the next afternoon as we drive out of the city toward the Bayou. Declan decided this morning that I was going with him to have dinner with the family. I've discovered that once Declan gets his mind set on something, talking him out of it is futile.

I admit, I'm curious to meet his family. I mean, it's not really that big of a deal. There will probably be a few other people there, and I can hold a conversation with just about anyone.

"I'm sure," he replies lazily and lifts my hand to his lips. "They're not scary."

"I'm not scared," I reply. *Much.* "It's just a bit early to introduce me to your family, don't you think?"

He slides his gaze over to mine, cocks a brow, then returns his attention to traffic. "What do *you* think?"

"I guess you wouldn't have invited me if you didn't think it was a good idea."

"Exactly. You know me well enough by now to know that I rarely do anything I don't want to," he says and kisses my hand again. "Have you been out here before?"

"No." I shake my head and gaze out at the trees, the swamps. "It's so different out here."

"You grew up here and never took a trip out to

the Bayou?"

"That's right." I wrinkle my nose. "Are there 'gators out there?"

"Most likely," he says. "I promise not to toss you in with the 'gators."

"Gee, thanks."

We settle into a comfortable silence, listening to satellite radio. We sing along to songs we know, and Declan shares stories about some of the musicians he's met.

"So you used to do studio work in Memphis?"

"Yes, ma'am." He nods. "Still do, sometimes."

"That's awesome, Declan."

"I prefer to perform live." He turns off the main road and points to his left. "There's the inn."

"Wow." I've never seen anything like it. It looks like something out of a fairy tale. Huge oak trees form a line with a brick path between them toward a large, two-story mansion with a deep front porch and a welcoming red door. "You grew up here?"

"In the summers," he confirms. "We stayed in the city during the school year. My youngest sister, Gabby, made it into an inn about four years ago."

"It's beautiful," I murmur as he pulls in to the driveway leading to the house. There are other buildings on the property, and from what I can see, gardens bursting with a riot of color. But it's the trees that have me transfixed. "These trees have to be hundreds of years old." To say they're massive is an understatement. They more than dwarf the house, and several of the long limbs are so heavy they rest on the ground.

"That they are," he replies with a smile, parks next to a row of cars that I assume are guests of the inn, and turns me to face him. "If at any time you're uncomfortable, or if you just want to leave, you say so and we'll go."

"Declan, it's a couple of people who happen to be related to you. I'll be fine."

He frowns. "It might be more than a couple of people."

"Let me guess, all of these cars don't belong to people staying at the inn?"

He shakes his head. "Gabby doesn't have guests on Sundays. You'll be great. You're used to dealing with strangers."

Yeah, but I'm not fucking the strangers' relative.

But rather than say anything, I smile and push out of Dec's car. He takes my hand when he joins me and leads me around to the back of the house. "Kitchen's back here," he says with a smile.

The smells coming from the house are amazing. "Do they hire someone to cook?"

"Hell no. Mama and Gabby do the bulk of it, but the rest of us pitch in too."

I didn't know real family dinners like this existed. I thought it was made up by Hollywood and romance novelists.

I take a deep breath as Declan reaches for the door, and then suddenly I'm led into a large, beautiful kitchen that is near to bursting with people and a dog that is currently leaping, trying to get the piece of meat that a little boy is holding high for him.

"Samuel Beauregard, take Derek outside, or you're grounded from the computer for a week!" a petite brunette yells.

"That's Gabby," Declan says. We still haven't been spotted by the crowd of people. "She's Sam's mom. Her husband, Rhys, is the guy holding their daughter, Ailish."

My gaze moves from the beautiful woman to her husband sitting at the breakfast bar with an adorable baby.

"You're here!" Sam exclaims and hugs Declan around his waist. "And you brought a lady!"

The room hushes as everyone looks over at us. Declan ruffles Sam's hair.

"I can't get anything past you," he says, then takes my hand and squeezes reassuringly. "I hope it's okay that I brought a plus-one."

"Of course it is," Gabby says and smiles as she wipes her hands on a towel and walks over to us. "Welcome. I'm Gabby."

"Callie," I reply and shake her hand, certain I've met her before.

"I'll introduce you to everyone," Gabby says as she slips her arm through mine and skillfully guides me away from Declan. "This is our mama."

"Pleasure," I say and smile at the lovely woman with eyes the same as all of her children.

"Oh no, child, the pleasure is all mine."

"This is my oldest brother, Beau." Beau is sitting next to Rhys, his eyes assessing but friendly. "And my husband, Rhys, is next to him, with our little one."

"She's precious," I reply and grin when Ailish leans over for me to take her, which I readily do. "Aren't you, princess?"

"She likes you."

"I like her too."

"The guy with his nose buried in the redhead's hair is my brother Eli, and that's his girlfriend, Kate. Charly's chopping the collard greens."

"I'd come shake your hand, but I'm a mess," Charly says with a smile. "But it's nice to meet you."

"And this is Savannah, Declan's twin sister."

My eyes immediately find Declan's. "Twin? That's great. Nice to meet you, Savannah."

"Call me Van," she says and shakes my hand. The

Boudreaux are a beautiful bunch of people, and they're obviously surprised that Declan brought me.

"So am I the first?" I ask the room at large.

"First?" Van asks.

"The first girl that Declan has brought to family dinner."

Beau laughs while the others simply smile. "You know him pretty well already," Beau says.

"It was just a hunch." I kiss the baby's cheek and take a deep breath, enjoying her baby smell. "And you're the most precious thing in the world."

She grabs my cheek and giggles.

"How old is she?" I ask.

"About five months," Gabby replies and takes her daughter from my arms. "And thanks. We think she's pretty great."

"My shoes!" Charly exclaims, pointing at my feet.

"Excuse me?" I glance down at my favorite red heels.

"You're wearing my shoes!"

"I knew I recognized you!" Gabby adds with a smile. "Charly owns Head Over Heels in the Quarter."

"The fabulous shoe store!" I nod enthusiastically. "I love that place."

"I sold you those shoes," Gabby says.

"Since when do you sell shoes?" Rhys asks with a frown.

"It was a long time ago," she replies, waving him off. "And they still look amazing on you."

"They're my favorite."

"I have all the new fall shoes in," Charly says as she finishes chopping the greens. "The girls are going to come by after closing next week. You should come too."

"Oh, I couldn't—"

"Yes. You could," Van says with a wink. All of the

Boudreaux are bossy. But I grin and nod.

"You're right. I could." I glance at Declan, to make sure this doesn't make him uncomfortable, but he just smiles and kisses my forehead as he passes by and hugs his mama.

"How can I help, Mama?"

"You always ask when it's all done," she says and shoos him away. "You've done that since you were a boy."

"I have to warn you," Beau says. "Declan's not a great cook."

I simply nod and smile as I remember having cereal in bed just yesterday morning. "I'll take that under advisement."

"Hey, stop trying to scare her off," Declan says and slips his arm around my shoulders.

"It'll take more than bad cooking to do that," I immediately reply.

"He's also not good at laundry," Eli adds.

"That did it." I move to walk out the door while everyone else laughs, but Declan catches my arm and twirls me back to him, plants his lips on mine, and right here in front of his mother, lays a kiss on me that makes my toes curl. "Okay." I swallow. "I guess that makes up for the laundry."

***

"That was fun," I say as we pull away from the inn into the dark Bayou. It was surprisingly easy. As rich and intimidating as the Boudreaux family can be, I found them to be welcoming and funny.

"They liked you," Declan says.

"It was mutual. Thanks for taking me."

He kisses my hand and rests our hands on his thigh. "That place," he says and points to a colorful plantation house, "is Laura. Another plantation here in the Bayou, it was one of the first built."

"Are you giving me a tour? In the dark?"

"It's not my fault that you women can talk for hours on end about shoes," he says defensively.

"If I'd known I was going to get a tour, I would have cut it short," I reply.

"Well, this will give you a start." He points out different homes and tells me stories about the families that originally homesteaded them.

"You know, if you ever lose your night job, this might fit you perfectly," I say when he pauses. "You know your history."

"A lot of this could be bullshit," he admits. "I'm just telling you what I've heard."

"Isn't that what most tales are?"

He's headed back to the freeway now and I turn the music up, singing along with an old Goo Goo Dolls song. "I met Johnny Resznik once," I inform him.

"Really? Do tell."

"It was at a Goo Goo Dolls concert. I got VIP tickets and got to pose for a photo with him." I giggle and shake my head. "So, I didn't really *meet* him, but I did get to touch him."

"He's a nice guy."

I turn in my seat and stare at Declan. "You *know* him?"

"I've just met him a couple of times when they recorded in Memphis."

I sit back in my seat and stare straight ahead. "You know Johnny Resznik."

"I've met him," he corrects me.

"That makes up for the lack of cooking skills."

Declan lets out a loud, surprised laugh. "I'm glad."

"Besides, I like your cereal breakfasts."

He sends me a naughty grin. "How about dessert?"

"We had dessert at your sister's house."

"I could go for second dessert."

I wrinkle my nose. "That's a thing?"

"Oh yes. It's a thing." Just as we enter the city, he pulls off the freeway and turns into the parking lot of a divey little diner. "And this place has the best peach cobbler in Louisiana. Wait here."

He jogs inside, places his order to go, joins me again and then lays the warm box in my lap.

"It's hot."

"Yes, ma'am. And there's a pint of vanilla ice cream in there too."

We're not far from his house, and he pulls into the driveway and escorts me to his door.

"I guess you're not dropping me off at home."

He turns the key in the lock and grins knowingly. "You're a good guesser. Let's go this way," he says when I would head back toward the kitchen. "I haven't had a chance to show it to you yet. I just finished it the other day."

He opens a door, and my jaw immediately drops. "Oh, Declan."

CHAPTER EIGHT

~Declan~

Her eyes are wide with wonder as she wanders around the music room, the dessert, and me, long forgotten. I hang back and gaze about the space with her, proud of the finished product. The walls are painted a soft grey with one wall lined with old grey barn wood. Antique brass instruments are hung on the walls, and the instruments I play are on stands, placed throughout the room.

But her eyes are glued to the piano in the corner, where wide windows look out over the back yard.

"You have a baby grand," she breathes and gently runs her fingertips over the top of it.

Every move, every sound she makes is pure sex. I want to boost her up and take her right here, on this piano, but I have to reign myself in.

"Can I play it?" she asks without looking back at me.

"Of course." I sit in a chair, giving her space, surprised that she plays. Not that I should be surprised; I never asked her. She opens the keys, settles her bottom on the bench the way she's comfortable, and then begins to play a song that I played at the bar a few nights ago.

Funny, I was thinking of her when I played it. But that was on the guitar. The piano makes it softer, more romantic. She's humming as she's playing.

Jesus, I've never seen anything sexier than Callie in this very moment. I'd wondered how I would feel about having her around my family. Would it be awkward? Uncomfortable? I'd never taken anyone to family dinner before, but it was none of those things.

Callie was gracious and friendly, despite being nervous, which she'll deny, but her sweaty palms didn't lie. She charmed my family almost as quickly as she charmed me.

Even Ailish went right to her, and if seeing Callie holding a baby wasn't a kick to the balls, I don't know what is. How can I barely know this woman, and already be thinking of something... *permanent?*

I don't do permanent.

While she plays, I pull the cobbler out of the bag, open it and the ice cream, and help myself. Good music and good food. I could live on this alone for about a week.

Suddenly, she stops and turns around.

"Hey! Don't eat it all!"

"Don't stop now, sweetheart. I'm getting food and a show. I'm never on this end of it." I grin and take another bite, but she gets up and joins me, kneeling between my legs. "Oh, you want me to share?"

Her lips purse as she tries not to smile. "Yes."

"Okay." I scoop up a tiny piece of cobbler and hold it up for her. "This is all you get."

She sticks that suckable lower lip out in a pout. "But I played you a pretty song."

"Okay." I add just a tiny bit more. "There you go."

She eats it off the spoon, then takes the utensil

from me, loads it up with a huge bite of cobbler and ice cream and holds it up for me to eat.

"Delicious."

"See? I was generous."

I nod and return the favor, then lean in and lick a drop of ice cream off the outside of her lips, making her purr in that sexy as hell way she does that makes my cock come to full attention.

Next thing I know, she's taken the whole damn thing and is running out of the room and toward the stairs.

"Mine!" she shouts and squeals when she hears my footsteps behind her. I could easily catch her, but I let her run, enjoying the way her ass moves up the stairs. She runs into the bedroom, to the bathroom, and shuts and locks the door.

"Does this mean you're not sharing?" I ask calmly, enjoying the fuck out of her.

"Not sharing," she confirms, panting. "Mmm, it's so good."

"Callie?"

"I'm sorry, Callie's not here."

I chuckle, pull my pocket knife out and get to work on the lock. It's easy to pick. Her eyes widen when I open the door. Her mouth is stuffed full of cobbler.

"I think you should share."

"I mox daf," she says around the food.

"I know you locked it," I reply, advancing on her. "I unlocked it."

"Rude."

"Yes, you are." She smirks and is about to put the last bite in her mouth, but I catch her wrist in my fist and quickly take the bite instead. "You're also a dessert hog."

"It's your fault for only getting one."

She wipes her mouth on a towel, stands, and smooths her hands down her shirt and jeans. "I'll be going home now."

I simply grin at her prim declaration. "No. You won't."

"No?"

I shake my head.

"What am I going to do then?"

I take her hand, the grin still firmly on my face, toss her over my shoulder, and slap her ass with a loud *whack*.

"Hey!"

"Did that hurt?" I ask, carrying her down the stairs.

"No. Where are we going?"

"You'll see."

"You're not taking me to bed?" I love that her voice sounds disappointed. I want her to crave me. To *need* me. Because I sure as fuck need to be inside her any chance I can get.

"Not yet."

"Declan!" The frustration in her voice makes me laugh, and then she's laughing with me. "You're such an ass."

"Yep." I stop out on the back porch and set her down, then turn her to face the yard. "I wanted to show you this too."

"Wow." The yard isn't huge, but the privacy fence keeps it quiet and free of prying eyes. "When did you do this?"

"I had it done last week while I was working on the music room. I'm not a landscaper, so I hired it out."

She nods, steps off the porch and walks into the yard. She's barefoot, and doesn't even think twice about stepping into the grass. "I love the pond back here."

"I'm going to stock it with koi," I reply, walking a few steps behind her, my hands in my pockets. Why am I so nervous about this? Why do I so desperately want her approval? It's not like I'm doing this for her. It's for me, and, at some point, it might turn a nice profit.

Regardless of the reasons, I do want her to like it.

"It's really beautiful, Declan. The crew you hired did a great job." To my utter surprise, she sits down, right on the bare grass. "Sit with me."

"Whatever the lady wants," I reply and sit next to her, leaning back on my hands. We're both looking up at the sky. "Even with the light noise of the city, you can see the Big Dipper."

"I bet the stars are amazing out at the inn," she murmurs. I glance over at her and take in the angle of her jaw, the curve of her neck as she continues to look up. Her shoulders are hunched up from leaning back on her arms. "I've never experienced a family like yours, Declan."

Her voice is suddenly soft, and not a little sad. I want to wrap her up in my arms, but I also don't want her to stop talking. "Most families aren't like mine," I murmur, eyes trained on the skies above.

"I didn't think they really existed," she says and I feel her turn her blue eyes to me. "I don't know what it's like to have that many people love me. And I don't say that to sound pathetic, it's just an anomaly to me."

"I get it." I shrug and pull my knees up, rest my elbows on them. "Having a big family is both a blessing and a curse."

"How so?"

"There's always someone else to blame when Mama gets mad," I say with a grin and tug on a piece of her soft blonde hair. "The bad thing is, you can't get away with *anything*. People are always telling on you."

"When you were kids?"

I smirk and shake my head. "All the time. They're all a bunch of pests."

"And you love them."

"Every last one," I agree and sigh. "I'm sorry that you didn't have the comfort of a loving family, Callie."

"My dad loved me," she says, carefully choosing her words. "And Mom did too, but when she passed away, Dad just couldn't deal with it."

"So you became the parent," I say softly, and she simply nods. "You have Adam."

"I do, and he couldn't be more of a brother to me if we shared blood. I'm loved, Declan, I've just never seen the Waltons up close and in person."

I laugh at the comparison and decide she isn't far off.

"I didn't know you were a twin," she says.

"We are three minutes apart," I reply, thinking of Van. "She's older."

"And you're close."

"We are," I reply, nodding. "We were even roommates in college, along with Kate."

"Eli's Kate?" she asks, surprised.

"She was our Kate first," I say and play with a strand of her hair. "She's one of my closest friends."

She's staring at the sky again. The pulse in her throat is steady and delicate, and I can't help but trace my finger over it softly, just to feel her skin.

"You're beautiful."

She rolls her head over to look at me with soft blue eyes. "You're not too shabby yourself."

"I want to fuck you, right here, under the stars, but I don't have any condoms on me."

She frowns. "I have the birth control covered," she replies, still looking me in the eye.

"Do we trust each other?" I ask. I've never, *ever*, had sex without a condom, and the thought of doing this with Callie… well, it would knock me off my feet if I were standing up.

She nods, a smile teasing her mouth.

"So, can I fuck you, here under the stars?"

"I thought you'd never ask."

***

She's still sleeping. She's warm and sweet, and snores like a lumberjack.

Bless her heart.

The sheets have slipped down to her waist, leaving me with a gorgeous view of her chest. Her breasts aren't large, but they're firm, and the nipples are small and pink. I brush my thumb over the tip and watch in fascination as it tightens.

Callie's legs shift, she rubs her nose and opens one ocean blue eye. "'Mornin," she mumbles.

"Good morning, beautiful."

"Did I snore?" she asks right away.

"Not bad," I lie easily. "And even if you did, it just means that you slept well, and that's good."

She frowns, her eyes still closed, and rolls toward me. "Need a shower," she murmurs.

"Let me hold you for a minute first," I whisper and wrap my arms around her, hugging her close. Her legs scissor between mine as she holds on, her nose buried in my chest. "You feel good."

"Mmm," she purrs. God, that purr of hers almost undoes me. "You're warm."

"Are you cold?"

"No, you're just warm."

I grin and plant my lips on her head, breathing her in. This not-so-little moment is one that I was talking to her about before. This is when I feel the most settled, where my spirit is calm, and the chaos of life is outside.

It's the closest thing to bliss I've ever experienced. It's even better than performing, and I didn't know that was possible.

"Hungry," she says against my skin.

"Get in the shower," I say, pulling back. "You're covered in grass stains."

A slow, satisfied smile spreads over her gorgeous face, and I'm tempted to roll on top of her and take her again.

Jesus, I can't get enough of her.

"I didn't mind getting the stains," she says, then rolls away and gives me a prime view of her naked ass as she saunters into the bathroom. "Find me food!"

"Yes, ma'am," I reply and pull on a pair of basketball shorts before padding downstairs to the kitchen. I really am a shitty cook, so it looks like we'll be eating cold cereal again, which she doesn't seem to mind, but it still feels lame. I should be able to provide a heartier breakfast than this.

As I move about the kitchen, the melody of the Adele song that Callie played on my piano last night is stuck in my head, so I decide to go play it. It's a beautiful ballad about being in love, and making the one you love feel it. It makes me think of Callie every time I play it.

The music room is washed in rich, gold sunlight this morning. I love this room. I sit on the bench and begin to play, and when the song is over, I start at the beginning and play it all over again.

The music washes over me, and I'm awash in Callie. Her smile, her laugh, her scent. Her skin.

God, her tattoos are beautiful. I want to know what they all mean, why she chose them, and why are they only on her left arm?

I hear a noise behind me, and without pausing, I

turn to see her standing in the doorway, wearing one of my button-down shirts in blue. Her eyes are happy. Shining. Full of lust and mischief.

She slowly walks across the room to me, and as I'm playing the bridge of the song, she stands on the bench at my hip, balances on my shoulders, and turns to face me, then plants her perfect ass on the piano above the keys, her bare pussy spread before me at eye-level.

Holy fuck.

I love that she knows exactly what she wants and isn't afraid to ask for it. Or demand it.

I take my hands off the keys, but she slowly shakes her head no, a half-smile on her perfect pink lips, so I continue to play, starting the song over again at the beginning. She spreads her thighs wide, and drags a perfectly manicured forefinger from her wet opening to her clit and down again, then licks that finger clean.

Jesus, I'm rock hard and yearning for her, but she's in control here. As my fingers move over the keys, she grips my hair in her fingers and guides me forward to her pussy, and I need no other invitation. I lick her, tracing the path of her finger a moment ago, then I suck on her clit, in tight, rapid pulses. Her fist tightens on my hair, and then it's gone, and she's leaning back on the piano, on her elbows, so she can still watch me.

She tastes so fucking good. Musky and sweet at the same time. I lick down to her lips, suck them in my mouth and fuck her with my tongue, lapping at her. Her head is thrashing and she's mewling, her noises moving through my body and straight to my pulsing cock.

My fingers fumble on the keys. *Fuck it.* My hands grip her thighs and spread her wider as I push my face more firmly against her. She's going to come. My hands scoop up her ass, pulling her against my lips, and she jerks violently, her heels making the piano shout loudly as she plants them on the keys and pulses against my mouth.

Finally, she melts back into the top of the piano, panting, moaning, shaking.

I pull back and watch my fingers gently pet her swollen pussy. She raises her head to look down at me, and seeing that look in her eyes sends me over the edge.

I stand abruptly, sending the bench over on its side, and I don't care. I need to be inside her.

Now.

"Fuck me, that was hot," I growl.

CHAPTER NINE

~Callie~

Hell yes, it was hot. Declan's given me some pretty amazing orgasms, but I don't think I've ever come like that.

I want to curl up in a satisfied ball and sleep like a kitten.

Instead, Declan grips my hips and pulls me off the piano, tugs me around to the side and bends me over it, so the very tips of my toes barely reach the floor.

I've never felt so small in all of my life. Because I'm *not* small. But Declan moves me around like I am, and I freaking love it.

"Do you have any idea," he growls against my ear as he pushes inside me, and grips my throat with his other hand, tipping my head back. "Any idea how fucking amazing you are? Jesus, I can't see straight."

He's keeping me pulled back against his chest, not choking me, just making sure I stay right where he wants me, his mouth is pressed to my ear, and he's fucking me harder than he ever has before.

"Never stop wanting you," he mutters, then groans when I tighten my pussy around him. He wraps my left leg back around his hip and finds my clit with his fingers, and proceeds to play it like he did when I was splayed before him, and that's it. I can't hold back.

"Ohmygod," I cry as I tighten further and, unable to control any muscle in my body, I come around him.

"Oh fuck," he growls and comes with me, pushing harder and deeper, until it just almost hurts, in the very best way.

He releases his hold on me and I collapse against the piano, gasping for air, drained of all energy. He's gripping my hips, still buried to the hilt. Finally, he places kisses on my spine as he pulls out, then leads me out of the room.

"Where are we going?"

"We both need a shower."

"I just took one." He grins back at me, completely proud of himself.

"You need another one."

***

"You're sure you're okay with this?" I ask for the fourth time in fifteen minutes and hate the uncertainty in my voice. Declan just smiles and kisses my forehead before I lower myself into my car.

"You'll have a good time. My sisters are fun. Plus, there are shoes involved, and for some reason, that makes women bond."

"Kind of like football for guys," I agree with a nod. "Okay, I'm gonna go, but just for a little while, so I don't seem rude."

"You have no reason to be nervous," he says reasonably as he leans on my door.

"I'm not nervous," I lie and square my shoulders. "It's just shoes."

"Exactly." He leans through the open window and kisses me in that way he does that makes my toes curl, then pulls away and waves as I drive away.

I'm still not sure that this is a good idea. I've only officially met his sisters and Kate once, and intruding on their shopping time feels... *odd*.

But then again, there will be shoes, so who am I to say no?

I find a parking space quickly and knock on the locked door of *Head Over Heels*. Charly has pulled curtains over the windows to block the view of us drooling and making asses of ourselves over shoes, I'm sure.

"Hey!" Charly says as she opens the door. "You came! I'm so glad. Come on in, we have wine and food and shoes."

"You just said my three favorite words," I say as I follow her inside. "Hi, everyone."

"Welcome! White or red?" Kate asks as she holds up two bottles.

"Red, please."

"You got it."

"It's good to see you again," Gabby says and pulls me in for a hug. For such a little woman, she sure is strong. Savannah waves with a big smile on her pretty face and then points down to her foot.

"What do you think of these wedges?"

"Hmm." I study them as I take my first sip of wine. "Too clunky for your foot."

"Told you," Kate says smugly and clinks her glass to mine. "Van, you should stick with the classic heels. Your feet were made for them."

"Maybe I don't want to be *classic*," she says with a frown. "Maybe I want to be daring and unusual."

"Those wedges don't say daring or unusual," Charly says, but pulls a red box out of a stack. "But these might work."

Van takes the box and smiles widely when she pulls out a pair of black peep-toe heels with little white skull and crossbones all over them.

"These are adorable!"

"The style fits you much better," Gabby agrees and we all sigh when she steps into them and walks around the room.

"Those are sexy," I say and sip my wine.

"Good. I'm going for sexy," Van says with a firm nod. "Put these in my pile."

"You got it," Charly says and sets them aside. "Callie, what are you looking for tonight?"

"Nothing specific," I reply. "I'm gonna poke through and I'll know it when I see it."

"Good plan," Kate says with a nod and sips her white wine. "I'm looking for something sexy to wear in bed."

"You wear shoes to bed?" Van asks in surprise. "Why?"

"Because they're sexy," Gabby says. "I never had before Rhys, but let me tell you, he's very thankful when I do."

"I don't have anyone to wear sexy shoes for," Charly says with a sigh.

"What happened to Harrison?" Kate asks, her nose wrinkled as if she smelled something bad.

"Not dating him again," Charly replies dryly. "I mean, he didn't even tap a toe when we heard Dec play."

"He was pretty uptight," Kate says with a nod. "Not really your type."

"What *is* your type?" I ask and pull a pair of pink patent leather sling backs out of a box and almost die at how pretty they are. "Oh God, these are hot."

"Put them on!" Gabby exclaims.

"My type doesn't seem to exist," Charly replies, eyeing the pink shoes on my feet. "Those, however, are *your* type."

"Oh yeah," I breathe and walk around the store in them, already in love. "These babies are going home with me. Now, back to you."

"Charly likes the assholes," Gabby informs me unabashedly.

"I do not," Charly disagrees with a frown. "I just seem to *find* the assholes."

"Tell me about this Harrison guy," I urge her. "What's wrong with him?"

"He wore khakis and a tie to your bar to watch Dec play," she begins and I automatically don't like him.

"Maybe he thought it would be a fancier place," Van says reasonably, but Charly shakes her head no. "That's just what he always wears."

"Always?" Kate asks and frowns when Charly nods yes. "I didn't like that he wasn't very gentlemanly. I mean, it was a first date, and he didn't hold one door for you or offer to pay for dinner or your drinks."

"I was mortified that Eli paid for everything," Charly says with a sigh.

"He didn't care about that," Kate says and pulls out a pair of royal blue heels, then passes them to me. "These would look great on you. He just didn't like Harrison."

"Well, then it's unanimous, no one likes him," Van says and zips up a super hot pair of black leather knee-high boots. "We do, however, like these."

"Indeed," Charly says, admiring the boots. "I'll sell out of those real quick."

I drain my glass and walk to the counter to pour more. "Does anyone else want more wine?"

"Me!" Gabby says with a giggle and joins me. "This wine is pretty strong."

"I hope you're not driving home," I reply with a smile.

"Nah, she's staying with me tonight," Van says and holds her glass out for more too. "We'll call Uber."

"Or Eli," Gabby adds. "He can take us home when he takes Kate."

"Yeah, that," Van says and takes a sip of wine, then waves a hand. "Oh! I forgot! I brought food." She runs into the back room, then comes back with a bag of chips and three containers full of different dips. "This will soak up some of the alcohol."

"Good idea! I still have some paper plates back here somewhere," Charly says as she disappears and comes back with a stack of plates and utensils.

For the next hour, we proceed to eat, drink and try on shoes. When all is said and done, I have four pairs picked out, but Van leads us all with six pairs.

"Now I need a man to impress with my new shoes," Van says with a pout.

"You're not ready for a man," Charly says.

"How do you know what I'm ready for?" Van asks, slurring her words and pointing to Charly's left. "Which one are you?"

"Over here." Charly moves Van's finger in front of her. "You told me you're not ready."

"I'm ready." Van sniffs, her nose dripping from the hot jalapeño dip, and flips her dark hair over her shoulder. "I haven't gotten laid in a long time, and maybe I just want to get laid. Laid."

"How many times are you going to say laid?" Charly says and drains a bottle, not bothering to pour it into a glass.

Atta girl.

"I'll say laid all day. Laid laid laid," Van says and then snorts. "Some of you are getting laid. Even Callie is getting laid."

All eyes suddenly turn to me. I look around, then simply drink the rest of my wine.

Oh God.

"You're fucking Declan," Kate says, pointing at me.

"Kind of," I reply. God, I can't feel my lips. What if they say stuff I don't want them to? Dumb wine.

"You don't kind of fuck, even I remember that," Van says with a giggle.

"Well, I mean, she could be kind of," Gabby says diplomatically. "I mean, maybe there's just oral."

"Oral doesn't count?" I ask, surprised. "I thought it counted."

"For the sake of right now," Charly says and plops right down on the floor, "we're gonna say it doesn't count."

"And please remember that he's our brother, so we don't want details, because *ew*," Gabby adds.

"Um, well, um… yes."

"Yes to what? Oral or everything?" Kate asks, leaning forward like she's watching a riveting TV show.

"Everything," I whisper. "Please don't hate me."

"Oh God," Van says and waves me off. "We know that Declan has sex, but he doesn't have sex with girls he actually *likes*. He's a man-whore."

"Savannah!" Kate cries and covers her face. "Don't tell her that."

"No, I know about his reputation," I say with a shrug. "But he's having sex with me, and he even takes me out on dates."

All four women stare at me with glassy, round owl-eyes, blinking slowly.

"Wow," Kate whispers. "So what are you gonna do?"

"Keep having sex with him?"

"No, like, after that," Gabby says, petting a pair of suede boots.

"Sleep?"

"Okay, focus," Kate says and takes me by the shoulders, looking me in the eye. "What is going to happen in the long term?"

"I don't know," I reply and frown. "That's scary to think about."

"Just be nice to him," Gabby says. "Of all our guys, Declan is the most sensitive. It's probably the artistic side of him."

"I'm nice to him," I reply. "I want to give him head, but he hasn't given me a chance to yet."

"Does he go downtown on you?" Charly asks.

"Hell yes. On pianos."

"Wow," they all reply in awe.

"Yeah. He has mad skills."

"So, we're a little drunk, and I really like you, but I have to say this part," Kate says and pushes her red hair back over her shoulders. "Don't be a bitch to him. Like, ever. Because we will kick your ass."

"You're pretty possessive for someone who isn't related by blood." I cock my hip out and brace my hand on it and try to look badass, but I'm pretty sure I'm failing.

"I like her," Van says with a smile. "She has gumption."

"I'm as close to blood-related to Declan as it gets," Kate says and mirrors my stance. She looks more badass than I do, I'm sure. "I've known Declan for more than ten years, and he's special to me."

"Okay. Got it."

"So don't be a bitch."

"But, what if it's sometimes just in my nature to be a bitch, but it's not on purpose?" I ask sincerely. "Because sometimes I just am."

"That doesn't count, because we all do that," Charly says. "She's talking about the on-purpose kind."

"Oh good." I sigh and smile. "I can do that."

"I don't want to stop drinking," Van whines. "I feel good and I want to stay this way."

"We can't go bar hopping with a bunch of shoe boxes," Gabby says.

"Leave them here and come pick them up tomorrow," Charly says. "That's easier."

"We can go drink at my bar," I offer without thinking. "On me."

"You don't have to give us free drinks," Kate says.

"But if you really want to, who are we to argue? Let's go!" Gabby grabs Van's and Charly's hands and leads us out of the shop.

"Wait! I have to lock up!"

We wait for Charly to lock the door, and then the five of us stumble down the sidewalk to my bar, just three blocks over. When we file in and walk to the bar, Adam looks up and grins.

"Hello there, ladies."

"Oh, you're cute," Van says and leans over the bar toward him, as if she's going to tell him a secret. "I haven't gotten laid in a long time, hot stuff."

Adam laughs and pats her hand as Gabby tries to pull Van off the bar.

"I'm sorry to hear that. You're too beautiful to not have all kinds of men knocking on your door."

"Really cute," Van says to Gabby and then giggles.

"Drinks are on us tonight," I inform him and gesture toward the stairs to the roof. "We're going up where it's private."

"I'll have Jessica stay down here and I'll go up and pour drinks for you guys," he offers, and I simply nod and lead the girls upstairs.

"Oh, it's so pretty up here," Kate says, taking a deep breath. "Look! Café du Monde is right there! I want beignets."

"Later," Charly says and plops down in one of the

plush couches. I turn on the gas fireplaces for light and heat and walk to the bar.

"Shall we keep drinking wine?" I ask.

"Shots first!" Gabby yells and runs to the bar just as Adam comes upstairs. "The hot guy can pour us shots."

"The hot guy can," Adam agrees and winks at her. "What's your poison?"

"Tequila!" all of the girls exclaim at once, and before I know it, we've all had three shots and are nursing glasses of wine.

"We should totally drunk text the boys," Kate says, pulling her phone out of her purse. "Eli will love it."

"Good call!" Gabby says and pulls her phone out. "I'm telling Rhys that he needs to go downtown on me on a piano."

I smirk and sip my wine, squirming a little in my seat as I remember the sex on the piano last weekend. Damn, Declan's good at the getting laid stuff.

Too bad I'm not seeing him tonight.

"That good, huh?" Charly asks as she sits next to me.

"You have no idea," I reply and clink my glass to hers.

"Been awhile for me too," she says with a sigh. "Men suck. And sometimes you get hung up on them, and can't have sex with someone new, and they still suck."

"Are you hung up?" I ask, watching as Van takes her phone out of her pocket, and with her tongue between her teeth, punches out a text, then puts her phone away with a satisfied smile.

"Unfortunately," Charly says. "Because men suck."

"They sure can," I reply. "Women can suck too."

"I don't swing that way," Charly replies, then we both erupt into giggles.

"You know I didn't mean it like that."

"I couldn't resist," Charly says, also watching Van as she retrieves her phone again and responds to a text. "This is fun. Thanks."

"Thanks for inviting me to play with the shoes," I reply. "I love shoes."

"Honey, if you didn't love shoes, there would be something fundamentally wrong with you."

"Eli!" Kate exclaims and then shimmies in her seat as Eli walks across the room to her. "You came!"

"Your offer was compelling," Eli replies and sits next to her, then scoops her into his lap and kisses her hard.

"What did you offer him?" Gabby asks.

"I just offered to blow him while he drove home."

"Good one," I murmur, longing to suck Declan's cock. I'm gonna do that the next time I see him, and there's nothing he can do about it. He's not gonna distract me with his lips and hands and cock.

Nope.

"Will you drive us home?" Van asks Eli. "I don't want to call a cab."

"No problem."

"Hey! Ben's here!" Charly says.

I watch as the hottest-man-in-the-known-universe, besides Declan of course, walks over and stands right in front of Van.

"Who's Ben?" I whisper to Charly.

"Long time friend of the family," she whispers back. "And he might be in love with Van."

"Does she love him back?" I reply and watch as Ben pulls Van to her feet, wraps his muscly arms around her and hugs her close.

"Do I have to stay with Charly tonight?" Gabby asks Van with a frown. "Are you guys gonna do some weird shit?"

Ben just chuckles.

"After everything she's been through, Van needs Ben right now," Charly says softly.

"What has she been through?"

"That's a sad story for another night," Charly says and pats my knee. "Let's not ruin this buzz. Come on, Gabby, you can stay with me."

Without a word, Ben leads Van to the stairs. She waves, then disappears behind him.

"I hope she knows what she's doing," Kate says with a frown.

"They're adults," Eli replies with a frown of his own. "They'll be fine."

We say goodbyes, and Eli ends up promising to drive Gabby and Charly to Charly's house. When they're gone, I join Adam at the bar.

"Declan's family?" he asks.

"Yep."

"Do I need to call him to come and get you, or are you actually going to sleep in your own bed tonight?" The words are meant to be teasing, but I sense a seriousness to them that I don't want to examine right now. I'm enjoying this buzz, from the alcohol and the good time with new friends.

"Awwww, do you miss me, Adam?" I ruffle his hair and then wrap my arms around his waist and hug him close. "Don't worry, I'll be home to tuck you in tonight."

"I think I'll be the one tucking you in," he replies with a laugh and kisses my head. "Did you have fun?"

"Mmm hmm."

"I'm glad you're making new friends."

"Thanks, Mom."

"I don't like seeing you lonely, Cal."

"Been lonely most of my life."

"I know." I feel him sigh, his hand is rubbing up

and down my back. I'm still buzzing good and man, I could fall asleep right here.

"But know what?"

"What?" he asks softly.

"You can be in the middle of a crowded room and still be lonely."

"I know that too," he replies, then tips my face up so he can look in my eyes. "Damn, you're toasted."

"Feels kinda good."

"I just want you to be happy, Cal."

"Happier than I've been in a long time," I reply, surprised that it's true.

"Good. Let's go tuck you in."

"Have to close the bar."

"Jessica can handle it."

CHAPTER TEN

~Callie~

Oh, dear Jesus, I'm dying. My head is pounding. I'm sweating. My mouth is dry and sticky.

And I'm wrapped like a mummy under something heavy.

I've already died and someone is trying to bury me. I swear, God, if you don't let me get buried, I'll never drink like that again. Ever. Okay, maybe not *ever*, but not for a very, very long time.

I'm gonna throw up.

I hate throwing up.

I moan and try to move, but I can't. Not only am I wrapped in the sheet and blanket as tight as can be, but something—or someone—is wrapped around me.

"Damn it, I know you tucked me in, but don't you have a bed of your own to go to?" My voice sounds raw, like the evil stepmother in Snow White.

"I know I didn't tuck you in last night," Declan says in my ear, making me grin. His voice sounds… musical, with its soft tone and slight accent. God, that accent makes me crazy.

"Don't worry," I whisper, still not opening my

eyes. "Adam took me to bed last night."

"This conversation isn't improving," he says dryly. "Maybe you should stop while you're ahead."

"Mm," is my only response as I snuggle closer to him and sigh in contentment. I didn't like falling asleep without him last night, wasted or not. I've gotten used to sharing a bed with him in the past few weeks, which surprises me. I've never shared a bed with anyone long-term, even Keith when I was in Denver. He didn't like to sleep over, and I didn't think I did either, but sleeping with Declan feels right.

"What do you want to do today?" he whispers into my ear. His fingers are combing through my hair gently, rhythmically. He's warm and safe wrapped around me, and I can feel the slight scrape from the scruff on his chin against my neck.

As soon as I'm done dying, I'm going to attack him.

"Stay here. Sleep."

He chuckles and bites my earlobe, but all that does is send sparks of electricity down my back. How in the ever loving fuck am I severely hung over and turned on at the same time? I didn't think that was possible.

Huh. Weird.

"You can't sleep all day."

"I can until I have to go to work. Just watch me."

"I want to spend the day with you," he says and kisses my cheek, then nudges me onto my back. "Open your beautiful eyes, darlin'."

"Don't have to."

"Are you always so chipper when you're hung over?"

I crack an eye open and glare at him. "Who says I'm hung over?"

"I do!" Adam yells from the doorway.

"God, he's annoying," I moan and bury my face in

my hands. "Just let me die in peace."

"I'm making you breakfast," I hear Adam say and then his footsteps as he walks down the hall.

"See? We'll feed you and then I'll take you somewhere fun."

"This is fun," I reply and smile sweetly.

"We'll do this later," he replies, brushing my hair off my cheek. "You're even gorgeous hung over."

And that's when it hits me; I must look insane. I squirm out from under the covers and rush into the bathroom, then cringe. "Oh, God."

"What's wrong?" Declan asks from the doorway, leaning against the jamb.

"Last night's smokey eye has turned into this morning's five-dollar-hooker eye."

He barks out a laugh and then shakes his head. "Fifty dollar hooker. At least."

I spread toothpaste on my brush and glare at him in the mirror as I scrub my disgusting mouth. "Bread haf be didguding."

"Your breath wasn't that bad," he replies, his hazel eyes shining as he watches me brush my teeth and then take a makeup cleanser to my face. "You're actually pretty cute when you're all messed up."

"You're not supposed to be here." I frown and stare at him as I wipe my face clean. "What are you doing here?"

He shrugs, but then he shakes his head, as if he's saying *fuck it* to himself, and he meets my eyes as he says, "I missed you this morning."

Oh. How am I supposed to resist that?

I toss the dirty cleaning cloth on the trash and walk to the impossibly tall, ridiculously handsome man and stand on my tip-toes to gently press my lips to his. I'm so much shorter than him when I'm not in my heels.

"What do you want to do today?" he asks me again, then brushes his knuckles down my cheek.

"I want to be outside," I reply with a smile. "But no strenuous activity. My stomach can't handle it."

"I know a place," he replies and kisses my nose. "You're short without your shoes."

"I was just thinking that."

"And you're gorgeous without your war paint."

"I was not thinking that."

"You're just beautiful, Calliope. I'll take you any way I can get you." With that, he winks and backs away from me. "Adam made breakfast."

"I can smell that bacon."

"Well, hurry up, or there won't be any left."

"You would dare steal bacon from a hung over woman?" I grip my chest as if I'm shocked and devastated, but he just laughs.

"It's not my fault that you're in a bad way this morning, sweetheart."

"It's your sisters' fault, so it's kind of your fault."

He shakes his head. "I'm not following your logic. Did you have fun?"

"I did." I nod and reach for a pair of denim capris and a blue T-shirt. "They're all nice girls. We bonded over shoes."

"I figured you would," he says. "Thank you."

"For what?"

"For hanging out with my sisters even though I know you were uncomfortable."

"It was fun," I repeat and walk away like it's no big deal. Because it is no big deal. I'm not making it a big deal. So I had wine and shopped for shoes with his sisters. It's not like we were picking out bridesmaids dresses or anything.

"I'm hungry," he says rather than pressing the issue.

"Me too. Go ahead, I'm gonna brush my hair and be right there."

Before I can turn away, he has be pressed back against the vanity, his hands planted on the countertop at my hips, and he's kissing me like his life depends on it. Only his lips are touching me, but I'm on fire *everywhere.*

How does he do this to me every single time?

Finally, he pulls back, smiles, and turns to walk away without another word.

I need a minute to catch my breath and gather my wits. Holy shit, that man can kiss.

***

"I love this park." I smile and lean my head back so I can breathe in the fall air. It's not cold here, the way it gets farther north in Colorado, but I can feel a difference in the air. And although the city always has tourists, it seems quieter now that school has started back up and families have returned home.

"You've been here before?" Declan asks as he takes my hand in his, threading our fingers.

"Of course. Audubon Park is famous. My dad used to bring me here and we'd feed the ducks."

"Coincidentally, I brought duck food with me," he replies with a smile and leads me down the path that circles through the park. "Do you know much about the park?"

"I know it's big and there are lots of oak trees," I reply with a smile.

"Those are both true. Do you want a history lesson, or is this boring?"

"So not boring," I reply sincerely. "Teach me, Obi Wan."

He snorts and then looks up at the oaks and begins his story. "These trees are more than two hundred and fifty years old. The land was originally settled by Native Americans, and then eventually by the first mayor of New Orleans. His name was Etienne de Bore."

"What was his name?" I ask, deliberately making him repeat it, just because I love the way the French rolls off his tongue.

"Etienne de Bore. Not only was he the first mayor, but he also founded the first granulated sugar plantation in the country."

"So he was smart."

"And rich," Declan says, smiling down at me. "Then, in 1850, the land was donated to the city. However, the Civil War began, and it was used as a Confederate camp and a Union hospital."

"Wow, both sides of the war on one site."

He nods, then points out a branch for me to walk around. "The cool thing is, in 1866, it was the site where the Buffalo Soldiers were activated from. So there is a lot of history where we're walking. After the turn of the century, the city put together a society to oversee it, and it eventually evolved into not only the park, but also a zoo, riding stables, sports fields, and other things too."

"You really should pursue that tour guide career," I say, impressed. "How do you know so much?"

"I love history. Especially Louisiana history. The music I love was born here, the people I come from were from here. I like knowing where I come from."

"What about where you're going?" I ask as he leads me to a bridge that arches over a lazy river full of ducks and swans. He digs in a bag slung over his shoulder and comes out with a half-eaten loaf of bread.

We've sent several pieces over the side of the bridge, and just when I think he's not going to answer my question, he continues. "I've never been so concerned about where I'm going."

"Really?"

He shakes his head. He continues to toss the bread, and I lean my back on the railing, watching him.

"I imagine that wherever it is I'm going, I'll get there eventually."

My eyebrows both climb into my hairline in surprise. "That easy?"

"Sure. Why does it have to be hard?"

I think back over the past ten years. "I guess all my adult life I've been worried about where I would end up, in what job, and who with. How I would get there."

"And you've ended up right back where you started," he says simply. "Not that you shouldn't work hard, because I do, but where I'm going has never been a question for me."

"And where are you going, Declan Boudreaux?"

He smiles down at me. "That's just it, Calliope. I'm not going anywhere. Not long-term, anyway. I'm exactly where I love to be."

And with that, he takes my hand and leads me across the other side of the bridge and to a deck that looks out over a pond nearby. There are wooden benches tucked perfectly in the trees. It's a cool place to sit and enjoy nature.

He leads me to a bench and reaches back in his bag, coming out with sandwiches. He hands me one, peels back the plastic on his and takes a giant bite.

We sit in silence for a while, chewing on our lunch, watching the birds and ducks. The last of the summer flowers are struggling to hang on, just a few more days. In the distance, a crew is setting up tables and chairs in a big stone pavilion, draped in pink and green. Someone will be getting married here later today.

And it's the perfect spot for it.

I sigh as I finish my sandwich and pass the wrapper to Declan. I move to stand, but he puts his hand on my arm.

"I have one more thing to give you," he says with a smile.

"More food? I'm full."

"No." He passes me an envelope, and inside are two tickets to see Seattle play football.

"Declan, you must have bought the wrong tickets. These say they play *in* Seattle."

"They're right," he assures me and drags his hand down my back.

"I can't just drop everything and go to Seattle."

"You're not. The game is two weeks away, and I know that business has slowed down enough that Adam can handle the bar for two days."

I shake my head, but inside, I'm jumping up and down like a little girl. He just stares at me, that smirk on his lips, until I finally throw my arms around him and hug him close.

"Thank you. I've always wanted to see Seattle."

"I can't wait to show it to you," he whispers into my ear.

Who is this man? This giving, sweet, affectionate man?

"What are you thinking?" he asks, tilting his head to the side.

"Nothing."

"Something just passed through that gorgeous head of yours."

I don't want to tell him. It makes me sound mushy and corny, but then I decide what the hell. "I was just wondering who you are, and how have you managed to make me feel so comfortable and easy with you? I trust you, Declan, and I don't trust easily."

Now he pulls me to my feet and wraps those long, strong arms around me. My arms are tucked against my chest, and I'm wrapped up in him. He sways us gently side to side, his mouth pressed to my head. I feel him inhale deeply, and then, finally, he whispers, "I'm Declan Boudreaux, and you trust me because I trust you, too."

Then he pulls back, kisses my forehead, and leads me further into the park.

***

"Thanks for swinging into Charly's with me," I say as he parks in front of Head Over Heels. "It's easier to grab my shoes now on the way home than later when I'll have to cart them to the bar."

"How many pairs did you buy?" he asks with a laugh and helps me out of the car.

"Four, I think."

"You think?"

"There was wine," I remind him and push inside the cool store. It doesn't smell like shoes. It smells like lavender and sunshine.

"Well, hello there," Charly says from behind the counter.

"Hi," I reply. "How are you feeling?"

"There's no need to yell," Charly says while holding her head, making me laugh.

"That good, huh?"

"Rough mornin'," she says with a sigh. "But so worth it. I have your shoes here." She lifts a big white bag full of shoe boxes off the floor.

"Can I have one more look at them?" I ask, eyeing the bag the way a kid eyes birthday cake.

"You can look at them all you want," she says and helps me get them out. "Those blue shoes are amazing."

I nod, looking down at my feet as I slide them into the blue pumps. They feel great, and will go with almost anything. "I love them."

"What about these?" Declan asks from the middle

of the shop. He's holding up a pair of grey suede pumps.

"I don't think I carry those in your size, little brother," Charly said, earning the middle finger from Declan.

"For Callie, smart ass."

Charly runs to the back to find my size, then returns a moment later with a box. "These are pretty," she says.

Declan takes the box from her, pulls the stuffing out of a shoe, then kneels before me and drags his hand down the back of my leg, behind my knee, to my calf. "Give me your foot, sweetheart."

I brace myself on his shoulder and offer him my naked foot, which he slips into the grey shoe. But before I can put it on the floor, he leans in and presses a kiss to my ankle.

I wonder how Charly would feel about her brother fucking me right here, in the shoe store? Because I'm about to climb him.

"Good eye, Dec," Charly says. "You know, if you're looking for a job, I'll hire you."

"Why is everyone trying to find me a new job? I have a job, thank you very much."

I step down on the shoe and, with his hand still cradling my calf, he looks up at me and gives me that half smile, then winks, and I know, without a shadow of a doubt, that I have fallen head over heels in love with this man.

As completely corny as it sounds, he's literally swept me off of my feet.

My heart pounds a bit as I step back out of his grasp, then stumble when I almost knock a designer display over.

"Are you okay?" he asks and reaches for my hand, but I pull it away and take another step away from him.

"Fine."

"Are they too tall for you?" Charly asks, her face creased in concern.

"No, they're great." I clear my throat and smile widely. "I'll take them." I fumble for my credit card. "In fact, I'll wear them out."

Declan is staring at me like I've suddenly grown a cucumber out of my ear, and I know I seem completely nuts right now, but I can't help it.

I'm in love with him.

Holy shit.

Charly's speaking, but I can't understand the words through the rushing in my ears. Finally, I sign the receipt—I don't even give one shit how much it all cost—and make a beeline for outside, dragging deep breaths of fresh air into my lungs.

Does everyone hyperventilate when they discover they're in love? Probably not.

"What happened in there?" Declan asks as he takes the bag of shoes from me and places it in the back of his Jeep, then waits for me to get buckled in before pulling out into traffic.

"I don't know what you're talking about."

I've never been a great liar.

"You looked like you saw a ghost, and when Charly asked you if you wanted to keep the boxes, you just smiled and said, *good for you.*"

"Oops," I murmur and stare out the passenger window.

"So what happened?"

"Must have been something I ate," I say and smile brightly. "I feel better now."

We stop at a red light and he sends me a look that screams *not buying it,* but he doesn't press me. And I'm glad because what am I supposed to say?

Sorry, but I just realized when you had your sexy hand on

*my leg and winked at me that I'm completely in love with you
and it gave me heart palpitations and I might have had a stroke?*

Probably not a great thing to say.

"I have to get ready for my gig tonight, so I'm
gonna drop you at Adam's. Is that okay?"

"Perfect."

"I'll walk you to your car at closing," he says.

"Great."

"You're sure you're okay?"

"Great."

He stops at the curb and before he can jump out
to walk me in, I grab the shoes out of the back and
wave, then rush inside to have my panic attack the way
any self-respecting woman would: by myself.

***

"Phone for you," Adam says later that day as he
pulls the cordless from his ear and holds it out to me.
We're both bustling behind the bar, him pouring drinks
for a party of twelve that just walked in, and me trying
to restock the beer before the evening crowd hits.

"This is Callie," I say and squat in front of the beer
cooler, mentally counting bottles.

"Callie, this is Ray Michaels. I'm a producer at the
Travel Channel."

I pause and frown at the Bud Light. "Okay."

"My associate was in New Orleans a couple of
weeks ago and had the privilege of being in The
Odyssey on a Friday night. He was so impressed with
the renovations on the place that we would like to
feature your bar on our travel show, *Ins and Outs*. Have
you seen the show?"

My mouth is gaping open by now, and my legs are
falling asleep from being in the squat position for way
too long, but I can't move. All I can do is nod.

"Callie?"

"Sorry. Yes, I've seen the show."

"Great. So the host travels around the country, and in a twelve-minute segment, features a different hot spot in the city they're visiting that week."

"And you want The Odyssey to be one of those hot spots."

"We do," he says. "I can email you with more information, and the legal formalities, but I wanted to touch base personally first to see if this is something you're interested in."

"O-of course I'm interested," I stutter and stand, then curse a million times in my head as the blood rushes back into my lower extremities. "I'd love to see the paperwork."

"Great. We'd like to film the week after next."

"That fast?" I ask and glance over to see Adam staring at me, unabashedly eavesdropping. I just shrug and put one finger up to say, *just a minute*.

"It's a last-minute addition because one of the other locations fell through. We're very excited to work with you."

"Thank you." I give him my email address, then hang up and simply stare at the top of the bar.

"Who was that?" Adam asks.

"A guy named Ray from the Travel Channel. They want to film in here and spotlight us on *Ins and Outs*."

"I love that show," he says with a grin.

"This is crazy." My hands are shaking.

"No, it's awesome. You worked hard and it's paying off. This will be excellent for business."

"*We* worked hard," I say absently and then smile and jump up and down. "The Travel Channel!"

"Okay, maybe it's a little crazy," he says with a laugh.

"It's a little crazy that I'll take," I reply and pour us each a shot. "Cheers!"

CHAPTER ELEVEN

~Declan~

She fucking blows me away. I'm sitting in The Odyssey two weeks later, watching as she sits for her interview with the Travel Channel crew. She's already given them a tour of the roof, and now she's giving them the history of the place. This is the part that I know is hardest for her, but you'd never know it. She's cool as a cucumber in her black skirt and white button-down, and she's wearing the grey heels I picked out for her. The blond hair that I can't seem to stop touching is piled on top of her head in a lazy knot and her lips are red.

She's pulled off the classy rocker-chick effortlessly. I know she was probably just going for classy, but she always has that edge to her, no matter what she wears.

And I fucking love it.

She's speaking of her father without blinking an eye, but she does fist her hand once, which tells me that she's not happy with this line of questions.

The fact that the freaking Travel Channel is filming in her place is amazing. Not that she hasn't earned it. Everything about the place has changed, not just because of the renovations, but because of the woman who runs the show.

And the producer is a smart man for recognizing that. The segment on the show will only be a little over ten minutes, but they've shot at least an hour's worth of coverage to make sure that they have enough footage to pull from. I'll be performing in about an hour, and they'll get more filming in then.

"She's doing great," Adam murmurs as he walks up beside my table. I purposely sat where I can keep an eye on my girl. Just in case.

"That she is," I agree with a nod. "Not that I thought she'd do otherwise."

"She's a pro," Adam says. "She deserves this."

"You both do." He shrugs, but I don't let it go. "You both worked your asses off, and continue to, Adam. She knows that, and so do you."

"It's her place," he insists, then pats my shoulder and returns to the bar, where he winks at a redhead and asks what he can get her.

Finally, Callie stands and shakes hands with the camera crew, waits patiently to have the mics taken off her clothes, and walks straight to me.

Good girl.

"You did so great," I say as I fold her into my arms and hug her tight. God, I love the way she fits just perfectly.

"I was so nervous," she admits with a sigh. "But my part is done."

"You were great," I repeat and tip her head up, my finger under her chin, to see her eyes. "You nailed it."

She smiles and squares her shoulders, claiming her power back, and I can't help but smile.

"What?" she asks with a grin.

"I love the way you shrug into your badass," I reply before kissing her forehead. "And I love that I'm the only one who gets to see you when you take it off."

"I—" She bites her lip and looks down, then just shakes her head. "Have a great set tonight."

"What were you going to say?"

"It's not important," she replies before leaning in and pressing a kiss to my collarbone. "Break a leg."

"I've never understood that sentiment," I reply as I turn toward the stage. The bar is filling up. I'll have a packed audience tonight. "We'll finish that conversation later."

She waves me off and walks away, and my eyes are drawn to the long, lean lines of her back and legs. Her ass is just perfect, and fits just right in my hands.

I can't wait to get my hands on her later.

But first, I have to put on a show for the bar patrons and the cameras. But this is what I do best, so I'm not worried in the least.

I'm just ready to have tonight finished so Callie and I can leave for Seattle tomorrow. Three whole days, with Callie all to myself without business to see to, sounds like my idea of heaven.

***

"I'm kind of in love with this hotel," Callie says as she checks out our suite at the Four Seasons Seattle. "I mean, look at this view!" She stands, face pressed against the floor-to-ceiling windows, and stares out at the Puget Sound before us. We're in the penthouse, and not only can we see the water, but we can see a good portion of the city as well. "I bet it'll be beautiful when it gets dark."

All I can do is stand and watch, my hands shoved in my pockets, as she looks at everything as quickly as she can, as if she can't decide what she should look at first.

"The tub is a freaking swimming pool!" she calls from the bathroom, then kisses me as she passes into the other portion of the suite. "Oh my God! There's a baby grand in here!" She pokes her head around the diving wall and smiles at me. "We like those."

"That we do," I reply with a grin, picturing her spread before me the way she was on my piano a few weeks ago. I would not complain if she wanted to recreate that particular fantasy.

"This kitchen is ridiculous!"

I follow her and silently agree. The massive gourmet kitchen is a bit much for a hotel room, especially given that neither of us likes to cook and room service will be our source of nutrition, but it is a beautiful added touch to the space. Finally, she spins and leans on the breakfast bar, facing me. "I know I'm silly, like a little kid who's never stayed at a hotel before, but I've never stayed in the penthouse before."

"You're not silly, you're cute."

She cocks a brow. "Cute?"

"Yes, ma'am." I nod and circle around the island, and when she would turn to face me, I take her shoulders in my hands, keeping her still. "Do you know what else you are?"

She tries to look at me again, but I hold her still. "Stay."

"You're bossy."

"I didn't ask you what I am, I asked you what you are." She's in jeans and a big sweatshirt with the neck cut out so it falls over her left shoulder, showing me her bra strap and lots of soft, delicious skin. Before I begin, I unbutton and lower her jeans, nudging her to step out of them, but I leave the sweatshirt.

I'm going to have fun with that.

"I don't know. What am I, bossy man?"

I grin and pull her loose blond hair back into a tail, tilt her head to the right, and lick, in one long motion, from her ear to the tip of her shoulder, then drag my lips back up the same path.

"You're sexy," I breathe. God, I love her neck. I scoop the hair that has escaped my hands out of my way and kiss and nibble the back of her neck, then over to the opposite side and pull the sweatshirt aside so I can taste her shoulder. "You're delicious."

She moans, and when she would tilt her head forward, I fist her hair and pull her head back, my grip firm, and kiss her cheek, then bite her earlobe.

"You're every fantasy I've ever had."

She fucking purrs as I push my hand into the neck of her sweatshirt and cup her firm breast in my palm. My cock pulses as her nipple puckers between my fingers.

I know she wants me to bend her over and fuck her here in the kitchen, but that's not the plan. Not right now.

Instead, I continue to nibble and suck her shoulder, her neck, more forcefully now. Both of her breasts are tight with lust. Her left hand slips back to grab my ass, but I catch it and press it against the counter. "Hands off."

"You're doing all the work," she whines, and only makes me smile against her shoulder where it meets her neck.

"Are you complaining?"

"No."

I bite her now, hard, and gasp as she pushes her ass against my cock in surprise. She's told me before that her neck is sensitive, and she wasn't lying. She's close to coming, and all I've done is touch her tits and ravage her shoulder and neck.

I drag my nose up her cheek, and then with my fist

in her hair once again, I turn her head so my lips can reach hers and I kiss her like a starved man. Tongues tangle, bodies heave, breath is ragged, and finally I feel her whole body tense and she moans against my mouth as she comes.

I slow down, soften my touch as she comes down from the high, and when her breath has calmed, I right her sweatshirt and simply walk away.

"Oh hell no," she says, her voice hoarse but determined. "You're not going to give me neck sex, make me come, and then walk away."

I turn to look at her and tilt my head. "I'm not?"

"No. You're not."

And there she is, the woman in control who knows exactly what she wants and isn't afraid to ask for it. She turns me on every fucking time.

She marches to me, completely naked from the waist down because, God bless her, she doesn't wear panties, and proceeds to push her hands against my chest and push me to a nearby chair, giving me no choice but to sit in it.

"I've been wanting to suck your cock for months," she announces, making me almost swallow my tongue. "And you keep distracting me with your damn mouth and cock and your hands, and you're not going to distract me today."

"I think I just did a fairly decent job of distracting you," I inform her and then hold my hands up in surrender when she simply glares daggers at me. "But I'm all yours. Do as you will."

She licks her lips and unzips my jeans, frees my cock, and without any hesitation, takes me all the way into her mouth, sinking down until her nose hits my pubis.

"Jesus, Callie!" My hips come up off the chair, but she holds me firmly, adds her hand to her mouth, and works my cock expertly, moving up and down, alternating between firm and soft. Just when I think I'm going to explode, she lightens her touch, both frustrating the hell out of me and making me want to yank her up and fuck the hell out of her.

She hums and cups my balls, licks me from root to tip, rubs her tongue in the slit in the head, and then sinks over me again, repeating the whole damn process over again.

"I'm not going to survive this."

She chuckles, and I notice that her shoulder is moving. Before my eyes cross, I glance down and see that she's not only getting me off, she's getting herself off at the same time.

"Mother fucker," I groan, unable to hold my orgasm back. Between her magic mouth and seeing her pleasure herself, I'm done for. "Callie, I'm gonna come."

Rather than back away, she hums her approval, and when I come in her mouth, she swallows, then leans back, a satisfied and proud smile on her face.

She moves to stand, but I stop her. "Don't quit touching yourself."

She tilts her head to the side, and with that smile still in place, she simply sits on her ass, spreads her legs right here on the hardwood, and runs her perfectly manicured fingers through her lips, pushes two inside her, then drags them up to her clit. It's a circle that she keeps following, slowly.

She's magnificent. Her face is flushed and goosebumps cover her arms. Her fingers are soaking wet from her pussy.

To my surprise, I'm already hard again, and I'm stroking myself while she watches, teasing her pussy, her lips, her clit. She puts her wet fingers in her mouth, licks them clean, then bites her lip as she puts on the show of a lifetime, and suddenly, she's coming again. Watching the way her muscles tighten is fascinating. Her body quivers. She cries out, and I'm coming with her, not even caring about the mess I'm making.

We're not touching, but this might be the most intimate moment of our relationship so far. Her blue eyes are lazy now as she catches her breath, watching me, and a slow, Cheshire cat smile spreads over her lips.

It's in this moment that I know I'm lost to her, forever. She doesn't just own my heart, she *is* my heart.

I love her.

***

"It's early," Callie pouts beside me the next morning as we walk from the hotel to the waterfront and Pike's Market. "We're usually going to bed right about now."

"That's an exaggeration, but it is early."

"So why are we out of bed? We had room service and sleep and sex back at the hotel."

"Because you've never been to Seattle, and I want you to experience it."

She frowns. "Okay. Can I experience it with coffee?"

"That's the first thing on my list," I assure her and take her hand, link our fingers, and squeeze reassuringly. Three squeezes, to be exact.

I love you.

Our first stop is the original Starbucks where we load up on probably way too much caffeine, then I lead her through the market. It's a little early yet, but vendors are already setting up their tables full of seafood, flowers, jewelry, just about anything you can think of. Callie is happy to slowly browse, stopping to taste some local honey, or accept a slice of apple.

A pair of earrings catch her eye. "We'll take them,"

I tell the man behind the table, who smiles and reaches for a box.

"Oh, you don't have to do that." Callie shakes her head and the man pauses with the box in his hand.

"Do you like them?"

"Of course, they're beautiful."

"Perfect." I nod to the man and he continues boxing her earrings. I pay him and she takes the bag with a thank you, and fifteen minutes later, when she still hasn't said a word, I decide to break the silence. "What's wrong?"

"Nothing's wrong. Thank you for the earrings."

"You're welcome." We walk further, tasting oils and vinegars with cut-up bread, and then finally stand and watch the guys who throw the fish put on a show. I wrap my arm around her shoulders, but she doesn't lean into me the way she usually does. "Spill it, sweetheart," I murmur into her ear.

"You're just a very take-charge kind of person," she says, her eyes pinned to the fish flying through the air. "And that's something I have to get used to."

"It's not a big deal. You like the earrings, so I bought them."

"And I like the Seahawks so you brought me to Seattle," she says with a nod. "You just—"

"I'm sorry if I crossed a line," I say and drop my arm. Am I coming on too strong? I don't see it that way. I love her, so I do nice things for her. It's really that simple.

"I've never been taken care of," she says softly and finally turns to look up at me. She takes my hand in hers and holds on tightly. "This is just new for me, and I'm not complaining, I'm just—"

"You're adjusting your sails," I finish for her, thinking of my father.

"What?"

"My dad used to say we can't control the wind, but we can adjust our sails." I lead her around the corner and sigh in bliss when I smell the tiny donuts being made. "So, you're adjusting your sails a bit, and that's okay."

"That's actually a really good way to put it," she agrees with a nod. "But nothing is wrong. *You* haven't done anything wrong."

"Okay. Just tell me if I do, because I probably will, and I won't even know that I'm doing it."

"Fair enough. Please tell me we're getting some of these donuts."

I grin and nod, already salivating. "This is the only reason I come to Seattle."

"You're kidding." She frowns as she watches the little pastries float in the cooking oil, then flop into the three-tiered cooking rack. "They're just donuts."

"You wound me," I reply, my hand over my heart. "These are not just donuts. These are Pike's Place Market donuts, and believe me when I say after you've eaten these, you'll never be the same."

"If you say so," she says. I order enough for two large brown paper bags full, take one out, still piping hot from the fryer, and pop it in my mouth, then offer her one. She chooses a cinnamon sugar one, takes a bite, and stops in her tracks. "Oh my God."

"I know."

"I mean, it's just... *so good.*"

"You're welcome."

"More." She takes the bag out of my hands and digs in, bites into another and sighs, moaning as if she's having really, really good sex.

"It's a good thing I bought two bags," I say with a laugh and open my own bag, but she reaches in and steals one. "Hey!"

"You took one of mine," she says primly, licking

sugar off her lips. "It's only fair."

I lean in and lick the sugar off her lips myself, then kiss her long and hard, right here for all of Seattle to see. "You can have all the donuts you want, sweetheart."

"Good, because we might have to make a trip back there before we leave."

"I was already planning on it."

"This is why I keep you around."

"Donuts?" I laugh and shake my head, leading her back toward the hotel where I plan to get her naked and in the enormous pool-size bathtub before we explore more of the city. "And here I thought you kept me around for my good looks."

"Well, before this it was for your oral skills, but now it's donuts."

I stop on the sidewalk and stare at her in surprise, then I bust up laughing and pick up the pace to the hotel.

"Are you in a hurry?" she asks.

"Yes."

"Why?"

"I want to hone my oral skills."

"Oh!" She speeds up, passing me. "Good idea."

CHAPTER TWELVE

~Callie~

"Come on! Are you fucking kidding me? Learn to throw the damn ball, Montgomery!" I scream down to the field. "I can throw better than that!"

"Easy, tiger," Declan says, pulling me back down in the seat.

"Did you see that?" I roar and glare down at Seattle's quarterback. "I mean, what the hell?"

"This is fun," Declan says calmly and finishes the last bite of his hot dog. We're almost at the end of the fourth quarter of the game, and Seattle is up, but only by three.

"What's fun? Watching the damn quarterback try to sabotage this game?"

He shakes his head and chuckles. "No, watching you lose your shit. I hope you never get mad at me. Actually, I take that back. You're sexy when you're on fire."

"If he doesn't start throwing like a damn

professional, you'll see an inferno."

He just continues to smile, running his hand over my ponytail and down my back.

"I like your outfit," he says as we wait for the commercial break to pass so the game can continue. "The team emblem on your cheek is especially hot."

I look down at my 12th man jersey, with my favorite player's name on the back, and grin. "I love this jersey. Thanks for buying it for me yesterday."

"I admit, I had ulterior motives," he says while he leans in and presses his lips to my ear. "I'm hoping you'll wear it and nothing else later when I continue to practice my oral skills."

"Is the game over yet?" I ask and glance at the scoreboard as Declan laughs and pulls his phone out of his pocket to check a text.

"I need to make a call," he says and stands. "I'll be right back. Are you okay?"

I'm soaking wet in the middle of a football game. What could be wrong?

"I'm great," I say, my attention returning to the field as the players assume their position for the next play. "Come on, guys," I mumble. "You got this. I came a very long way for this game. You can do it."

I cross my fingers and hold my breath during the next play. They're at the fifty yard line, directly in front of me. I don't know how he did it, given that the home games are sold out for the season, but Declan got us some kickass seats.

Montgomery calls the play, the ball snaps, and he throws to my favorite player, Sanders, who catches it perfectly and runs it in for a touchdown.

"That's right!" I scream and jump up, clapping. "Woohoo!"

Declan returns, also clapping and smiling.

"Everything okay?" I ask.

"Yep, nothing to worry about."

I nod and grin at the field. There are only thirty seconds left on the clock, and unless there's some miraculous act of God, Seattle is gonna win this game. With just a few plays, and Seattle's defense killing Pittsburgh, Seattle is victorious.

Declan and I stay in our seats, waiting for the majority of the stadium to empty.

"Traffic is going to be a bitch as it is. We might as well just wait," Declan says and fidgets with the neckline of my jersey. "Did you have fun?"

"It was great," I reply and lean in, intending to give him a quick kiss, but it swiftly turns into a long, hot kiss, the way it always does where Declan is concerned. We don't seem to do anything softly or gently. It's always passionate. Eager. Hungry.

And I love it. I love that I can just be me with him. My sexual requests don't seem to startle or repulse him. And when we're together, just hanging out, we can talk about anything, or simply sit and enjoy the quiet.

We're comfortable, in the best way.

He reaches down and takes my hand, giving it three squeezes. Finally, when most of the place is empty, we stand and he leads me up and out of the stadium and into the parking garage, where we can catch a cab back to the hotel.

But when we get inside, Declan rattles off an address I don't recognize.

"Where are we going?" I scoot as close to him as I can and rest my head on his wide shoulder.

"You'll see."

In control, as usual.

"I'm not a huge fan of surprises, you know."

"Actually, I don't know that," he replies and kisses my forehead, then turns to look out the window and into the already dark evening. We're quiet as the cab maneuvers through the game traffic. My ears are still rushing from the noise, my throat raw from screaming. When the cab passes the exit to our hotel, I tip my head back and kiss Declan's cheek.

"Where did you say we're going?"

He smirks. "I didn't. Don't worry, you'll like it."

"I hope it's not fancy," I say before yawning widely. "I'm not dressed for it."

"Not fancy," he assures me and tips my head back, his finger under my chin, and kisses me sweetly at first, and then more deeply, as if he hasn't touched me in weeks.

We drive outside of the city, where lights are fewer and fewer, making the dark settle in. We seem to be following the coast. The cab pulls off the freeway, and then turns onto a smaller two-lane road that meanders for a few miles before ending at a huge iron gate.

"Stop here," Declan says and disentangles himself from me. "I'll be right back."

Before I can say anything, he jumps out of the car, walks to the speaker box and talks into it. The gate begins to roll away as he joins me.

"This is all very 007 of you," I say, my curiosity piqued.

"It's not that dramatic," he says with a laugh as the cab pulls through and stops at the entrance of a beautiful two-story stone house. It's craftsman in style, spread out and simply breathtaking.

I wish I could see it in the daylight.

I can hear the ocean not far away. "Are we near the beach?"

"Yes," Declan says with a smile after he pays the cab and leads me to the door. "This house is on cliffs that sit above the Sound."

"Wow."

The door swings open and a pretty, small blonde

woman smiles widely. A tall, slender, tattooed man is standing right behind her. He has a sleeve that runs down over his hand and to his fingers, and I'd recognize that face anywhere.

"Hi! I'm Samantha. You must be Callie. Declan has told us a lot about you. This is my husband—"

"Leo Nash," I reply for her and feel myself blush. "Sorry. I'm a fan."

"And I'm flattered," Leo replies and shakes my hand. "Hey, Dec."

"Hey," Declan says and the two do the man-hug thing that I don't understand in the least, as Samantha leads us all into the heart of the home: the kitchen.

"Your home is beautiful, Samantha." I'm trying to absorb it all at once, and it's impossible. The style is contemporary, with little pops of rustic and shabby chic thrown in here and there. The combination is both homey and eye-catching.

"Thanks. You can call me Sam," she says with a grin. "We just finished building it about a year ago. I think we just about have it the way we want it."

I nod, just as the doorbell rings, and rather than waiting for someone to answer it, the door is opened. "Hey guys! We're here."

"Oh good," Sam says and all I can do is pray to God that I don't have the stupid dog look on my face. Because Will Montgomery just walked through that door.

"Will, this is the friend I told you about, Declan Boudreaux," Leo says. "And his girlfriend, Callie."

"It's good to meet you both," Will says, shaking our hands. "This is my wife, Meg."

I shake myself out of my stupor to see a beautiful redhead standing next to him. She's rocking a boho chic style of clothing that I wish with all my might I could pull off. She also has tats on her arm, and she's smiling kindly.

"I'm not a cook," Sam warns us all as we congregate in the kitchen. "I didn't want to risk killing any of you, so I ordered in from Palomino downtown."

"And I picked up some cupcakes from Nic's bakery," Leo adds. "I helped."

"Yes, you were an integral part of the process," Sam says and rolls her eyes.

"Nic is our sister in law," Will-mother-fucking-Montgomery informs me. "She owns a bakery in Seattle. And I hope you got a lot of them because I'm hungry as hell."

"You're always hungry," Meg says and shakes her head. "Feeding him is the same as feeding a third-world country."

"Best cupcakes in the world," Sam says as she pulls warming dishes out of the oven and sets everything out in her gourmet kitchen buffet-style.

"I like your jersey," Will says to me with a smile. "Except the wrong name is on the back."

I'm beginning to relax now, not exactly sure how I feel about having dinner with a rock star and a football hero, but at least I can breathe.

Kind of.

"No, it's not," I reply and link my fingers with Declan's as I lean against the kitchen island.

"It doesn't say Montgomery," Will says, as if I'm slow.

"No. It doesn't. Sanders is my favorite player," I reply with a laugh.

"What?" He covers his heart, as though he's been stabbed and is dying a slow death. "This hurts."

"Sanders is an excellent running back, and when you managed to throw the ball at someone on your own team today, he's the one that ran it in for a touchdown."

Silence descends on the room for several long seconds, and then everyone, including Will, busts up laughing.

"I like her," Sam says, wiping tears from the corner of her eye. "She can stay."

"Well, despite the abuse you're slinging at me, I had the team sign the game ball for you today." He jogs over to the entryway and returns with the ball, then passes it to me.

"Wow, thank you. You didn't have to do that."

"Declan said you're a big fan, so I thought I'd send you back to New Orleans with something special."

"Thank you." I grin, turning the ball in my hands, looking at all the signatures. Then I surprise even myself when I throw it over to Will, who catches it easily and throws it right back.

"Good arm. Looking for a job?"

"No." I laugh and set the ball aside. "So how do you and Declan know each other?" I ask Leo. "I'm assuming it's through music."

"You're right," Leo says with a nod. "Declan helped write and produce several songs on a few of our albums."

"Wow." *Stop saying wow.* My gaze turns to Declan, who's watching me with happy hazel eyes. "Impressive."

"Hasn't he told you who he's worked with?" Meg asks, while loading up a plate. "I used to play with Leo, before Nash went nuts. He's my brother. Well," she clarifies with a shrug, "the closest thing I have to a brother anyway."

"Who have you worked with?" I ask Declan, who just shakes his head.

"Lots of people."

"Okay, he's being modest," Leo says with a grin. "I'll tell you. He works with us, but he's also worked with Bruce Springsteen, Adele, Coldplay, just to name a few."

My eyes are trained on Declan, who won't meet my gaze. If I'm not mistaken, he's blushing.

He's embarrassed.

"That's something to be proud of," I murmur and kiss his shoulder. "What do you do, Meg?"

Taking the focus off of Declan makes him relax, and I learn that Meg is a nurse at the children's hospital and Sam is a magazine editor.

I love, *love*, that these women are married to important, wealthy men, but have maintained their own careers, their own identities. I have a lot of respect for Sam and Meg.

Dinner is delicious, but I can't eat much. I'm too nervous and excited to eat. After dinner, Meg, Leo and Declan wander into the sunroom/music room off the kitchen to play songs and talk music.

Sam, Will and I are cleaning up from dinner, which is easy given that dishes go in the dishwasher and the food just needs to be recovered and put in the fridge. We take our cupcakes, Will grabs four of them— grumbling when Meg yells out that he can't have six because other people want to eat them too—some coffee, and sit in the living room. We can hear the music and murmurs from the next room, but we can still talk.

"How did you meet him?" Sam asks right away and bites into a lemon cupcake.

"I own the bar that he plays in a few nights a week," I reply and take a bite of my own chocolate cupcake, and just about die in ecstasy. "Oh my God, these are *so good*."

"Best ever," Sam agrees. "Nic is a genius when it comes to cake."

"Nic is my new favorite person," I say as I stuff

the rest in my mouth, not even caring that I'm not by myself.

Will smiles proudly. "Atta girl."

"I was just teasing earlier," I say to him and shift in my seat. "You played a good game today. I really am a Seattle fan."

"It's okay, Callie. I played like shit today. I've had a lot on my mind."

"Oh?" Sam asks with a raised brow. I'm still not sure how Sam and Will are connected, except through Leo and Meg, but something tells me that it goes deeper than that.

"Everything is perfect, and I'll fill you in in just a bit."

"Okay." Sam nods and sips her coffee.

"Okay, I have to ask, and forgive me for being rude, but I am dying to know how all of you know each other. I mean, I know Meg said that she and Leo grew up together, but you've also mentioned a sister-in-law Nic."

"Oh God, this is going to be confusing," Sam says with a laugh and looks at Will. "You tell her."

"I got this," Will says confidently. "Sam's brother is Luke Williams."

"The movie guy?" I ask with surprise.

"That's him," Sam says with a nod. "And he is married to Will's sister's best friend, Natalie."

"But like Leo and Meg," Will continues, "Nat and Jules are more like sisters. I sure see her as a sister."

"I also have another brother, Mark," Sam says, "and he's married to his high school sweetheart, Meredith."

"Where does Nic fit in?" I ask, already confused, my head swimming.

"Nic is married to my brother, Matt," Will says with a smile.

"Do you have other siblings?" I ask.

"Luke and Mark are it for me," Sam replies and sits back into the deep couch, grinning at Will.

"Jules is the baby of the family, and she's married to Nate," Will says. "My oldest brother, Isaac, is married to Stacy. My brother, Caleb, is married to Stacy's cousin, Brynna."

"I'm so confused," I cry out, but Sam laughs and shakes her head.

"He's not done yet."

"I also have a half-brother, Dominic, who is married to our event planner, Alecia."

"This is a huge family." I sit back and stare at them both, glassy eyed. "I thought Declan's family was big, but that's nothing compared to yours."

"We are big," Will agrees with a nod, then smiles and stands. "Follow me."

Sam and I look at each other, shrug, and follow Will into the music room where Leo is playing guitar, Declan piano, and Meg is singing a sweet song that I recognize. I sit next to Dec on the piano bench, leaning on his shoulder as he plays. Sam sits next to Leo, and Will simply lifts Meg, sits in her seat, and settles her in his lap. We listen until the song is finished, and erupt into applause.

"That's a great song," I murmur, only loud enough for Declan to hear.

"So, I have to tell you something," Meg says and suddenly looks nervous. Will wraps his arms around her and kisses her forehead.

"What's wrong?" Leo asks immediately as tears gather in Meg's eyes.

But she shakes her head, swallows, and with a watery smile, says, "I'm going to have a baby."

Will smiles proudly and lets go of Meg as she's pulled out of his lap by Leo, who wraps her in a gentle hug, rocking her back and forth, his own eyes wet.

"That's so great," Sam says sincerely. "Congratulations."

"It's gonna be a boy," Will announces.

"You know the sex already?" I ask with a frown. "She isn't even showing yet."

"It's too early," Meg says with a sniff. "He's hoping."

Declan laughs and begins to play Braham's Lullaby on the piano.

"So happy for you, Meg-pie," Leo says to her.

"I'm celebrating with more cupcakes," Will says, already on his way back to the kitchen.

"Bring the whole box," Meg calls out to him. "He'll eat the whole thing."

"I bought two dozen and hid the other one," Leo assures her, which makes us all smile.

This is... *nice*. Watching their connections with each other, their genuine love for each other, reminds me of my relationship with Adam.

It reminds me of Declan's family too, with all the siblings, and the laughter and the chaos.

I watch as Will and Declan fight over the last lemon cupcake, and Leo and Sam bicker about the landscaping she wants to be done in the spring. Meg is happy to nibble on her cake and snuggle up to her man, glowing with a life growing inside her.

It makes me yearn, in ways I never have before. But I know one thing: I'm so happy to be a part of it, no matter how small.

I grip Declan's hand in mine, and he squeezes it, three times, and smiles down at me, his eyes happy, and it makes me happy that I'm the reason for that smile.

Life sure doesn't suck right now.

***

"I can't believe I had dinner with Leo Nash and

Will Montgomery tonight," I say with a gusty sigh as I walk into our hotel room.

"Umm, who am I?" Declan asks with a laugh and pulls me against him for a long, deep kiss. "I've been waiting to do that for—"

"About five minutes, since you almost had sex with me in the elevator," I say with a laugh.

"Not my fault that the elevator is so fucking slow in this place," he grumbles against my neck. I know that if I let him, he'll drag me off to bed and give me another night that I won't soon forget, but I'm not ready for that.

Yet.

"Sit with me?" I ask, gesturing to the fireplace. I flip it on and sit on the sofa, in the middle, so no matter where he chooses to sit, I'll be smashed up against him.

He sits, wraps his arm around me, and I lean into him, my cheek on his chest, and watch the fire. I can feel his lips brushing back and forth on the top of my head. His fingers dance softly up and down my arm.

"Are you okay?"

"I'm so much better than okay, I don't think there's a word to describe it," I answer him honestly. "Thank you for today. For this whole weekend."

"It's completely my pleasure," he replies and tips my face up to meet my lips with his own.

"I started getting tattoos on my arm when I was seventeen," I blurt out, surprised that I said the words aloud. Declan shifts so he's still holding me, but I'm facing him now, and he can see every emotion that crosses my face.

This is far more intimate than anything we've ever done while naked.

"Go on," he says softly.

I swallow hard and try to decide where to begin.

"Start at the beginning," he says, as if he can read my mind.

"I've never been a cutter," I say, my eyes trained on the neckline of his plain white T-shirt. "Hurting myself never appealed to me, but I can understand why people do it, Declan. Sometimes life just hurts, and if you can control any of the pain, it makes you feel like, even for those few moments, you're in control.

"My childhood was challenging. I grew up fast when Mom died and Dad found solace in a bottle. I was an adult far sooner than I could vote. Life didn't suck, but it was a struggle, and when I was seventeen, I met a tattoo artist who didn't ask for ID when I lied and said I was eighteen."

Declan tilts his head to the side, listening intently. He's not just listening, he's *hearing* me. And that gives me the strength to keep talking.

"So I started up here," I say and pull my sleeve up so he can see the ball of my shoulder. "I'd heard that it hurt really bad up here, and I wanted it to hurt. I know that sounds crazy and stupid—"

"You are neither of those things," he says. His voice is calm, but his eyes are on fire.

"It did hurt," I continue. "I wanted the calla lilies because those were my mom's favorite and pink for breast cancer awareness."

He reaches up and traces the lines with just the tip of his finger, making me break out in goosebumps.

"As you know, tattoos can become addictive, and for a while that was my drug. I had the whole arm done, from shoulder to mid-forearm, in the span of about two years. The artist I was seeing wouldn't go down to my wrist because he said I was young and one day I might have a job that I would need to cover it for, so he said to just think on it."

"You never added to it," Declan says.

"No." I shake my head and watch his fingers tracing the lines, the vibrant colors of my ink. "I stopped getting tattoos altogether when I was twenty."

"Why?"

I take a deep breath and bite my lip. "Because I liked it too much. The pain. I would have gone every day if I could afford it, and when someone suggested I pierce my nipples, and I seriously thought about it, I knew it was time to stop."

"Lots of people have piercings," he says logically. "Your navel is pierced."

"They do, and the navel happened around the same time as the tattoos, but if I'd taken that step down that road, I would have mutilated my body, Declan. I didn't, and don't, want that. I like the ink on my arm; the navel is enough. I don't need anything else."

"Thank you for trusting me with this," Declan says, his voice rough.

Tell him you love him!

"I do trust you," I say instead and point to his own ink. "What does yours mean?"

"I was a young musician in college," he says with a sly grin. "You do the math."

CHAPTER THIRTEEN

~Callie~

"I don't know," I murmur, walking from room to room in the unusual farm-style house that my new realtor, Peggy Lewis, has found to show me. I thought, and Declan agreed, that it was a good idea to find a new realtor, given that Pete didn't seem to understand that *help me find a house* didn't also mean *let me take my pants off for you.*

"This house has everything you asked for," Peggy reminds me, following close behind me with her hands clenched at her waist. "Actually, each of the three homes I showed you today do."

"Mm hmm," I hum and ignore her. In the two weeks since we returned home from Seattle, I've been even more anxious to find my house and begin renovations. Maybe it was seeing how Sam and Leo decorated their house, and all of the ideas it inspired in me, or maybe it's that, despite being thankful that Adam's given me a place to stay, I'm tired of finding a different strange woman in the kitchen each morning, and it's just time to have my own space.

"It's nice," Declan says from across the room, giving me space to pace and think. Unlike Peggy, Declan gets me. "High ceilings, big rooms."

I nod, staring out of a window so big it practically spills out into the spacious back yard. I do like the space, and with a minimal amount of work, it would be gorgeous in no time.

But I can't picture myself living here. No matter how I try, I can't envision how I'd decorate it, what color of paints I'd use, which walls I'd knock down.

None of the three we've seen today speak to me, and it's frustrating me. Even if I'm not looking for a house for me to live in, I can usually picture how the house should be rehabbed in my head.

But today? Nada.

"Maybe I'm just not in the right mood," I say with a shrug and a sigh, then turn to Peggy. "I appreciate your time."

"So, did these just not fit what you had in mind?" Peggy asks, and I know she's just trying to do her job. She wants to find the right property for me, but damn it, I'm irritable, and I don't even know *why*.

"No, you did a great job. I'll definitely think about it."

"Well, just give me a call if you have any questions, or if you'd like to see more."

She ushers us out of the house and locks the door as we walk to Declan's car. Peggy waves as we pull away.

"Talk to me, baby," Declan says and takes my hand, squeezing three times.

"I don't know what to say," I reply.

"You're out of sorts today."

I nod and look out the passenger window. Geez,

I'm moody. Hormones? Probably. Or, I'm just a girl.

That's usually reason enough to get teary, but I don't like to cry, so that just makes me even crabbier.

"I liked the last house," I say after I clear my throat.

"But you didn't love it," he guesses correctly. "It's okay, you'll find it. You're not in a huge rush."

"Right." Except I am in a rush. I want my space. I want to get elbow-deep in a project and make something ordinary beautiful. I want that.

Soon, Declan pulls into his driveway, but rather than get out of the car, I turn to him.

"Dec, I'm not great company tonight. You can just take me home."

He frowns, his hazel eyes seeing too much as he cups my cheek and lightly brushes his thumb over my jaw. "I don't want to be without you tonight."

I lean into his touch, turn my face to kiss his palm, and nod. "Okay. Let's be lazy tonight."

"Do you know the definition of *lazy*?" he asks with a laugh and unlocks the house, gesturing for me to go ahead of him.

"The bar has been slow enough for me to take a couple of days off a week," I remind him. "I can be lazy." *Kind of.* "Why aren't you working tonight?"

"Broken sewer line," he says with a cringe. "Happens in buildings more than a hundred years old."

"Yuck." I shudder and glance to the empty room on my right. It's between the library and music room. I'd open it up with wide windows and make it a sunroom, and spend every morning with my coffee in there.

And my imagination chooses *now* to wake up. Great.

Once in the kitchen, Declan says, "What would you like for dinner?"

"A big burger and Tavern Tots from Highland Tavern." I sit in a stool and brace my chin in my hand on the island.

"I don't know where that is."

"It's in Denver. I've been craving it like crazy." I shrug. "Really good burger joint."

"Huh, well, I can go grab burgers here, but it's going to take time to get your Highland Tavern, and I'm hungry now."

"I don't want to go anywhere, and I don't want you to go anywhere. Let's just order pizza."

He nods and circles the island, then just hugs me. "Sure you're okay?"

"Yeah, I'm just thinking about the houses we saw today. I think I'll pass on all three."

"We'll find you something."

I nod and smile, tired of moping, and being a Debbie-downer. I do my best to shake off my mood and playfully grab Declan's ass.

"I'm hungry too. Are you gonna feed me, or what?"

"I'll feed you," he says after kissing my chin. He pulls his phone out and dials the pizza place we both like, places our order, and reaches out for my hand. "Let's eat and lounge upstairs. We can watch Netflix and be lazy."

"Perfect. I'm gonna take my pants off."

"That is an excellent plan," he says with a laugh. The main stairway in this house is grand and dramatic. I'd refinish the banister and hang a more modern chandelier over the landing.

There are four empty bedrooms upstairs, and I'd love to knock down a couple of walls, make the spaces bigger.

Stop it! This is not my house!

I have to stop renovating Declan's house in my

head. I don't live here, and I probably never will.

Declan's right; I'll find my place.

The pizza arrives faster than we expected, so he fetches it while I shimmy out of my jeans and climb in bed, under the covers and everything. I grab his pillow and bury my face in it, breathing him in.

I fucking love the way he smells.

"Okay, despite my better judgment, I had them add mushrooms because I know you like them," Declan announces as he returns to the room. He stops on a dime, in the middle of the space, holding a big box of pizza, sodas and a bag of bread and just stares at me.

"What?"

"I—" He takes a deep breath and shakes his head, then walks the rest of the way to me. "You're just beautiful. Sometimes you take my breath away."

I blink at him, completely thrown. Declan is a mellow man, but he's also an artist, and with his artist's heart comes a romantic side. He has a sweet habit of knocking me back a step with it because I never know when it's going to show up.

"Thank you."

***

"The show comes on in fifteen," Adam announces and changes the channel on the big TV in the back of the bar to the Travel Channel.

"I can't believe they were here only a month ago, and it's already going to air." The Odyssey isn't packed this evening, and that's okay with me. It's a Monday, after all, and deep into autumn. I'm nervous about the show, how I'll look, how the bar will look. Having a huge crowd here would only make it worse.

I grin down the bar at Declan. Of course he came to watch it with me. He calms me. I've never told him that, but I'm pretty sure he knows.

He checks an incoming text on his phone and

frowns, replies, and lays the phone face-down on the bar. I cock a brow when he looks at me, but he shakes his head, as if it's no big deal.

Must be work.

A large group comes through the doors, laughing and chatting, catching all of our attention, and I feel my jaw drop as I realize it's the entire Boudreaux family, even Declan's mama.

"Hi everyone!" I smile at them all and then look questioningly at Declan, but he just smiles. "What are you all doing?"

"Well, we came to watch the show, of course," Dec's mom says and winks at me. "This place sure is beautiful. No wonder they wanted to put it on television."

"Thank you."

"We mostly want to watch Dec make an ass of himself," Beau says as he claps Declan on the back.

"That's your job, big brother," Declan replies.

"Well, have a seat wherever you like, and I'll have my cocktail waitress come get your drink orders."

I walk over to Declan and lean in so only he can hear me. "Did you know this was happening?"

"I told Beau and Eli about it when we worked out together yesterday. I didn't know that they used the family phone tree to fill everyone else in, but I think it's nice."

"It's better than nice," I reply. "I just didn't expect it."

"They like you," he says simply, kisses my cheek and joins his family just as the opening credits of the show begin.

The room grows quiet as we watch, and I'm thankful The Odyssey is the first bar showcased in the show because waiting until the end would be pure torture.

"Lookin' good, Callie!" Rhys calls out to me when I first appear on camera, and the other boys whistle and cat-call.

"I'll break your fingers," Declan says in that smooth way he has, as if he was saying *the weather sure is nice.*

"You should have let Charly do your makeup, Dec," Eli says when it's Declan's turn on the screen. "You might have looked prettier."

"Boys," their mama says sternly, and all three of them pout as if they're tiny children again, making me laugh.

"You wore the shoes!" Charly exclaims.

"Of course," I reply. "I love those shoes."

When our segment is over, which feels like it was three seconds and three hours all at once, we all applaud and cheer. I'm happy with the results. They made the bar look hip, fun and classy, and that's exactly the atmosphere I'm looking for.

Having Adam with me, and Declan's family too, is just icing on the cake.

***

"Everyone's gone," Declan says after coming back in from walking his family to their cars. "And they had fun."

"Me too." I grin, and catch a look that passes between Declan and Adam.

"Hey, Callie, I think there's something on the roof that needs your attention," Adam says.

"The roof? The roof is closed."

"Well, the movement sensors went off, so you should go see what's up."

I frown and cock my hip, my hand braced on it. "You're too chicken shit to go up to the roof, so you're sending a musician and his girlfriend to check it out?"

"Hey, I may be a musician, but I can kick serious

ass when I have to," Declan says.

"I can too," I reply with a wink. "Okay, let's check it out. I've told you for years, Adam, this place is haunted."

We climb the stairs, and I find nothing out of place in the bar area, and then when I step out onto the terrace, I stop cold.

One of the firepits is lit, and on the table is a spread of food from my favorite restaurant.

The Highland Tavern.

"Declan," I breathe and rush to the table. "How?"

"I have resources," he says with a smile. "I also have cupcakes from Nic's shop in Seattle."

I turn and simply look at him, my arms hanging limply at my sides. He did this for me. This took planning and work, and he did it for me.

"Thank you."

"You're welcome." He takes my hand and kisses my knuckles. "Let's eat before it gets cold."

"It's hot?" I grab a burger and bite into heaven. "Oh, my God."

"Of course it's hot," he replies with a smirk. "You can't eat cold burgers."

"Seriously, this is ridiculous," I say around a huge bite of burger.

"That it's hot?"

"No. Yes." I laugh. "It's ridiculous that you had this flown in."

"You wanted it." He shrugs as if it's no big deal and takes a bite of his own burger. "Wow. That's amazing."

"Told you."

"I'll have this flown in every week," he says, reaching for a tot.

"That's excessive," I reply with a laugh.

"No, I think it's necessary."

We fall into a comfortable silence as we munch on our food, and when all that's left is oily wrappers, he pulls me to him and snuggles me close.

"Delicious," I say with a contented sigh.

"Yes, you are," he murmurs while nibbling on my neck.

"The food."

"That too."

"I want cupcakes."

He smiles, reaches for a box on the floor and hands it to me. It's a plain white gift box with a red ribbon wrapped around it.

Inside are a dozen cupcakes, all different flavors, and a note.

"Would Nic send a note?" I ask, but Declan just shrugs. He's no help.

Calliope:

I'm so proud of you. Tonight should be special. You've earned it. Thank you for spending it with me.

Thank you for being mine.

Yours,

Declan

Oh my.

"Declan, I—"

I slip the note back in the envelope and lay it on the table.

"You what?"

Tell him you love him! Now's the best time.

But I'm such a damn wimp.

"Tonight wouldn't have been half as special without you. And not just because of all of this, which I love, but because when I'm with you—"

He kisses my hand and squeezes it three times. "When you're with me?"

"I just feel better. I feel *more.*" His eyes widen and then darken. "Emotions are brighter, and that's the only way I can describe it."

"I think that's a beautiful way to describe it," he whispers before he pulls me in and kisses the hell out of me. "You *are* more, Callie. We're more."

I nod and brush my fingertips down his cheek, his neck. "I like it."

A slow smile spreads over his sexy face. "I like it too."

CHAPTER FOURTEEN

~Declan~

I wake up needing her. I'm not jolted awake out of a dream, or because of a noise in the house.

It's because I *need her*, and I'm not only hard as stone, but I'm sweaty with it.

I roll over. The moon is shining in the window, casting a blue glow over the bed, and there she is, with her back to me, curled up in a ball, sleeping peacefully. Her arm is over the covers, the bright colors of her ink perfectly lit up by the moon.

I became addicted to the pain.

That there was ever a time in her life that she needed the pain as an outlet for her feelings pulls a sorrow, a longing, from so deep inside me it almost renders me breathless. And the fact that she pulled herself together and became what she is now makes me burst with pride.

I reach over and trace the ink with the pad of my forefinger, smiling when she lets out a soft moan. Her noises are the best music I've ever heard. The way she breathes when I'm inside her, the way her muscles tighten around my cock, around my body.

I've never been with anyone like her, and I know I never will be again. She's *mine*. Callie is it for me, and I know it's going to take patience while she comes around to the idea, but she'll get there.

I'm nothing if not patient. Some would call me too laid back, or even lazy, but the truth is, I just know how to bide my time.

I smile as she leans back into my touch, still sound asleep. The connection we have can't be explained with words. It just exists, like electricity, or the moving of the tides by that bright moon.

God knows I feel both the energy and the pull of her, even when we're not together.

I let my hand drift around to her chest and gently roll her already hard nipple through my fingers, then slide down her flat stomach and firmly urge her onto her back so I can part her legs, brushing my knuckles over the soft flesh of her thighs.

"Mmm," she moans and cracks her eyes open. "Time is it?"

"No idea," I whisper and kiss her belly as I work my way down. She threads her fingers through my hair, over and over again, with a sweet touch, and when I open her center to me and place a deep kiss over her pussy, those fingers clench in my hair, not pulling me closer but holding on while the first jolt of pleasure bursts through her.

"Oh my," she breathes, then catches her breath again when my lips close over her clit and suck, not hard, but in a persistent rhythm. My face is rocking against her, and I can't get enough of her. I love the way she tastes, her scent, all of it. I could camp out here all night.

But I need her. I need to be inside her, to claim her. It's primal, and 100% male ego, and I don't fucking care.

"Love you," she whispers, just as I push two fingers inside her, and my world just tilted on its axis.

"Love you too," I reply softly, but she's whimpering, her lip caught between her teeth, already in that incredible place she goes when the pleasure takes over. It's the damnedest thing to watch.

I kiss both her thighs, her flat stomach, then over to her side. Sex with Callie is usually fierce and passionate, fast, hard, maybe a little dirty. But tonight I want to savor, enjoy.

Love.

My body covers hers, her legs are hitched around my hips, and her arms are wrapped around my back. Her clean face is sleepy and happy, and as I slip inside her, we both sigh at how damn good it feels.

"It's always different," she murmurs. "Just when I think I know exactly how you'll feel, you surprise me."

I grin, seated inside her to the hilt, and kiss her neck, then drag my lips up to her earlobe. "I want to keep surprising you."

She cups my cheek and guides my lips to hers, and for several long minutes, I move at a slow, leisurely pace in and out of her while I make love to her mouth. I link my fingers with hers, squeeze, and pin her hand over her head, using it as leverage as I pick up the pace, just a bit, adding a little more force to each thrust.

Not to change the tone of the moment, but to kick up her own need just a notch because I don't know how much longer I'm going to last. Jesus, she's sweet. Tight.

Mine.

"Love the way you feel," she whispers and grabs my ass with her free hand, pulling me against her, and I can feel the tension building. Her back arches and her pussy tightens around me, making my eyes cross. "Your pubic bone hits me in just the right damn spot."

"Callie, go over, baby."

She cries out, then whimpers softly as she surrenders to the orgasm and pulls me over with her. We're quiet, the room is hushed as we fall apart, then cling to each other and fall back together, catching our breath.

I brush the hair off her face and kiss her softly, then roll us to our sides, wrap her up against me and kiss her forehead.

"Sleepy," she mumbles, and before I can reply, she's slipped away, back into sleep.

I want this, every night.

***

Over the past year or so, my brothers, plus Ben and Rhys, have started getting together a couple times a month for a guy night. Mostly, we play pool, drink beer, and rag on each other.

It's generally a good time, and as much as we all love our women, it's nice to not have any estrogen around for a little while.

Not that we'd ever admit that to them.

Tonight, we're in a dive bar a few blocks from the Quarter, playing pool and watching Monday night football. We usually gather at Ben's, but he's having work done on his place—mine's not ready, and the others have that estrogen I mentioned earlier.

So, dive bar it is.

"Nine ball, corner," Eli says and takes his shot, easily sinking the ball.

"So you're moving into town?" I ask Beau as he watches Eli survey the table. Beau has lived on the inn property since Gabby opened, to keep an eye on things there, and to protect Gabby and Sam.

"Yeah, I'm moving into the loft next to Eli's townhouse," he confirms. "There's no need for me to be out at the inn now that Rhys is there."

"We told you a hundred times," Rhys says and smirks when Eli misses his next shot. "We don't mind if you stay. Your house is separate from the inn, you're not in anyone's way."

"It makes sense to move into town," Beau says. "I won't have to commute to work anymore. The loft will do just fine until I find something else to buy."

"Are you looking for a house?" Ben asks. "I think I saw a house about a block from me come up on the market."

"Not yet," Beau replies. "Although I do love the garden district."

"How's your house coming along?" Rhys asks me.

"It's coming, one room at a time," I reply with a shrug. "No hurry."

"Declan's never in a hurry for anything," Eli says, but he smiles over at me with affection. It's not a dig; it's the truth.

I simply shrug just as my phone rings.

"This is Declan."

"Hey, man, it's Adam. Are you available to chat?"

"Sure, what's up?"

"No, I mean in person."

"Is Callie okay?" I ask with a frown.

"She's great. I'd just like to talk to you in person."

Ben raises a brow, but I just shrug. "Sure. I'm at the Big Boy, it's a bar in—"

"I know it. See you in ten?"

"See you then."

I hang up and frown.

"What's that about?" Eli asks as he takes a shot and misses, then swears a blue streak when Ben laughs at him.

"Not sure. Adam, Callie's friend, is on his way to *chat*."

"Uh oh," Rhys says and pats my shoulder. "Good luck with that."

"What does that mean?"

"Means he's gonna want to have the same chat with *you* that we all had with Rhys last year," Beau says.

"You guys didn't scare me," Rhys insists.

"You didn't have any reason to be afraid," Eli replies. "What did you do, Dec?"

"I didn't do anything," I say and cross my arms over my chest, lean back against the bar and watch Eli at the table.

"I'm glad we get to watch this," Ben says and cracks his knuckles. "Just so you know, if he takes a swing at you, we have your back."

"Maybe," Beau says. "Depends on what he did."

"I didn't do anything," I reply, my voice hard just as Adam walks through the door, surveys the room, then walks toward me when he sees me at the bar in the back of the place. He doesn't look angry. His face is calm, his walk loose and relaxed.

"Doesn't look mad," Rhys murmurs, reading my mind.

"Hey, Adam," I say and shake his hand. "You remember my brothers."

"I do. Hi, everyone." He nods at them, then turns to me. "Can we talk?"

"You bet."

He glances at the others and then at me.

"We can talk in front of them," I tell him. "They're a vault, and I don't have anything to hide."

"Fair enough." He sits on a stool to my right and shakes his head at the bartender when asked if he wants anything to drink. "I'd like to talk about Callie."

"Told you," Beau says, earning a look from me

that says *shut it*.

"Shoot," I say and lean against the bar, facing him.

"Look, her dad's gone, and I'm the only man in her life that gives a fuck about her. You and I have been friends for a long time, and I like you, but I love her." He stops and frowns, looking down at his hands, and I suddenly respect my friend more than I ever have. "You have a history, Declan."

"He's a man whore," Eli says from across the room.

"Not helping," I say mildly.

"No, he's right," Adam says with a chuckle. "You are. So am I, so I know it when I see it."

"And you want to make sure that Callie isn't just another notch in my bedpost," I say, nodding.

"She's better than that," Adam says simply. "She's better than any of us."

"Damn," Ben whispers. "I like him."

"Honestly," Eli says as he sets his cue down and walks toward us, "I've been wondering what's going on there too."

"I think we all have," Rhys says. "I know I haven't been in the picture for long, but even I know that you're not a one-woman kind of guy, Dec."

I frown, suddenly ashamed of myself for the first time in my life where women are concerned. In the past, I always made it clear that if I was with a woman, it wasn't going to be long term. We had fun together, and went our separate ways, no harm, no foul.

But it never occurred to me that it could have caused hurt feelings, and that leaves a bad taste in my mouth.

I glance around at the guys I respect most in the world, and then let out a gusty breath. "The truth?"

"No, lie to us, moron," Beau says and rolls his eyes.

"I love her," I say, enjoying the way the words roll off my tongue. "Adam's right, she's better than any of us. She's probably too fucking good for me, but I'm so damn in love with her, I can't breathe."

"Well, that's just the sweetest thing," the bartender says, wiping a tear from her eye, eavesdropping unapologetically.

"Adorable," Adam agrees, but he's not smiling. "But that doesn't really ease my mind."

"What do you want from me?" I ask.

"I want to know where you plan to take this. Is she fun for now and when you decide you're *not* in love with her anymore you move on to the next thing?"

"I should fucking deck you for that."

"It's a fair question," Ben says quietly.

"Look, Callie and I have known each other for about four minutes. It's early, way too early to put a ring on it. Especially for Callie. She doesn't trust easily, and she definitely doesn't make life-changing decisions in just a few months' time."

"You're evading," Adam says. "And you forget that I know her. I agree, if you dropped to one knee and pulled out a rock, she'd run screaming into the night."

I frown, hating that he's right.

"But," he continues, "that doesn't mean that you haven't already thought about what you want."

"I want her. All of her." I stand and pace to the pool table, then back to Adam. "I am in love with her. Not for a month, or until she irritates me. For good. I plan to make her mine, but damn it, it's not as easy as just deciding it and expecting her to fall in line. She has a say."

"You're damn right she has a say," Adam replies, smiling now. "And you've told me all I need to know."

"You're going to make a good dad someday,"

Rhys says to Adam. "I hope you have a girl."

"No kids for me, pal," Adam replies, then shudders and takes a swig of my beer. "Unlike Declan, I'm a player for life."

"That's what I thought, man." I clap him on the back and motion to the bartender, who's smiling at me with bonafide heart eyes, for another beer.

"I think we've all thought that at some point," Eli adds with a shrug. "And then you meet the person that turns your life upside down, and you can't remember why you thought that way in the first place."

My brother is one smart bastard.

"Not me, man," Adam insists, less forcefully now. "I'm out of here. Y'all are too mushy for me."

"We're not mushy," Ben says with a frown. "We're respectful."

"Hey, I respect women," Adam says. "They're the strongest creatures on this earth. I just don't intend to have to choose among the three billion of them on Earth to be with forever. There are too many to enjoy."

Adam waves and leaves, and the five of us grow quiet for a moment. "I like my choice," Rhys says honestly. "And I have no problem choosing her every day, for the rest of my life."

It's the best choice there is, and Callie is my *only* choice.

***

I never nap. It's not productive, and when I wake up, I'm grouchy as fuck and disoriented, but I fell asleep on the sofa in the music room the next day. My ringing phone wakes me, and I fumble it as I push myself into a sitting position.

"'Lo," I say, not even checking the caller ID before answering.

"Holy shit, you're actually answering," the woman on the other end exclaims, making me wince.

Should have checked the fucking caller ID.

"Hi, Beth," I mumble and rub my hand over my face. "What's up?"

"Don't try to pretend that you haven't been dodging me for the past two months. I've sent texts almost every day, and I've called at least twice a week."

I know, and it annoys the shit out of me.

"Well, you caught me now. I only have a minute," I lie and settle in for the tongue lashing I'm sure to get.

"I guess you don't have some woman sitting next to you right now," Beth says, her voice dripping with censure. "If you did, you'd be ignoring me again."

"Is there a point to this call?" I finally ask.

"I haven't seen you in three months, Declan. That's not okay. I know you're busy with gigs, and probably with a whole harem of women, but a lot has happened. I have important news. You won't like it, but you need to hear it from me. In person."

I sigh and shake my head. Beth's always been overly dramatic. "I honestly don't have time to meet up with you, Beth. Can't you just tell me over the phone?"

"I need one hour of your time, Declan Boudreaux, and I'm not hanging up until you agree to give it to me."

She's also like a pit bull when she sets her teeth in. Knowing this is a losing battle, and seeing that I really do have to meet up with Callie in less than an hour, I cave.

"Fine. I have Wednesday night off. I'll meet you for drinks."

"Dinner," she insists. "Come on, you know you miss me."

Right. Like I miss the flu.

I laugh in frustration, pacing the room now. "Fine. Dinner. But you only get one hour, Beth, and then I walk away."

"Fine." Her voice is smug and I can just picture the smile on her medically-enhanced lips. "I want to go somewhere good."

"You're pushing it. I'll text you Wednesday to confirm."

"You better, Declan. No more dodging me. You can put the flavor of the week on hold for one hour."

"That's enough, Beth." My voice is cold and hard. "I said I'd meet you, and I will. If you keep insulting me, I'll simply tell you to go to hell."

"Right." She laughs, setting my teeth on edge. "You'd never tell me to go to hell, Declan. You love to hate me too much."

"The *hate* part is close enough. Goodbye, Beth."

I want to punch a wall. Few things make me truly angry in this world, but Beth is right at the top of the list. Knowing I need a half hour in the gym, punching the fuck out of a bag to relieve some of this energy before I see Callie, I shoot her a text.

Hey babe, gonna be a little late.

A few moments later she replies.

No problem. See you soon.

Just seeing those five words from her helps to calm me. I grab my gym bag and lock up, then jog out to my car.

Some time with the punching bag is still in order. Better yet, maybe Eli will spar with me. Kicking someone's ass always feels better than the punching bag.

CHAPTER FIFTEEN

~Callie~

I'm scrubbing the kitchen floor on my hands and knees, like a woman on the edge. Because I *am* a woman on the edge, and that just pisses me off. And what do I do when I'm pissed off?

I clean.

Because I'm a normal, red-blooded American woman, and that's what we do. The same way we go all soft over babies and cry during Hallmark movies and enjoy flowers. And sometimes we say *I love you* during the sweetest, most intimate sex ever.

I cringe and sit back on my heels as I dunk my rag in the bucket of warm soapy water. I can't believe I *did* that! I mean, it wasn't entirely my fault. I was half asleep, and it was so *good* and the words just slipped out. I didn't even remember or realize I said it until this morning when I woke up, but then it hit me: he didn't say it back.

It's embarrassing. And I have to see him in a little

bit and try to act like everything's normal, when it definitely isn't.

Just as I'm calling myself every kind of moron in the book, my phone pings with a text from Dec. *Hey babe, gonna be a little late.*

Great. We'll just prolong the misery. The bathroom needs a good scrubbing.

I quickly text him back and am glaring at the backsplash behind the stove, wondering how in the bloody hell the marinara sauce ended up on the tile—doesn't Adam use a lid when he cooks?—when the man himself comes sauntering through the front door, a smile on his handsome face. He stops cold when he sees me.

"Uh oh," he says.

"What?" I snap, still frowning at the tile. Why is dried tomato sauce so hard to get off?

"You're mad."

"I'm cleaning," I reply.

"Which means you're mad."

I shrug, still not looking at him.

"Wanna talk about it?" he asks.

"No," I reply immediately, then quit scrubbing and spin around to face Adam. "I don't get men."

"So you *do* want to talk about it."

"I mean, I guess it's not really his fault, and if he's not in the same place I am, it's okay, but damn it, I'm embarrassed that pisses me off more than anything."

"Back up," Adam says, shaking his head while he takes a seat at the breakfast bar. "What happened?"

I twist my rag in my hands and frown. "Did you hear the part where I said I'm embarrassed?"

"You can tell me. It can't be that bad."

"I said *I love you* and he didn't say it back."

Adam's eyes get big, then he clears his throat. "Wow, you said the L word?"

"Yeah." I drop the rag in the bucket, then lean on the counter and bury my face in my hands. "I'm so dumb."

"You're not dumb," he says. "How did you say it?"

"While we were having sex," I mumble into my hands. "Jesus, he must think I'm an idiot."

"You don't have anything to be embarrassed about," Adam says, confidence in his voice.

"I don't?" I look up from my hands and he's smiling. "Why?"

"If you said it during sex, it doesn't count." He smiles proudly, but I just stare at him, frowning in confusion.

"Is that guy logic?"

"You were in the moment, Callie. Maybe you said, *Oh, I love that*, or something. Maybe he didn't hear you."

"That's stupid," I announce and begin pacing around the kitchen. "I didn't really *mean* to let it slip out, but I was still half asleep, and he was going down on me, and he's *so good* at that, and I couldn't help it. But he didn't say it back, and now he has to think I'm stupid. Or, I've freaked him out."

My phone buzzes with another text from Declan.

Sorry to do this, but something came up. Been a rough day. I'll definitely be there to walk you to your car after work. Sorry babe.

"See!" I show Declan the text, knowing that I sound like a crazy woman, and not caring. "He's blowing me off. He's never blown me off before. I've made everything weird."

I don't bother to respond to Declan. I just toss my phone on the counter and grab a rag to feverishly scrub down the cabinets.

"You're a pig, by the way. This kitchen is disgusting."

"I don't cook in it," he replies, smiling at me. "The girls I bring home sometimes do."

"Well, they're pigs then. And why are you grinning at me?"

"Because you make me smile."

I frown, leaning on the broom handle. "Why are you so calm? What do you know?"

He shakes his head. "Nothing. I just think you're overreacting."

"If you told a girl that you loved her—" He scoffs, but I ignore him and keep going. "And she didn't say it back, didn't say *anything* back, are you telling me that you wouldn't feel like a jackass?"

"Look, all I'm saying is, maybe he didn't hear you. Or, maybe it really just has been a bad day. There could be a million reasons why he had to cancel on you today. I mean, why do women always assume the worst?"

"Because we think about stuff," I reply, as if he's being an idiot. "This is important, Adam."

"I get it." He holds his hands up in surrender. "I'm just saying, you're *over* thinking it, and this is exactly the reason that I don't get involved with only one woman."

"No, you get involved with every woman in the United States and hurt everyone's feelings," I snap, and then feel bad.

"Hey, they know the score," Adam says in his own defense.

"Sorry." My voice is soft, and now I'm pissed because I'm on the verge of tears. "I just didn't want to make it weird. Maybe he's just not in the same place as me, and that's okay."

"I'm going to tell you a secret about men, and you can't tell anyone I told you because if you do, I could lose my man card. Men really aren't that deep. We generally say what we mean, so when he said it's been a tough day and something came up, that's probably the truth. And if he didn't say it back, he either didn't hear you, or he thought you were talking about the sex. Or his mouth was busy." He's ticking items off on his fingers, his eyes pointed at the ceiling while he thinks.

"But you don't think I made it weird."

"I don't think so, no."

"Okay." I take a deep breath and tighten my pony tail. "You just saved me from having to clean the bathroom."

"I wouldn't be mad if you cleaned it anyway."

"You should clean it," I reply and prop my hands on my hips.

"I don't do bathrooms."

"You need a maid."

"I have you," he says and smirks, knowing that I'll beat the shit out of him for that remark. "I'll just nudge Declan into pissing you off more often."

"You *are* a jackass."

"Yep." He grins and walks toward his bedroom. "I'm gonna take a nap before work."

"Okay." He disappears and I empty the bucket, then put the cleaning supplies away and go to my own bedroom. A nap before work doesn't sound too bad. Since I don't get to see Declan this afternoon, I have time for one.

I lie down and sigh. Maybe Adam's right and I'm just overreacting. Maybe he didn't hear me. Did I whisper it? I try to remember, but all I know is that he was making me see stars with that amazing tongue of his.

It'll be okay. I'll see him tonight, and follow him home after he walks me to my car the way I always do, and things will go back to normal.

I hope.

***

It's been a slow night at work. Weeknights usually are this time of year anyway. It's hurricane season, and the weather is less predictable, so the tourist crowds slow down. We'll get another rush around Christmas time, so for now we really depend on the weekends to get us through.

But that means that during the week I have too much time to think. I usually plan drink specials, but I'm eager to see Declan.

"Stop it," Adam murmurs as he passes me on his way to the beer tap. "You're doing the girl over-thinking thing."

"I am not," I lie and elbow him in the ribs. "You are not a mind reader, you know."

"When it comes to women I am," he says and wiggles his eyebrows.

"Ew." I shiver. "TMI."

Finally, the night comes to a close, but Declan hasn't shown up. He usually gets here about a half hour before closing, but he's not around when Adam leaves out the back, locking up on his way, and I go through the front.

I lock the door and turn to walk to my car and about jump out of my skin when I see Dec leaning against the building, the way he used to when we first reopened.

"You scared me!"

"Sorry," he says with a grin. "I just got here, figured I'd wait outside."

"You're like a ninja." I turn on the sidewalk and he falls into step beside me, but he doesn't take my hand like he usually would. "So you had a bad day?"

"Yeah." He nods, but doesn't explain further, and we fall into an uneasy silence. He seems distracted.

"Are you okay?" I ask.

"Fine."

I nod, the knot in my gut growing. I *did* screw up. I knew it. I hate this new tension. It's never been here before, not once, even when we tried to do the just friends thing before, and the thought of that makes me nauseous, because if he suggests we go back to being friends, I won't be able to do it. Not with Declan.

I'm just too in love with him.

Not touching him is killing me. Finally, unable to stand the silence any more, I blurt, "I cleaned today."

I cleaned today? That's the best I can come up with? But he looks down at me, truly looking me in the eyes for the first time tonight, and smiles softly. He grabs my hand and squeezes three times as he says, "You're so sweet."

And for that second, my world is right again.

But he lets go and looks away, and we're right back where we were.

I'm so damn confused!

Finally, we reach my car. I just want to get back to his place so we can make love and I can ask him what's really wrong. I want to talk this out, and make it better. I *need* to make it better.

I need him.

When I reach for the handle of the door, he leans in and brushes his lips over the edge of my mouth and backs away. He doesn't kiss the hell out of me, or threaten to fuck me right here for the whole French Quarter to see the way he usually does.

He just backs away, and without meeting my eyes, says, "I'll talk to you tomorrow."

Oh. So I'm not invited back to his house.

Thrown, and at a loss, I just nod and get in the car, and without looking back, I pull away, driving blindly while tears form in my eyes. What in the ever loving hell just happened? He brushed me off, that's for sure, but was he brushing me off for good?

Who was that?

Because it certainly wasn't the man I know and have grown to love.

It's a good thing it's the middle of the night, and that traffic is pretty much non-existent because I'm not sure how I get back to Adam's. I'm on autopilot as I park and drag myself into the condo, which is dark and empty. Adam must have gone to someone else's place, which suits me just fine. The last thing I need tonight is to hear him fucking some girl in the next room.

This way I can have a temper tantrum in peace.

I drop my bag on the couch, kick my shoes off, and take my clothes off, dropping them as I walk into my bedroom. I don't give a shit that I've just left a path of clothes from the living room to my room.

I'll pick them up eventually.

I fall into my bed, pull the covers up to my chin, turn on my side and let the tears come. I've screwed everything up. Declan is so uncomfortable around me that he can't even *look* at me, let alone touch me. He doesn't want me around tonight, and I *always* go back to his place after work.

I've stayed in this room maybe a half a dozen nights since I started seeing Declan. So the fact that the tension was so thick I could cut it with a knife, and he doesn't want me at his house, says that this is pretty much over between us.

And, oh, how it hurts.

My whole body aches as I cry it out, and when I've shed all the tears I have inside me, I start to get a little mad.

Or a lot mad.

I've had to walk on eggshells around men my whole life. I refuse to do it now. If Declan can't handle my feelings, that's not my problem, and I can't regret telling him that I love him, because I do. So much.

I have to be true to myself. I deserve that, and damn it, I'm going to keep being honest with myself and everyone else in my life. I'm done pussyfooting around.

So screw Declan and his weird mood and his brushing me off.

I guess the bathroom is going to get scrubbed after all.

I climb out of bed, throw on my ragged old sweats and a T-shirt, fill my trusty bucket and get to work on the bathroom.

By the time Adam rolls through the door approximately three hours later, the rest of the condo shines.

"You're here," he says in surprise. His eyelids are heavy, his clothes rumpled, and his hair a mess from someone's fingers.

"Nothing wrong with your eyes," I reply, finally tired.

"And judging by the smell and look of the place, last night didn't go well, huh?"

I sigh and shake my head, rinsing out the bucket. "No, it didn't."

"Wanna talk about it?" he asks with a yawn. He scratches his chest.

"No. I really don't, Adam. But thanks."

"Wanna snuggle?" he offers as he hugs me, but I can smell another woman on him, and although he isn't mine, I still don't like it.

"No, you smell like sex," I say, pulling away.

"I'll shower."

"I really want to be left alone."

He nods. "Okay. I'm sorry, Cal."

I shrug. "You win some and you lose some."

Despite the exhaustion, sleep doesn't come easy. I toss and turn for what feels like hours before I get up and take an allergy pill that isn't non-drowsy, and then when I do sleep, it's fitful.

I dream of Declan, but he's mean. He's laughing at me as he takes another woman by the hand and walks away from me. I don't know who the girl is, and it doesn't matter. He wants her and not me.

Then Keith is there, saying, "I told you I'd never love you, Callie. You're fun, but not the kind of girl someone loves."

I shake my head, trying to run away, but my feet won't move. Why won't they move? I can hear people laughing, but my head is heavy. I can't look up from my feet. I can only see lots of feet, of people standing close together, and they're laughing.

Finally, I fight to raise my head, and everyone's there. Adam, my father, Declan and all of his family. Keith, and the people I used to work with in Denver.

And they're all laughing at me. I'm so embarrassed. I want to run, but my feet still won't move, and when I look back down, I'm naked. Oh, my God! Why am I naked?

I push away from a brick wall that's just appeared, and I slowly float into the air, but my feet are heavy, and I land just a short hop away, but there's a pole, and I try to hide behind it.

Holy shit, I'm naked! And they're laughing. And I can't get away.

I'm sweating, and Adam keeps saying, "Stop it, Callie." But then he laughs again, and points at me. My face is wet. Is it raining?

"Callie."

I'm shaken awake, and Adam is in the bed with me, holding me against him. "Come on, baby, wake up now."

"Stop laughing at me," I whimper, hating the weakness in my voice. The sun is up, shining in my window. I forgot to pull the blinds when I went to bed.

And Adam is wrapped around me. He took a shower, because he smells clean. I burrow into him, crying harder than I have in *years* as his hands rub circles on my back and he kisses my head.

"It's okay, sweetie. You're okay. It was just a dream."

"It was horrible."

"Shhh." He's brushing my hair back from my face. Half of it is stuck to both dried and wet tears on my face, and it feels good when he brushes it back. "Just a dream."

"So cruel."

"Who, baby?"

"Everybody." The tears come harder. "Laughing at me. Telling me that I'm not lovable."

"Well, that's a load of shit," he says and kisses my forehead. "Because I love you."

"I love you too," I whisper. God, it feels good to hear someone say it. "I feel so ashamed."

"For loving me? No need, I'm lovable too."

"No," I say, smiling despite myself. "Because of Declan."

"Stop it right now, Callie." He takes my chin in his hand and tilts my head back so he can see my face. "Stop beating yourself up. Calm down and go back to sleep for a few hours."

"Will you stay?" I ask, holding onto him like he's a lifeline.

"Always, you know that."

We both sigh as we cling to each other, and I feel him fall asleep, his chest moving rhythmically with each breath, and that makes my eyes heavy, and I follow him into a dreamless sleep.

CHAPTER SIXTEEN

~Callie~

I haven't seen him at all since he walked me to my car Monday night. He's called twice, and texted a couple of times, but that's it.

He's backing away, and I feel so powerless because there's nothing I can do to stop it. He feels the way he feels, and that's that. We have a standing dinner date on Wednesdays, so I'm looking forward to seeing him and really talking. It's always been so easy to talk to him, this shouldn't be any different. Is it going to suck? Yes. But damn it, this sucks too, and I'd rather have some answers.

I'm at the bar before noon to go over the books and to take a look at the space next door that just went up for sale. I've done well enough in the past three months that I am seriously considering an expansion. I'd like to add a dance floor and maybe even a full kitchen for a menu.

It'll be expensive, and would require quite a

renovation, which excites me. Adam arrives around one to look at the other space with me. I don't say much to the realtor as we look, but I can picture it all perfectly in my mind.

It's going to be badass.

When we say goodbye to the realtor and return to the bar, I turn and give Adam a wide smile. "I loved it."

"It's going to be a ton of work," he says, returning my grin. "And I agree, it would be awesome. Can we afford it?"

"Here's the thing." We sit at one of the tables. "I don't think I can afford it alone. I can probably get a loan, using the bar as collateral, but I'd rather not have to do that."

"Callie, I have plenty of money," Adam says. "I'm happy to loan it to you."

"I don't want a loan, Adam, I want a partner."

He sits back and narrows his eyes. "A partner."

"Absolutely. You're just as invested in this place as I am. Probably more, actually." I lick my lips and tuck my hair behind my ear. "I can't run this place without you, and we already bounce ideas off of each other like partners. Let's just make it official. I told you from the beginning, my dad should have left it to you."

"Are you sure this is what you want? Absolutely positive?"

"I'm sure." I nod and smile at my friend. "So, are you in?"

"I'm in." We shake hands and then laugh, excited all over again. "Call the realtor chick and tell her she has a sale."

I make the call, and she assures me that she'll get the paperwork started right away. Just as I hang up with her, a text comes in from Declan.

I won't be able to make it to dinner tonight. I'll see you later.

And just like that, my bubble is burst. I sigh in disappointment, but before I can think on it too hard, my phone rings with a number from Denver.

"Hello?"

"Hi, Cal," Keith says, making me raise a brow. "It's good to hear your voice."

"Okay," I reply, not sure what else to say. "What's up?"

"Well, I'd like to see you," he says, and I pull the phone away from my ear and stare at it.

"Wait, you called Callie Mills. You know that, right?"

"You're exactly who I meant to call, Callie," he says, a smile in his voice. "I know it's been a few months."

"It's been eight months," I reply. "And I don't have time for this."

"I'll come to you," he says. "I know you're busy with the business. I don't expect you to clear your schedule for a trip."

"How kind of you," I reply and roll my eyes. "But the answer is still no, Keith."

"Callie—"

But before he can say anything else, I hang up.

"He has nerve," I say as I join Adam behind the bar. "I don't care enough about Keith to give him even five minutes of my time."

"Good girl," Adam says with a smile. "Where are you and Declan going for dinner tonight?"

"We aren't." I sigh. "He just cancelled."

He cocks a brow. "How do you feel about that?"

"You know, I'm just getting impatient. I wish he'd just talk to me so I can tell him to get a grip and if he can't handle me, he doesn't deserve me."

"I like it when you're badass," Adam says with a grin. "It's hot."

"Damn right it is," I reply and wink, just as Kate O'Shaughnessy walks through the door. "Hi, Kate."

"Hi! I know the signs says you're not open yet, but the door was open."

"No worries. What's up?"

"Well, Eli's out of town tonight for business, and we live just a few blocks over. I was thinking I could take you out for dinner tonight? We haven't had a chance to really talk."

"Actually, dinner just opened up for me tonight," I reply with a nod. "I'd like that."

"Great, I'll come get you at about six. I have to get back to the office. Have a great day!"

She rushes out and I turn back to Adam. "Maybe out of all of this, I'll have made some of those girl friends you've been wishing for," I say to him.

"As long as some of them are hot and single, I'm good with that."

"God, you're disgusting."

***

"So," Kate says with a smile after the cute waiter at Café Amelie takes our drink orders and walks away. "What are your intentions with Declan?"

I choke on the water I just sipped, and when I can finally breathe again, I laugh. "Just gonna get right to it, are you?"

"Why not?" Kate says with a nod. "I like you, and Declan is one of my very best friends, so I want to know the scoop."

"Well." I sit back and look at Kate and decide what do I have to lose? Maybe she'll have some new insight. "Things were going great. Declan is attentive, encouraging, sexy, fun… all the things I could ask for in someone."

"He is all of those things," Kate agrees. "But?"

"But." I take a deep breath. "A few nights ago, we

were making love, and I blurted out that I love him. He didn't say it back. Since then, he's been blowing me off. He's distant and distracted, and I'm honestly just embarrassed. I think I screwed up."

"You didn't screw up by loving him," Kate says, then smiles at the waiter as he sets our drinks down. "Thanks, Joe. We're talking for now, but will you put in an order of the Brussels sprouts for us?"

"You got it."

"He's hot. You know him?" I ask, watching the hot Joe walk away.

"Just from here," Kate says with a laugh. "Anyway, loving someone isn't the wrong thing, Callie."

"Maybe he wasn't ready to hear it," I reply. "I'm confused. He's always been so tender and affectionate. *Loving*." I shake my head and shrug. "I mean, I did say it in the moment, and I was half asleep too, but the more I think about it, the less I regret it. It's how I feel, Kate."

"Then it's definitely not a bad thing that you said it," she says emphatically and sips her lemon drop.

"Except, since then, he's barely spoken to me. He walked me to my car Monday night, like always, but he didn't even touch me. I usually go home with him, but he made sure tsay goodnight and he'd talk to me later."

"Weird," Kate says, frowning.

"Very weird. I think I freaked him out."

"I don't know." Kate twirls her cocktail glass, still frowning in thought. "Declan is a sensitive guy. It's not like him to avoid someone. If anything, he's *too* insightful. Even if he didn't feel the same way, it's not like him to ignore it."

"I'm so confused about it all. He's not the guy I fell in love with, that's for sure. But maybe this *is* the real him?"

"No. What you're describing is *not* Declan. Trust

me, I know him. There has to be something else going on with him."

"If there is, he's not talking about it."

I lift my drink and glance to my right and the world falls out from under me. I can't hear Kate's voice. I can't feel anything except my heart beating erratically in my chest, as I see Declan, sitting across the room with another woman.

His profile is to me, and he's smiling at her, and to my utter horror, she reaches across the table and... and I stand up. I should go over there, but I just... *can't*. I'm so exhausted by all of this, so over the drama of it, I just need out of here.

"I'm sorry, Kate." I can't feel my feet as I step away from the table. "Declan's here with a woman." Is that *my* voice? "I can't do this."

And without looking back, I escape. I walk as quickly as my heels will allow, out of the restaurant, through the courtyard to the street, and to the bar.

I'm panting, my feet are screaming at me, and I'm just seeing red.

He's already moved on without even talking to me?

I stomp through my place and behind the bar.

"I thought you were with Kate," Adam says, his eyes widening when he sees my face. "What happened?"

"I saw Declan with his new girlfriend. Or flavor of the week," I clarify, pacing behind the bar. I don't even care that half of the place is empty, and I'm putting on quite a show for the others.

"Wait. What?"

"Yep." I nod and begin washing dishes, just to do something with my hands. "He was at the restaurant Kate took me to. Didn't see me, I don't think."

"And he was with a *woman*?"

"That's what I said, isn't it?" I snap.

"Hi, Callie."

I look up. "Fuck you, Keith," I reply, then just simply laugh. "Oh great, let's make it a fucking party, full of men who are a royal pain in my ass."

"I know you said no on the phone earlier," Keith says, "but it was important to me to see you."

"Take it in the back, Cal," Adam says, and I'm just *so fucking pissed off.*

"Fuck you too, Adam."

He grips my arm and pulls me to him and whispers in my ear, "I know you're hurt and you're pissed, but this is your *business.* Take that motherfucker in the office and have it out, then get him the hell out of here. I'm here if you need me."

I pull my arm free and gesture for Keith to follow me, leading him to the office. He shuts the door behind him.

"I want you back, Cal."

"You can't have me," I reply immediately. "And how the fuck *dare you* come into my place, after all of these months, and just say that?"

"Wow," he says and shakes his head, as if he doesn't know what to say. He's in his usual suit. His blond hair is perfect, his tie straight. He looks exactly the same as he did the last time I saw him. And I realize, for the first time, that I feel... *nothing.* I never loved him, that's for damn sure. I felt affection, sure, but now with the months of no contact, there is nothing left.

"Why are you here?"

"I told you, I want you back."

"In what capacity, exactly?" I ask, crossing my arms over my chest.

"I want everything we had before," he replies and shoves his hands in his pockets, standing firm.

"You want me to run your club?"

"Yes," he says with a nod.

"And you want me in your bed." It's not a question.

"I do. I miss you."

I look at him, impassively, for a long minute, then just shake my head. "Why would I do that?"

"Look, I saw the show on TV—"

"That's why you're here," I interrupt, it all making perfect sense now. "You saw that I made something good here, and you knew you made a mistake letting me go."

"I'll give you a raise."

I cock a brow. "I'm not for sale."

He blows out a breath and rubs his forehead, a sign that he's agitated. "Look, I know I'm an asshole for doing this. The club has suffered since you left. None of your staff is still there; they quit when they learned you weren't coming back. I've gone through two managers."

"This isn't my problem." And I don't feel even a little sorry for him.

"No, but I'm asking for your help."

"And you think that if I came back to get the club up to par, I'd fall back into bed with you too?"

"We always were good in bed, baby."

"Don't call me that," I snap. "I'm not a whore. You can't buy me."

"I didn't call you one," he replies, his voice calm, but his eyes... his eyes are turning dark with both frustration and lust. We always had the best sex when we were pissed at each other.

"Don't."

He tilts his head, glances at my desk. "Wouldn't be the first time I fucked you blind on a desk."

"I'm not interested in you touching me, or in helping you with your club, Keith."

And that's when he changes. His stance, the fire in his eyes, even his hands come out of his pockets. He's no longer hunting me, he's just examining me.

"You've changed."

"Really?"

"You're stronger." He frowns, thinking. "And damn if it doesn't look good on you."

"I've always been strong, Keith. You just didn't give me the chance to show you. You were too busy micromanaging me in the club, and making sure that I knew that you'd never fall in love with me and that sex was all you wanted to see past the heels and blonde hair."

"Maybe," he replies, nodding. "And that's my fault."

"One hundred percent," I agree. "And as pissed as I was to see you tonight, maybe it's good that you came to see it, and remind me of it at the same time."

"I'm proud of you."

My jaw drops at this declaration, and then he continues. "This bar is amazing. I was in earlier, looking for you, and took a look around. You've done a stellar job."

"Thank you."

"And you may have been strong in Denver, Cal, but it's been doing this, living here, that's brought out the best in you. Asking you to leave is wrong. You're better here."

Being with Declan has made me better.

I bite my tongue and soak in his words, not even realizing that I needed them. But I did. I do.

"You look good," I say, calming down and seeing that he is making an effort.

"You're beautiful, but you always were," he says with the smile that got him in my pants in the first place.

"You're not charming me," I say with a chuckle. "I'm sorry that the club is struggling. Can I give you some advice?"

"I can't guarantee that I'll take it, but go ahead."

"Stop being an asshole, and stop sleeping with your staff." He shuffles his feet and frowns. "Yes, you do both of those things."

"I don't sexually harass anyone."

"No, but you have to stop hiring women who will fall into your bed easily. In fact, maybe you should stop hiring women altogether."

"Let's not go crazy," he says with a smirk.

"If you fuck them, they start expecting special treatment. And when that doesn't happen, they quit." I know I've hit my mark when he glances down and frowns.

"I didn't have that issue before because you and I were exclusive," he says.

"I know. But now you're messing around, and enjoying it. But stop pulling from your staff, Keith. Because they won't respect you, or be loyal to you, after you've gotten them naked."

"Point taken."

"You'll be fine. You're a smart man; you'll turn it around."

"I'm obviously an idiot for letting you get away so easily."

"Well, that goes without saying," I reply with a smile. "We all make mistakes."

"Yes. We do. You're mine." His face sobers. "I was wrong, about a lot of things." He steps toward me, and just when I think I'm going to have to kick him in the neck for coming on to me after telling him no, he simply folds me into his arms and hugs me tightly, gently rocking back and forth. "I was so wrong to tell you I'd never fall in love with you. I *did* fall in love with you, Callie. And I'm sorry if I ever hurt you."

With that, he kisses my forehead, and pulls back.

"Thank you for that," I say, smiling up at him. "You were an important part of my life for a long time, and I won't forget that."

He smiles, brushes his lips over my cheek, and turns to leave. As he moves away, I see Declan standing in the doorway, his eyes hard and trained on me. His whole body, usually loose and calm, is tight, every muscle on high alert, as Keith brushes past him.

"Sorry, man, she's all yours," Keith says, having no idea who he's talking to. He looks back at me, "Take care, sweetheart."

And with that, he's gone, and I'm left squaring off with the man I'm hopelessly in love with. I have nothing to feel guilty for. I'm not the one who was out at dinner with someone new.

Neither of us says anything. We simply look at each other, both of our faces completely impassive, not giving away what the other is thinking.

I'll be fucking damned if I let him see me cry. Hell no.

I simply fold my arms over my chest and wait. And after what feels like forever, Declan simply shakes his head and walks away.

CHAPTER SEVENTEEN

~Declan~

"So what's your news?" I ask Beth. She's sitting across from me at Café Amalie, decked out in a red dress that shows off her curves and her long blond hair. She smiles slyly and leans an elbow on the table.

"We'll get to that. First, how are you?"

"Great." I'm short with her on purpose. I don't want to be here. I want to be with Callie. I haven't seen her in days.

"Okay, I see how this is going to go," she says with a sigh. "Look, Dec, I know you weren't thrilled to be stuck with me when Laura retired and left the firm."

"I've never made that a secret," I reply, agreeing whole-heartedly.

"I'm a good agent," she stresses.

"You're a decent agent, and if I hadn't been under contract to stay with the firm, I would have left immediately. That contract is up in six months."

"I know." She nods and sips her drink. "But I've

managed to keep you busy with work—"

"*I've* kept me busy with work," I reply coldly. "You're too busy trying to get in my pants."

She blushes and looks at the candle flickering on the table. "Okay, let's talk about that. Why not me?"

"Excuse me?"

"Oh come on, Declan, we all know your reputation." She reaches out to touch me, but I catch her wrist in my fist.

"Don't touch me."

"I've made it clear that I'd like to sleep with you, and you never once took the bait. Why?"

"Two reasons. Because I'm not stupid enough to mix business with pleasure, Beth, and I'm not attracted to you."

Shock, dismay, then indignation cross her face, but before she can speak, I continue.

"If you think I'm stupid enough to have a very brief affair with someone I do business with, you don't know me very well. I am an artist, but I also come from an influential business family, and I'm a smart man, Beth. It's your job to get me work, not get me off."

She clears her throat. "I see."

"Finally."

"What in the bloody hell?" I glance up and see Kate stomping to our table, her furious face firmly in place.

"Oh, is this the flavor of the week?" Beth asks.

"Shut up," Kate snaps at her. "I want to speak to you without the bimbo listening in."

"Hey, who are you calling a bimbo, sister?" Beth demands, ready to go to war.

"Stop." My voice is firm and clipped. "I'll be back."

I stand and escort Kate out of the restaurant and to the sidewalk outside. "What the hell, Kate?"

"Oh no, you don't get to be mad at me," she says, shaking her finger at me. "What are you doing out on a *date* with someone other than Callie?"

"I'm not on a date. Beth is my agent."

Kate frowns, and then her shoulders deflate as she lets out a sigh. "Oh."

"It's okay. Say you're sorry for biting my head off. Where's Eli?"

"Eli isn't here," she says, worry suddenly settling over her. "I was here with Callie."

And now dread settles over me. "Oh, God."

"Yeah, I asked her out to dinner because Eli's out of town tonight, and we were in the middle of talking about you being an idiot when she glanced over and saw you getting all cozy with Beth the *agent*." She props her hands on her hips.

"This is a business meeting, Kate."

"I know that now, but it didn't *look* like that. Let me put it this way: remember when you picked me up to take me to the airport when it was time for me to return to Denver last year?"

"Yeah."

"And we saw Cindy leaving Eli's house, and I was devastated because I thought he'd spent the night with her?"

"I hate Cindy," I mutter.

"Yeah, well, that's what it looked like to Callie."

I rub my hand over my mouth, dread settling in my belly. "Look, I have to finish this dinner, but I'll talk to Callie tonight and clear it up."

"You'd better," she says. "And you'd also better explain to her why you've been a douche bag lately."

"I've been a douche?" I ask, completely thrown. "I haven't even *seen* her in days."

"Exactly," she says. "Fix it." And with that she turns on her heel and walks away. Jesus, what a shit show. Women confuse the hell out of me. How could I have screwed up? I've barely spoken to Callie.

I walk back to the table and find a pouting Beth when I get there.

"Jealous?" she asks.

"Cut the bullshit, Beth, and tell me what you need to tell me. I don't want to be here all night."

"I'm leaving the firm," she says, and my heart bursts with joy, but I keep my face and voice passive.

"Good luck to you, but you could have told me this via email. There was no reason to blow my phone up and demand a meeting."

"Well, I was hoping that once I told you, you'd want to go home with me."

She leans on the table, showing off her cleavage, and I just stare at her face. "If you don't have any other business to talk about this evening, I'm leaving. Right now. I've told you I'm not interested. I can't make that any more clear."

"Fine. A girl can ask," she says irritably. "I do have some business to talk about. There's some recording work coming up in Memphis you might be interested in, and some song writing requests came in last week."

It takes an hour to discuss all of the business details. Honestly, when Beth is in professional mode, I don't hate her. But I take a deep breath when the meeting is over and I can head straight over to The Odyssey to see Callie and straighten all of this out.

When I walk through the door, the place is mostly empty. Adam is behind the bar.

"Hey," I say as I approach. "Where's Callie?"

"In the office, but—"

"Thanks," I say, cutting him off and hurry to the back of the bar, then stop short when I open the door and find another fucking man with his hands on my girl.

He's pulling away from her, as if he just kissed her. I can't see Callie because the dude's back is to me, completely concealing her.

When he does move to turn away, she's smiling up at him in the special way that she smiles at *me*, and it sets my teeth on edge.

Tall, Blond and Handsome bushes past me. "Sorry man, she's all yours." *Damn right she's all mine.*

And just when I think he's going to leave, he turns back to her. "Take care, sweetheart."

I should punch him, just out of principle, but I can't take my eyes off of Callie. God, she's a sight for sore eyes. I've had a shitty few days, and all I want is to pull her in my arms and hold on tight, but her eyes are emotionless as she stares back at me. She crosses her arms and cocks a brow, and I read her loud and clear.

Fuck off, Declan.

She's mad at me, and I don't even know what I did wrong, but I can see anger and frustration written all over her. So I'm going to leave her be, let her cool down, and then she and I are going to have a coming to Jesus about who's allowed to put their fucking lips on her.

Because I'm the only one on that list.

I shake my head and walk away, through the bar and to the street, when Adam catches up with me.

"Hey!" he yells. "What the fuck, man? Were you really out with another woman tonight?"

"It was a business meeting," I reply in frustration.

"So things are good with you and Callie?"

"She's upset," I reply, shaking my head. "She needs to calm down, so I'm going to give her some space."

"Knowing Callie, that's probably a good idea," Adam says with a nod. "Just don't make me regret trusting you with her."

"It's a misunderstanding," I reply and clap him on the shoulder. "We'll figure it out."

***

Someone is leaning on my doorbell, making it go off over and over again. I stumble out of the music room where I spent the night writing songs for the job Beth gave me last night and open the door.

"What's wrong with you?" I ask Savannah, glaring at her.

"You didn't hear it the first three times," she says, breezing past me and into the kitchen, where she proceeds to brew a cup of coffee, then glances over at me. "You look like shit."

"Thanks." I slide onto a stool, longing for a cup of that coffee. "Didn't sleep much."

"Kate called me," she says, eyeing me over her mug. "Did you get it all straightened out with Callie?"

"Not really," I reply and scratch my head. "I saw her, but she was pissed, and I decided to give her time to cool down."

"You're an idiot."

"Wait. What?"

"She's upset, thinks you've been out with another woman, and you walk away to let her *cool off*? You're such a man."

"First of all, I don't like the way you call me a *man* like it's a bad thing."

"It can be," she says, but I keep going.

"Second, I know Callie pretty well by now, and I think she needed some space."

"How much space are you going to give her?" Van asks.

"A day," I reply. "I miss her."

Van barks out a laugh, rinses her mug, and turns back to me. "If you miss her, go see her. You know, women aren't as difficult as men believe. Hug us, tell us we're pretty, and we're happy."

"Not true," I reply, shaking my head. "Y'all are complicated as fuck. Trust me, she's not hurt; she's pissed. I know what I'm doing. I *want* to see her, but I'm respecting her space."

"Whatever," she says. "There was a reason I stopped by."

"Aside from giving me awesome relationship advice? Great."

"Smart ass." She glares at me. "I have a hearing for the divorce next week."

"I'm there," I say immediately. Van will never have to be in a room with that asshole alone ever again. She nods and fights tears, and I stand, circle to her and pull her in for a hug. "It's going to be okay, you know."

"Why is it taking so long?" she asks. "It was supposed to be over long ago, but he keeps appealing everything."

"His lawyer is a dick, but ours are better," I assure her, rocking her back and forth. "He can legally appeal all he wants, but it'll eventually lead to a court date and it'll be over."

"It could take a long time," she says and sniffs.

"It's okay. It's all going to be okay." I'm not sure who I'm trying to convince, her or me, as I rock us both back and forth.

***

She won't take my calls or answer my texts, and the last time I tried to call, I went straight to voice mail.

She turned her damn phone off.

It's been a good thirty-six hours since I last saw Callie in her office, and I'm done giving her space. I need to see her, hold her, and put this whole mess behind us.

But I can't find her. She won't answer the phone, and she's not at the bar. She has to be at Adam's.

I surprise Adam when I burst into the apartment. He's in the kitchen, eating cereal dry and out of the box.

"Hello," he says mildly and tosses some Lucky Charms in his mouth.

"Where's Callie?" I ask on my way to her room, then return to the kitchen when I don't find her.

"I don't know," he replies with a frown. "I assumed she was with you."

"I haven't seen her since the other night."

The frown turns into a scowl as he glares at me. "What the fuck, man? You said you were going to give her space, not disappear!"

"A day and a half is space."

"Two hours is space," he argues and tosses the cereal on the counter. "She hasn't been here since yesterday morning."

"Well, where is she?"

Adam shrugs. "She hasn't even mentioned your name. I assumed y'all kissed and made up and were fucking like rabbits at your place."

"Did you tell her I was giving her a chance to cool down the other night?"

"Now, why would that be *my* job?" Adam asks. "You didn't tell me to relay a message."

"I just figured you would!"

"Well, I didn't know I was supposed to be Dr. fucking Phil this week," he shouts, just as frustrated as I am. "She didn't come to work last night."

"Great." I pace the living room. "I don't know where she would have gone."

"You know, I should deck you. I trusted you with her, especially after we had the talk where you assured me that you love her and want to be with her forever."

"I meant every word of that."

"But you hurt her, and then you walked away

without a word."

"I didn't walk away for good. I walked away in the moment. I'm not interested in anyone but Callie, damn it. If I can just find her, I'll explain everything and fix this."

"Well, I don't know where she would be," he replies. "Keith's probably left town by now."

"Who the fuck is Keith?"

"Her old boss from Denver. The guy who was in the office with her the other night."

"He was from Denver?"

"Oh, right, you left without *talking*, so you don't know what went down there. He wanted her to come back to Denver." Adam's eyes widen as mine narrow. "She wouldn't have gone back to Denver without telling me."

"No, but would she be staying in some hotel with the fucker?" I ask, fury at the very thought running through my veins.

"No," he says, shaking his head. "Definitely not. She's too hung up on you to fall back in bed with Keith."

"*Back in bed?*"

"They were a thing, but that's been over since she moved home."

We stare at each other for a long time. "Call him."

"I don't have his number."

"Find it."

"I know the name of his club in Denver that Callie used to manage," he says, waking his laptop up and loading Google. He finds the number to the club and calls, but curses when they're closed. "It's morning. No one's there."

"What's his name?"

"Keith Marron," he replies, "but I won't be able to find a cell number for him. We'll have to wait for the club to open."

"Damn it," I mutter, the very idea of her being with him now eating a hole in my stomach. But then I remember her, in my arms, telling me she loves me, and everything in me just... *calms*. "You know what? She's not with him."

"She's not?" Adam asks.

"No. I know her better than that. Damn it, Adam, I love her. She may be pissed at me, but she's not fucking some other dude."

"You're right."

"So where is she?"

"Fuck if I know."

***

As night falls, I'm exhausted and worried out of my mind. Adam and I looked everywhere we could think of for Callie, and couldn't find her. She obviously doesn't *want* to be found.

And that just pisses me off. It's not fair for her to worry us this way. Even a text to let me know she's okay is all I need.

My phone rings in my hand and I answer before it can ring a second time. "Yeah."

"It's Charly," my sister says. "What are you doing?"

"I just got home. I've been looking for Callie."

"Can't find her?" she asks.

"No, and I'm really worried. Do you know where she is?"

"Yep," she says, totally throwing me. It never occurred to me that my own sisters might know where she is.

"Where is she?" I demand, standing and grabbing for my keys.

"I'm not telling."

"Excuse me?"

She clears her throat at the sound of my voice. "She's safe, Dec, but she's hurt, and she just needs some time to think."

"I've given her two fucking days," I growl. "I'm tired, worried, and I need to see her."

"And you will," Charly says. "I'll call you in the morning and let you know where you can find her. But for tonight, she needs to be left alone."

"Fuck that, Charly. This is all way more dramatic than it needs to be."

"For you," she says. "You can be the knight on the white horse tomorrow. She just wants to be left alone for today."

I sigh and sit back down, scrubbing my hand over my face. Christ, I can't sleep without her.

"This isn't fair, Charly."

"Neither was not speaking to her for days, then going out with another woman," she says. "I love you, and you will always have my loyalty, but the woman meant for you wants one more night to think, and you're going to give it to her."

"Does she hate me?" I whisper.

"She's so in love with you she's stupid with it," she says. "I think you'll figure it all out, and one more night won't kill you."

"Thank you for being there for her." I love that my sisters like Callie. It's important to me that they do. Because they're going to have her in their lives for a very long time.

"I like her," she says simply. "We all do."

"I do too."

"All I'll say is this: when you do talk to her tomorrow, really listen to her. Okay?"

"Okay."

CHAPTER EIGHTEEN

~Callie~

Two Days Earlier…

I can't believe he walked away. I mean, he didn't even say anything; he just walked away.

I'm lying in bed the next morning. Actually, I think it's almost afternoon now, and I just keep replaying the last twenty-four hours in my head, over and over again.

It's beginning to feel like it didn't really happen to me, and instead it was a bad movie.

But it *did* happen. Declan blew me off, and then went out with someone else, and instead of talking to me about it, he walked away.

Un-fucking-believable.

"Cal?" Adam says from the other side of the door, knocking softly. "Are you awake?"

"No."

"Okay, I'll tell Declan's sisters to leave on my way out," he says and walks away.

Damn it.

I peel the covers back and wince when I see the outfit of leggings and an old, stained cami, and then decide, who cares? I'm sure they own the same outfit.

They're women, after all.

I walk out to the kitchen, and there they are, looking way too much like their damn brother.

"Hi, guys."

"Hey, Callie." Charly raises a brow and looks me up and down, then grins. "I have the same outfit."

"It's the standard girl outfit," Van says, nodding. "So, I talked to my brother this morning, and—"

"I don't want to know," I say immediately, holding up a hand, already on the verge of tears. "I can't do this."

And now the tears do come, and I *hate it.*

"Ah, honey," Charly says as I pace away and wipe furiously at the tears on my cheeks.

"I just *can't.*" I take a deep breath. "I love him, but damn it, it's been a shitty week, and I don't want to talk about him. Just thinking about him *hurts.*"

"He's a moron," Van says, shaking her head, and I just nod in agreement.

"You know what you need?" Charly asks.

"A lobotomy so I can forget how great we had it for a little while? Because it was so great." I hate myself for falling apart like this. I sit on the couch and hang my head in my hands, just crying. "He was so sweet and I miss him, you guys. I miss his hands, and I miss the way he wouldn't touch me when I was sleeping so I didn't get too hot."

"Wow, I love it when a guy does that," Charly says.

"I just can't get the image of him with that woman out of my head," I continue. "I mean, he hadn't even broken up with me yet before he moved on."

"What if I told you that it's not what you think?" Van asks. "And that he loves you, too."

"I'd say I don't know," I reply honestly. "I just don't know. I thought I knew him, and then he just... *threw me*. So frankly, I don't know what I want. I have a lot on my plate right now, and I just feel overwhelmed. I definitely don't want him to see me like this."

"No," Charly agrees. "I think I have a good idea. You should get away, even if it's just for a couple of days. Take some time to *think*. Think about what you want, for *you*. Then come back and have it out with Declan."

"I don't think he'll want to wait that long to talk to you," Van says.

"Well, it's not all up to him, is it?" I reply. "I wanted to see him all week, and he blew me off. So he can wait."

"Atta girl," Charly says.

"But I don't really have anywhere to go," I add.

"We do," Van says. "I'll call Gabby. You should go to the inn for a couple days. It's quiet there, and it's out of the city."

"You guys do remember that it's *your brother* that is no longer my boyfriend, and that the thinking I have to do involves whether or not I want to even see his face again?"

"I wonder whether I ever want to see his face again all the time," Charly says, waving me off.

"We love Declan, Callie," Van adds, "but I really think he's messed up here. I like you. I want you two to work it out because I think you're really good for him. But whether you end up together or not, you're our friend, and we'd make the same offer to any other friend that we care about."

"What she said," Charly says.

God, I'm an emotional mess. What did I do to

deserve these sweet women? I bite my lip, but can't stop the tears from flowing as I simply nod and then say, "Thank you."

"You're welcome. Go pack a bag."

Charly's already dialing the phone. "Hey Gab, we're sending Callie to you. Declan's being a man."

***

Van was right; it's very quiet at the inn. I've been here for two days. I'll go home later today, and I've loved every minute that I've been here.

"Your cinnamon rolls are the best, Gabby," I say as I watch her knead the dough for the delicious pastries for the next morning.

"Thanks," she says with a smile. "It's my mama's recipe, and it's usually a big hit."

"I think I've gained ten pounds in the past two days, just from eating too many," I reply, patting my belly.

"I don't see any pounds on you, but it does look like a few might have been lifted off your shoulders," Gabby says and sets the bowl of dough aside to rise, as my phone begins to ring incessantly, just like it did yesterday.

"I had to turn this damn phone off yesterday, and it looks like the same thing's going to have to happen today." I glare down at Declan's name as another text comes in. Without saying a word, Gabby reaches over and takes it from me, then sets it in the fridge.

"Trust me," she says. "It works."

"It stops ringing when it's cold?" I ask.

"No, you can't hear it when it's in the fridge," she replies with a laugh. "Just don't forget that it's in there. I've done that. Not a good idea."

I laugh and shrug. Hey, I could use a couple of quiet hours, without the ringing phone in my hand.

"Where's the baby?" I ask, itching to get my hands

on her again. She's such a sweet little thing, and she smells so good.

"Mama took her last night," Gabby says with a sigh. "Sam was off to school this morning, and I had two whole hours alone with my husband. It was bliss. But I miss the little stinker. Mama should be back with her soon. You're sure good with babies."

"I love babies," I reply and grin. "I know, I don't look like the type."

"Why? Because you're a strong woman who dresses like a badass? Seems to me you'd be a great mother and wonderful role model for any child."

I blink at her and have to swallow hard. "Thank you."

"How are you feeling?" she asks kindly.

"I'm... better."

"Come to any conclusions?" She grabs two oatmeal raisin cookies and passes one to me.

"I guess I can't really make any decisions without talking to him," I reply and bite into the cookie as she nods in agreement.

"Probably a good idea," she replies. "I tried to figure out my situation with Rhys *without* Rhys, and boy, did he ever put me in my place when he got his hands on me." She smiles smugly. "I guess that if a decision is being made that involves another person, they should be in on that decision too."

"I agree, but he's the one who shut me out last week."

"Daddy always said, *two wrongs just means that you're both stupid.*" She laughs. "He was a blunt man."

"Sounds like it." I sigh and take another cookie when she offers it. Yep, I'm going to need some serious time in the gym when I leave here. "Maybe he's right."

"He usually was, much to my chagrin." We both

look out the window above the sink when we hear a car pull up. "There's Mama now."

"I'll be sure to say hello to her before she leaves. But in the meantime I'm going to enjoy my last couple of hours here and take a walk."

"Have you seen the old slave quarters out back?" Gabby asks. "Rhys and I also added a confederate army camp site out back too, where we think the original site was."

"The confederates camped here?" I ask, amazed.

"They camped just about everywhere along the Mississippi," she replies with a nod. "Best I could tell, from old diaries that the women kept, we got it right. And let me tell you, it wasn't a hardship to watch Rhys work with his shirt off, digging some holes and setting up the tents."

"I'm sure that wasn't a horrible thing to watch." I laugh. "I love that you're still so much in love."

"It's only been a year. And honestly, I fall more in love with him every day. I know, it sounds corny, but I can't help it."

"It doesn't sound corny. I think that's how it's supposed to be. Okay, I'm going to wander out there, then through the garden."

"Perfect day for it. Fall's settling in."

I nod, wave, and while chewing on the last of my cookie, I wander out back, down a path that leads me through several huge old oaks, like the ones out in front of the house. There are several small cabins lined up that Gabby has preserved in their original conditions, with genuine artifacts that were found around the grounds where the cabins originally stood. Plexiglas covers the windows and doors, so guests can look in without disturbing anything.

Plaques stand near each cabin, describing what slave life was like here on the plantation two hundred years ago. She's included photocopies of original sales receipts when her ancestor bought or sold each slave. The documentation is striking and amazing.

How incredible is it that all of this was preserved and saved all of this time? It's a true treasure for the family. How would it feel to belong to a history as vast and as old as this one? To know that no matter where you end up in the world, this is where you belong?

And maybe that's what I've needed to figure out all along: where I belong. Because I'm just not sure. I never have felt like I truly belonged anywhere. I left New Orleans as soon as I could, but Denver wasn't home any more than Louisiana was. And now that I've been back for a while, I thought that I was starting to feel like this is home, but I'm not sure. I still feel restless.

I wander through it all, soaking in the history, picturing how it must have looked then. When I find myself near the rose garden, I hear footsteps behind me and turn to find Declan's mama coming out to join me.

"Hello, Mrs. Boudreaux," I say with a smile.

"Oh, you can call me Mama," she says with a chuckle. "Just about everyone does."

"Thank you," I reply as she takes my hand and walks beside me. Mama is a petite woman, like Gabby, with salt and pepper hair that she keeps in a short cut. Her makeup is perfectly done, and despite being easily in her sixties, she's in excellent shape.

I like her.

"It's a nice day for a walk," she says and takes a deep breath. "The air always was fresher out here."

"It's a beautiful place," I agree with a nod. "I've enjoyed being here."

"It's a good thinking spot," she says. "And I expect you've had some thinkin' to do."

"I have."

"Sometimes you can do too much thinkin'," she says as we make our way through the garden and over a beautiful stone bridge that carries us over a creek. "You'll just think your way into circles."

"I might have done some of that too," I reply with a laugh. We fall into an easy silence. I can tell that she wants to ask me questions, but she doesn't push. Instead she points out places in the trees where her boys built tree houses in the summer, and where her husband proposed to her.

"He proposed out here?" I ask.

"He did. He courted me for a few months, and talked me into taking a drive out here to his family's summer home. Walked me through the gardens, like we are now, although Gabby's really brought them back to life. And then we sat under that magnolia tree and had a picnic lunch, and he asked me to marry him."

"That's sweet," I murmur, picturing a younger woman sitting under the tree with her handsome man, him slipping a ring on her finger.

We walk just a bit farther, and we're at the entrance to a cemetery, and I can't help but feel sudden guilt. I haven't been to either of my parents' graves.

And right now, in this moment with Declan's sweet mother, I miss my own mama, and I wonder what advice she would give me about Declan and this whole mess.

"You can talk to me, you know," Mama says as she sits on a bench, under an oak tree, and pats the seat beside her.

"Oh, I don't know where to start."

"I always find that the beginning is as good a place as any," she says with a kind smile, and I find myself suddenly spilling all of it to her, about how Declan and I first met, how he would walk me to my car after work, helping him with his house, all the way through until this week and how confused I am.

She sits patiently, listening, nodding, and when I'm finished and wiping tears from my cheeks, she simply reaches over and grabs my hand in hers and squeezes gently, three times.

And that only makes me cry more.

"What?"

"Declan squeezes my hand like that."

She smiles. "How lovely. Ask him what it means sometime."

"It means something?"

"Just ask him." She sighs. "Oh, you poor sweet child. My Declan is a smart man. I think that out of all of our children, he's the most like his father." She points to a headstone, and I'm surprised to find that we're sitting right in front of Declan's father's grave.

Beauregard Francois Boudreaux
1947 ~ 2012
Beloved Husband & Father
I've adjusted my sails.

"I've adjusted my sails," I read softly. "Declan told me once that I've adjusted mine."

"We're always adjusting our sails," Mama says with a smile. "My Beauregard was a very smart man. He had a cunning business sense, and our Beau and Eli both inherited that love of business, carrying on an empire that was once just a very profitable business. But my husband wanted more than that. He wanted to take the family business and make it *more*. You see, my husband was also a dreamer, and that's what I see in my Declan. I see a very smart man who is also a dreamer. That's the artist in him.

"That boy could pick up an instrument, spend ten minutes tinkering with it, and before you knew it, he was playing it like he'd been taking lessons for years."

"Declan's never had lessons?" I ask, surprised.

"No, ma'am. It's a God-given gift, the way he can hear the music in his head. We knew early on that the family business wasn't meant for Declan, and that was just fine with his father."

"Your husband sounds wonderful," I tell her, almost envious that she had such a solid, dependable man in her life.

"He was wonderful. And there were plenty of days that I wanted to hit him with the cast iron skillet I fry chicken in."

She laughs when I stare at her with surprised eyes.

"Oh, honey, no marriage is easy. We had more than forty wonderful years together. But any relationship is work. And one important thing that I finally learned, after a few very frustrating years, is no one can read minds."

I frown and stare ahead, reading over and over again, *I've adjusted my sails.*

"I had to learn to talk to my husband, to tell him what I needed. And with time, he learned the same. He was a smart man, but he was still a man, and men have that pride gene that seems to make us women madder than a honey badger."

"Yes, they do have that gene."

"But we have the *he should know what I'm thinking* gene that just confuses the dickens out of them."

Is that what I've done?

"I don't know what's happening between you and my boy, but I want to tell you that the first time he brought you out here to dinner, and I saw the two of you together, I saw a connection there that just doesn't happen every day. I've known about Declan's reputation, and as his mother, it didn't necessarily make me proud. But when he looked at you, it reminded me of the way his father looked at me. And I can tell you,

226 | KRISTEN PROBY

the Boudreaux men, when they love, they *love*. It's black and white for them. There is no grey area.

"And it's the best thing that will ever happen to you."

"I'm not so sure he loves me," I murmur, remembering that morning that we made love. "And I also don't know if we have anything in common."

"You have one very big thing in common," she says, nudging me with her elbow. "You're crazy about each other. And if you doubt what he feels for you, well, you're not nearly as smart as I thought you were."

"Thank you."

"For what?"

"The walk. Listening to me."

"Oh, dawlin', it was my pleasure. I like you, Callie."

We stand to walk back to the house, and come face to face with Declan, as he walks toward the fence bordering the cemetery.

"Well, seems you're not done talking for today," Mama says and pats my arm. She walks to Declan, kisses his cheek, and walks away, leaving us staring at each other, just like we did the other night.

CHAPTER
NINETEEN

~Callie~

He's standing, hands in the pockets of his jeans, looking back at me with those hazel eyes. But instead of impassive, they look... *sad.*

I cross my arms over my chest. I want to run right to him, wrap myself around him and hold on.

But I don't. Maybe I inherited that damn pride gene too.

Thanks a lot, Dad.

Declan pulls his hands out of his pockets and flexes them in and out of fists at his sides, as if he's itching to touch me, and after a long moment, he curses, and begins to pace in front of his dad's grave.

"I fucked up," he begins and pushes his hands through his hair, then stops and looks back at me.

"I'm listening," I reply and cock a brow.

"Look, I'm not perfect."

"I don't want perfect," I reply and drop my arms to my sides. "I want honest."

"I've always been honest with you. The thing is, Callie, I *don't know how* I fucked up. I don't know what happened." He looks truly haunted as he stares at me, unconsciously rubbing his fingers against his thumbs.

God, I want to feel those hands on me again.

He can't read your mind, Callie.

"Okay." I nod and lick my lips, gathering my thoughts.

"God, you look so fucking good," he growls. His eyes have darkened and they're pinned on my mouth. "I feel like I haven't seen you in months."

"You saw me the other night."

"What, exactly, happened the other night?" he asks.

"That's my question," I reply, already getting frustrated. "Wait. It started before that."

He rubs his hand over his mouth and waits for me to keep talking.

"You pulled away from me," I say, my voice suddenly quiet. "You blew me off several times last week, and that's not like you. At all."

"I didn't mean for it to feel like I was blowing you off," he says, his voice also calmer, and he's starting to look like *my* Declan again, which gives me the strength to keep talking.

"It did. And I realize now that I should have just spoken up, but it threw me. And then on Wednesday, you did it again, and when I went to dinner with Kate—" I have to pause and shake my head, the horror of it making me sick all over again.

"Keep going," he says and takes another step toward me.

"I saw you with another woman," I say and bite my lip so I don't cry. "It just… it killed me, Declan. I assumed you were done with me, and had already moved on."

"No."

"And then later, back at the bar, after Keith apologized to me and left, you were there, and for a moment I thought, *Oh good. He's here to explain things.* But you didn't. You left." I shake my head and pace away.

"Don't walk away," he says, his voice firm. "Look at me, Callie."

"*You* walked away," I reply and turn back to him, my anger back in place. "You didn't fight. I needed to believe that you want this as much as I do. I needed you to fight for me, and you didn't. You *left*."

"Callie, you were upset, and I didn't know what in the hell was going on. I thought you needed time to calm down. I went looking for you the next morning to figure it out."

"I didn't want to figure it out the next morning."

"Maybe I needed a little space too," he replies softly.

"Why did you need space?" I ask, but he just shakes his head and shrugs, as if he can't figure it out himself. "Do I look like an idiot to you, Declan?"

"No, you look like the rest of my life."

I stop and simply stare at him, all of the mad leaving my body. It's replaced with nothing but hope and so much love for this infuriating, frustrating man.

"I needed to hear that," I whisper, my eyes glued to his gorgeous face.

"What else do you need?" he asks. I frown, not understanding where he's going with this. "What do you need from me? What do you need in *life*?"

"I need you to talk to me," I reply without even thinking. "I need affection, and I need you to support me when I've had a bad night at work."

"That's a good start," he says, his voice tender. "Go on."

230 | Kristen Proby

I begin to pace as I think about the question. "I need my business to be a success, and I need to renovate houses because it makes me happy."

"And you're fucking good at it," he adds, but I'm on a roll.

"I need you to communicate with me. If you're having a bad day, or if you're just busy, or whatever's happening, just let me know so I don't do the girl thing and over-think it, making it into more than it is."

"I've learned that lesson, sugar," he says with a smile. "What else?"

"I need to feel like I belong somewhere," I say quietly. "I don't think I ever have before you. I feel like I belong with you."

"Because you do," he murmurs.

"What do *you* need?" I ask.

"It doesn't matter; you're the one who matters," he replies.

"Fuck that," I bark, suddenly frustrated. "I'm not the only one in this relationship, Declan. Don't throw that macho bullshit at me. What do you need?"

He sighs and rubs his fingers over his mouth.

"I need you to talk to me too," he replies softly. "I need your brutal honesty, always. I need your body against me every day, and I need to be inside you more than I need my next breath."

"That sounds good to me," I whisper.

"I need music, Callie. It's my soul. It's been my only constant, until you."

"You're damn good at it," I reply, echoing his words. "What else?"

"I need your friendship. Your patience. I need my family, even if they are a pain in my ass most of the time." He smiles. "I need to protect you, keep you safe. And I know this is going to piss you off a little, but I need to take care of you."

"I don't think that's a bad thing. I mean, I like taking care of myself because that's all I've ever known, but I'm adjusting my sails, and getting used to you taking care of me."

"Good." He sighs, the tension finally leaving his tall, lean body. "I just need you, baby."

"Who was she?" I ask. I need to know before I run into his arms and never let go.

"My agent. Beth. She asked for a dinner meeting." He's looking me right in the eyes, unwavering. "I'll never lie to you, Callie."

"Why didn't you just tell me that, when you cancelled? If you'd said something, I wouldn't have jumped to horrible conclusions!"

"Because when I'm stressed out, I pull in, I shut down, and Beth stresses me the fuck out."

"And she's why you had a shitty week."

He nods.

"Okay, I need you to not shut me out, Declan. Even when you're stressed out, just tell me so I know what's going on."

"I'm sorry, baby. I'm learning here. Can you forgive me?"

I nod, swallowing against the tears that want to flood my eyes. I'm relieved and happy, and I feel so stupid for jumping to conclusions when I know in my heart that he would never lie to me.

Declan isn't a liar.

Finally, he steps to me, so close that I can feel the heat from his body, but he doesn't touch me. Not yet, and it's killing me.

"I need you to understand that I will never knowingly disrespect you, Callie. Lying to you, betraying you, is disrespectful, and that's not the kind of man that I am."

"I know," I reply with a whisper. "I know that."

"You know *me*. You know me in ways that no one else ever has, or will, and the last few days have been an utter hell."

"I'm sorry."

He drags his knuckles down my cheek, and for the first time in a week, I take in a long, deep breath and close my eyes, reveling in his touch.

"Let me start over with you," he says.

"I don't want to start over," I reply. "Everything we've had has been so great. We had a bad week, and a communication breakdown, but I don't want to start it all over again." I take his hand in mine and kiss it. "I just want you."

"You have me."

He wraps his arms around me and holds on tight, hugging me so close, I can't tell where he ends and I begin. I love being tangled up in him. I'm not ready for him to let go when he kisses my forehead and pulls back, just a few inches, so he can look down into my eyes.

"Come home with me. Lie down with me. I want to talk about nothing with someone who means something."

I smile and nod. He takes my hand, squeezing three times, and leads me toward the inn.

I'll ask him what it means later.

***

I've learned in the past two days that makeup sex *is* all it's cracked up to be. I'm pretty sure he's fucked me against every wall, on every surface in his house, more than once.

I have muscles screaming in places that I didn't know I had muscles.

But today, we've taken a break from the crazy sex, and actually put real clothes on to paint the sunroom downstairs.

The new windows are in, and I'm in love with them. They're floor-to-ceiling, and each is split into nine panes, giving the house the original charm it would have been built with almost two hundred years ago. The hardwoods will go in after we paint, which is good because Declan is a messy painter.

"You've dropped more on the floor than you've managed to roll on the wall," I comment lazily and continue to paint the trim around the window, my back to him.

"I'm sorry, did you say something?" he says, just as lazily.

"You heard me."

"You want to criticize my painting?" he asks. He's closer to me now, but I resist the urge to look over my shoulder to see what he's doing.

Bad move.

I suddenly feel two drops hit my head and I whirl around, my brush out, and paint a perfect stripe over the middle of his chest, also getting one arm marked as well.

He looks down, then up at me and cocks a brow.

I'm in trouble. *Think fast.*

"You dropped paint on my head."

"You painted my chest."

"And your arm," I add, then bite my lip so I don't laugh.

"This was my favorite T-shirt," he says, stalking after me as I back away from him.

"You have a hundred black T-shirts," I point out reasonably, but his eyes narrow, and I know that unless I think fast, I'm going to end up with paint rolled down the front of me.

So I stop backing away and stand my ground. I drop the brush on the floor and hold my hands up. "I'm not armed."

"Have you ever looked at someone and thought, I just want to treat her like no one else ever has?" he says softly, completely throwing me for a loop.

He lowers the roller to his side, but continues to stare at me, as if he's trying to decide what to do with me, but he doesn't have a chance to follow through because I pull myself together and step forward, press my breasts to his chest and slide my hand under the waistband of his jeans, grinning when I cup his cock and find him already hard.

"Me painting you turns you on?" I whisper against his lips.

"You just breathing turns me on," he replies softly, then closes his eyes as I pump him twice before unfastening his jeans and letting them drop to his ankles.

"How convenient," I say as I squat and lick him from root to tip. "No underwear."

"I do what I can," he replies and drops the roller. Paint spatters on my pants and arm, but I don't care. "I had you an hour ago, and I want you all over again." His voice is hard. I glance up as he buries his hand in my hair and tightens his fist, holding it firmly.

"I haven't done this in at least a day," I reply and take him deeply into my mouth, sinking down until the tip reaches the back of my throat, and I swallow, massaging him and making me growl in pleasure.

I grip the shaft with my lips and pull up, drag my teeth, barely touching him, over the head.

"Fuck."

"I am," I reply with a nod and make the motion again. I cup his balls in my other hand, massing all of him now, balls, shaft and head, and suddenly, he reaches down, pulls me to my feet and spins me around, pinning me against the wall.

His face is intense now, my playful man replaced

by someone I've only recently found. He's possessive. Intense.

And makes me instantly wet.

In the blink of an eye, he has my jeans unfastened and peeled off my legs, and he's pinned my hands above my head with one of his larger ones.

"I never stop wanting you," he says, his lips grazing over my mouth. "I want you everywhere, in any way I can have you."

"You can have me anytime you want," I reply and take his lip in my teeth, tugging hard.

His free hand slides between my legs. "This is mine, Calliope." His fingers push through my wet lips and into my pussy as his thumb presses on my clit. "Mine."

"Yours."

"No one has ever wanted anything more than I want you," he says and drags his lips down my jawline to my neck. My back arches as he nibbles on my sweet spot. Jesus, the things this man can do with just his hands and lips should be illegal in Louisiana.

But thank the good Lord they're not.

"I want you just as much," I reply, panting now as he drives me mad with that magical hand. Before I know it, I'm shattering into a million pieces, and the only thing keeping me upright is his body and hand, playing puppet with my pussy.

"Incredible," he murmurs, nibbling at my lips. "Now it's time to stop being lazy and get back to work."

"You're not going to fuck me?" I ask, surprised.

He smiles widely. "Disappointed?"

"No," I lie, but he catches my chin in his fingers and lifts my gaze to his.

"No lying. Ever."

"Not disappointed," I reply. "Surprised."

"Trust me, I'm going to fuck you later."

***

It's almost closing time. Adam's out overseeing the cleanup, giving the servers direction while I sit in the office, staring at my dad's ledgers.

I found them in a drawer that I hadn't bothered to open before. They go all the way back to when he and Mom bought the place until the week he died. Dad always was old fashioned, so having a computer to keep these records in wouldn't have occurred to him.

Every inventory entry is here, in his precise handwriting. As the years passed, and his drinking got worse, the entries are a little wobblier. It all seems pretty standard, except the amount of Chivas Regal Scotch he had on order every month.

A bottle will last me a month here in the bar, given how rare and expensive it is. Dad was ordering a case every month.

A mother fucking case.

I always knew that that was his drink of choice, and that he could go through quite a bit of it. I hate the smell of it. I used to have to rinse out buckets when he would throw up into them after drinking too much of the scotch.

I've never been a huge fan of math, but I go through and add up what he spent on it, from the time Mom died until the day he died, and feel more than a little sick to my stomach at the total.

My God, Dad.

Declan pokes his head around the doorjamb. "Ready to go?"

"Yeah." I frown and close the ledger, then follow him out into the bar, where I look over the place, say goodnight to Adam, and lock up.

"Did you have a good night?" Declan asks and weaves his fingers with mine, keeping me close to his side.

"Mmm hmm," I reply with a nod.

"What's wrong?"

"I really don't want to talk about it," I say and sigh. I don't know *what* to say.

"No," he says, pulling me to a stop on the sidewalk. "We are not having a repeat of last week. You told me that you need me to support you when you've had a rough day, and that's what I'm trying to give you, but I need you to talk to me, sweetheart."

"Okay." I sigh and nod. "You're right, but I need a minute to gather my thoughts."

"That's perfectly fine." He kisses my hand and is quiet as he leads me the few blocks to my car. I'm so fucked up in the head right now. I'm so disappointed in my dad.

And I guess that's a good place to start.

I stop us when we reach my car and face Declan. "I found my dad's old ledgers tonight," I begin. "I found them in a drawer I'd never bothered to look in before. I'm not sure why." I frown at that, but shrug it off.

"He didn't keep records on a computer?" he asks.

"No, he had hand-written ones. His records are complete, showing exactly what he ordered and when, how much he made, how much he paid his employees, everything."

"Okay."

"And I found out exactly how much whiskey he was drinking." I shake my head. "My dad died of acute ethanol toxicity."

"He killed his liver," Declan replies with a sigh.

"He *destroyed* his liver. Dec, he was drinking a case a month." I shake my head again, still not believing what I saw. "And it wasn't the cheap stuff. No, my dad loved the Chivas Regal."

"Jesus, he was drinking a case a month?" Declan asks, as shocked as I was.

"Every month, from the time my mom died until the week he died," I confirm. "I did the math, Dec. He basically financed over one hundred and forty thousand dollars to kill himself. And when I saw it all, his handwriting, seeing how as the years passed the writing is more wobbly and unstable, I don't know, I was just twelve years old all over again, and I could hear him, *smell him*, and I'm so fucking *mad at him!*

"But he's dead. I can't yell at him, or tell him how he made me feel for all of those years. I can't tell him, Declan. I don't know if I would even if I could, and even that pisses me off."

"Hey," Declan says and pulls me in against him, letting me cry the tears I didn't even know had been falling down my cheeks against his chest. "You don't have to do this alone, Callie. That's what I'm here for."

"I just didn't know what to say because it messes me up, and that surprised me. I thought I was better. I was gone for so long that I didn't have to be reminded like this, and it just surprised me."

"I know. And it's okay. Come on, let's go home."

"I want to go home with you," I say, almost desperately. "I don't want to sleep alone tonight."

"Neither do I."

CHAPTER TWENTY

~Declan~

I'm never awake this early, but I'm drawn to her. We don't cuddle through the night because we get too hot, but in the early morning, with the chill from the air conditioning, I want her in my arms.

Who am I kidding? I want to be fucking *inside* her.

She's on her back, snoring like crazy, which only makes me grin. I sleep better when she's snoring next to me.

I am just *better* because of her.

I drag my fingertips down her cheek, her neck, between her perfect, firm breasts and down to her belly, where I circle one fingertip around her navel, and the piercing there. She stops snoring, clears her throat, and breathes silently, but doesn't open her eyes.

She's not fooling me.

I take my hands off of her and move to roll away, but she reaches out for me.

"Don't stop now, sexy man."

"I figured you'd want to sleep," I reply, teasing her. I roll back to her and lean in to pull her earlobe between my teeth, my cock twitching when she gasps and then moans softly.

"I like sleepy sex," she replies sweetly. God, I love all of the facets of her. She's so damn sweet, but can be fierce and tough as fucking nails. Life is never going to be boring with her.

I can't wait.

"Mmm, me too," I reply and slide my hand down her side to her hip and grin against her neck when she opens her legs, silently asking for my fingers to slide into her and drive her crazy.

But I have other plans.

I cover her, my body touching hers, and slide down, kissing every inch of her as I go. Her hands plunge into my hair, her fingers threading through the strands and not pushing me, rather just holding on tight as my mouth plays her skin like an instrument.

"You're good at that," she breathes. Her hips shift, pressing against me, trying to ease the throbbing there.

"You taste good," I reply and nudge the piercing in her navel with my nose, then place open-mouthed kisses down her lower stomach, over her pubis, and finally lick over her clit, down to her opening, and take as much of it as I can into my mouth, moving my head back and forth slowly, devouring her.

"Oh, my God," she moans, pulling her knees back to give me more access to her. I groan against her and suck her lips into my mouth, and slowly fuck her with my tongue. I press my thumb on her clit, and she pushes up on her elbows, watching me. Her eyes are still glassy with sleep and lust, and she's pulling on one of her nipples, which only makes my cock throb harder.

Jesus.

I want to fuck the hell out of her, just pound her into the mattress until she can't remember her own name, but that's not how this morning is going to go.

I reach up and slide my hand under hers, tweaking that nipple myself, and grin against her pussy as she lies back down with a long, satisfied groan.

I fucking love the way she sounds.

I move up and concentrate on her clit while pushing two fingers inside her, and watch in rapture as she pushes her hips against me and the orgasm gathers so tightly that she's blind with it.

She lets go and calls out as it moves through her. The muscles in her core tighten like a vice around my fingers, and as she relaxes back against the bed once more, I kiss my way back up her gorgeous body and simply slide right inside her, making her gasp once again.

Her muscles ripple around me, making me sigh and tip my forehead against hers. She wraps her arms and legs around me. "Roll us over," she whispers.

I immediately comply and suddenly she's sitting on me, and she takes over, riding me in slow, deliberate strokes. She sits up straight, reaches behind her to cup my balls in her hand, and I swear to Christ my eyes cross as she grinds down on me and squeezes: her hand, her pussy, her thighs.

"Oh my God, Callie," I growl and grip her hips tightly, and then take over, guiding her up and down.

"No fair," she pouts, but then sighs as I lift my hips to meet hers. "Oh God, that's deep."

And yet, it never feels deep enough.

She braces her hands on my chest and surrenders to the ride, moving those hips in sync with mine, until we both come so hard I'm pretty sure the house has folded in around us.

She collapses on top of me, panting. My hands

glide down her back to her ass, and we lie like this, me still seated deep inside her.

"God, I love you, Callie."

She stills, and then jerks her head back to look at me with wide, tear-filled blue eyes.

"What's wrong? That makes you sad?" I ask as I wrap my arms around her and hug her close, completely confused as to why she's crying.

"No," she replies and buries her face in my neck, clinging to me. "It's just, I said it once before and you didn't say it back." She sniffs. "I thought I screwed up and made everything weird."

"You mean when we made love that morning?" I ask, brushing her hair off her face. She nods and sniffs.

"I said it back," I reply and turn us onto our sides so I can see her better. "I've been saying it, every day."

She frowns, not understanding.

"When I hold your hand and squeeze?"

"You squeeze three times," she says, nodding. "Your mom said it means something."

"It means *I love you*," I reply and kiss her forehead. "My dad used to do it to Mom and us kids because he wasn't always good with the words."

"I like it," she says with a watery smile. "I like it a lot, actually. But I like the words too."

"Ah, baby, I'm sorry. Callie, I'm so in love with you I can't see straight."

"I love you, too," she whispers.

"I'm in love with all of our little things," I say softly, wiping tears from her cheeks.

"They're not so little," she replies, and grins.

"I love the big things, too," I say and simply stare into her eyes. She nods and yawns happily, cuddled up beside me.

"Can we do this all day?" she asks.

"What, have sex? I suppose, but I need to catch

my breath, baby."

She giggles. "No, stay in bed."

"Most of the day, but we have dinner at Mama's house tonight."

She nods happily. "Okay." She shifts her legs and grimaces. "I need a shower. I'm sticky."

"Good idea." I scoop her up and stalk into the bathroom, start the shower, and set her in the tub, climbing in after her. "I love your body."

"I love your body," she replies and grabs the soap, lathers up a wash cloth, and begins cleaning me up. "I love your chest and arms. The muscles are defined perfectly." She glides her hands over me. "Your abs are perfect. Hard, but not airbrushed."

I bark out a laugh, and then swallow thickly when she moves down to my semi-hard cock.

"And this is just… perfect for me. It fits," she says simply.

"Fits where?" I ask.

"My mouth, my pussy, my hand." She smiles up at me sweetly, then slips behind me. "And your ass makes my mouth water."

"You're welcome to bite my ass anytime."

So she does, hard. I glance back at her, and she just smiles innocently while she washes my ass cheeks, then up my back, and finally I can't take it anymore, I turn the tables on her, stealing the cloth from her and begin running it all over her body.

"You make me crazy," I murmur. "Your breasts are the perfect size, and so responsive to my fingers and mouth." At my words, they pucker, making me smile. "I love your firm body. Your height. Your strength."

Her body is all soapy now, and she's watching me with humor-filled eyes. "I love your pussy, baby. Sliding inside you is the closest I'll ever get to heaven."

I move out of the way of the water so she can rinse, and she reaches down and clenches my cock in her hand, immediately bringing me right back to attention.

"It seems you've caught your breath," she says.

"This shower isn't conducive to me fucking the hell out of you," I growl, turning off the water and lead her to the vanity. I cage her in and kiss the hell out of her, then spin her around, bend her over and push inside her. "I love how tall you are," I growl, my eyes closing as her warmth surrounds me.

She leans on the mirror and pushes back against me. "Fuck me hard," she demands.

I slap her ass, on both sides, then grip her hair in my hand and pull.

Hard.

She gasps, but her face in the mirror is pure bliss.

"I've wanted to pull your hair like this since the first time I saw you," I say, my voice rough. Her head is tilted up, exposing her long neck, and I lean forward to bite, then suck on it, making her moan. I know she loves it when I go for the neck.

She reaches down and rubs her clit vigorously, and quickly pushes back against me and comes spectacularly.

She squeezes me so hard, I can't help but follow her over. I try not to rest my weight on her as I come, leaning my hands on the counter on either side of her.

"I'm sticky again," she says with a grin.

"The first priority on our list is renovating this bathroom," I say as I pass her a towel. "We need a better shower, and a bigger vanity. I think we almost broke that one."

"*We* do?" she asks, one brow cocked.

"Yes. We." I toss my towel on the floor and take her face in my hands, touching her gently now. "Stay here, with me."

Her eyes widen. "For good?"

"For good." I nod and smile, enormous butterflies suddenly trying to beat their way out of my gut. "I don't want to sleep away from you. I want you to help me renovate this house. It's *your* house, Callie. I didn't know it when I bought it, but it is."

"I love this house," she whispers.

"I don't want to ever be without you again," I whisper. "I need you. Be with me." I kiss her forehead. "Marry me."

"*Marry* you?" She's completely shocked.

"Marry me. You are it for me, Callie. You are everything I've ever wanted, and I'll be yours until I take my last breath."

She's watching me with those wide eyes, and finally, she blinks and says, "I'll marry you under two conditions."

I narrow my eyes. "Name them."

"One, I want a bench in our shower. It'll make things very interesting in there."

I pretend like I'm thinking it over, weighing my options. "I think I can do that. What's the next condition?"

She swallows hard, but squares her shoulders, never afraid to ask for what she wants. God, I love that about her. "I want to make one of the bedrooms a nursery."

"Are you—?"

"No." She shakes her head and smiles. "But I want babies with you, Declan."

I pull her to me and kiss her softly but thoroughly. "I can definitely live with that."

***

"'Bout time you got here," Charly says as Callie and I walk into Mama's house. Everyone is here for dinner, just the way Mama likes it.

Speaking of Mama, I need to find her. "I'll be back." I kiss Callie's hand as she nods and sits with Charly and Kate to discuss shoes.

I love that she loves my family and they love her too. Family is important to all of us.

"Hello, sweet boy," Mama says and tips her cheek up for me to kiss it.

"Hi, Mama. I need to talk to you."

She looks up into my eyes, then hands the spoon she's stirring something with to Beau. "Mind this for me, Beau."

"Sure thing," he replies and smiles at me.

Mama leads me out the back door to the back yard. "What's up?"

"Remember when you told me, long ago, that I could have Nannan's ring when it was time for me to propose?"

Her eyes immediately fill. "Oh, baby. I love her for you."

"I love her for me too," I reply and nod. "And I'm keeping her."

"I hope you word it differently than that when you ask her," she says with a laugh, reminding me how I asked Callie out in the first place.

"I've already asked, and she said yes."

"I'm so happy for you, son." She pats my cheek, the way she did when I was small. "She fits you."

"She does."

"I'll fetch the ring from the safe," she says as we walk back inside.

***

Dinner is loud and chaotic, which is pretty usual for our clan. There's always lots to say, and it seems we all want to say it at once.

"I'm telling you," Savannah says to Charly. "You

should go."

"Go where?" I ask.

"So there's this guy, Simon Danbury."

"Sounds British," Beau says, interrupting her.

"He is," she replies and wiggles her eyebrows. It's fun to see Van's sense of humor returning. She's healing, and that makes my heart happy. "He has the sexy accent to match. Anyway, he's a motivational speaker, and I think that Charly should go to one of his workshops."

"Why me?" Charly asks with a frown.

"Because I can't go, and I want to know what it's all about," Van replies, as if it's the most reasonable request in the world. "It'll be fun. You might learn something."

"I don't think so," Charly replies. "I have a business to run."

"You're no fun," Van grumbles.

"I'm learning stuff in school," Sam says.

"What kind of stuff?" Eli asks him.

"About bugs and stuff." Sam shrugs, as if it's no big deal. "And there's this girl, Amanda, that says she likes me."

"You're nine," Gabby says, panic lacing her voice. "No girl talk until you're at least thirty."

"Right." Sam shakes his head. "I didn't say I liked her back. Plus, she keeps throwing these stupid notes at me, then running away."

"What do the notes say?" Rhys asks, obviously enjoying his wife's discomfort.

"Stupid stuff, like, *Do you like me? Check yes for yes and no for no.* As if I can't figure out what to check."

"What did you check?" Van asks.

"I didn't check anything." Sam shakes his head. "My best friend Louie likes her, and I don't poach on another guy's girl."

"Where did you hear that?" Gabby demands, glaring at her husband, as we all laugh.

"Dad says not to poach on another guy's girl," Sam says and Rhys nods.

"I did. It's good advice." He looks at the rest of us guys for back up, and we all nod.

"Good advice," Beau agrees. "So you didn't say anything to her? You just left her hanging?"

"I told her I'd take it under advisement, but that as of right now, I'm not accepting any applications for a girlfriend because I don't like girls very much."

"He's going to make an excellent CEO one day," Beau says proudly as the rest of us laugh.

"I have something to say," Eli announces, tapping his water glass with a spoon.

"You always have something to say," Savannah says sweetly, but Eli just smiles and turns to Kate.

The room quiets as we all watch as Eli clears his throat, looking nervous for the first time in… *ever.* "I love you."

"I love you, too," she replies cautiously.

"You know," he continues, "It's amazing how someone can come into your life, and you expect nothing out of it, but suddenly, right there in front of you is everything you'll ever need. I don't need much in this life, although I've been blessed with more than I'll ever want. But at the core of it all, it's quite simple. I need my family, and I need you, Mary Katherine O'Shaughnessy."

Kate swallows hard, unable to look away from Eli's face.

"Oh my," Charly says with a sigh.

"I spoke with your father this morning, and he gave me his blessing. I also had a long talk with Rhys." He glances at our brother-in-law, who smiles and nods as he rocks his sleeping daughter on his shoulder. "So,"

Eli continues and lowers down to one knee as he pulls a blue box out of his pocket. "I'm going to ask you, here, with every person who means the most to me in one place, to be my wife. Grow old with me. Build a family with me. As long as you're mine, I'll have everything I'll ever need. And I promise you this: I will protect you, respect you, and love you every minute of every day."

Tears spill onto Kate's cheeks as she smiles up at Eli. Finally, she nods vigorously and launches herself into his arms. "Of course. I'm already yours."

"Yay!" Sam yells and as the others applaud, Mama slips something in my hand, then winks at me. I glance down and see the antique sapphire with diamonds sparkling in my hand, then reach over and silently slip it on Callie's finger. She looks up at me in surprise.

I lean in and whisper in her ear. "We'll share our news later, but I want you to have this. It was my grandmother's, and her mother's before her. And now it's yours."

She looks down at it, touching it reverently, then looks over my shoulder and smiles. I glance back in time to see Mama smile back, and nod, proudly surveying the table where her family is all gathered, and so much happiness lives.

I wish Daddy was here to see it. He'd be bursting with pride.

CHAPTER TWENTY-ONE

~Callie~

Six Months Later…

"Oh my God, I'm so damn nervous." I'm standing in a room in the inn, shaking my arms out at my side. "I can't feel my fingers."

"You're going to be great," Savannah says, smiling as she adjusts my veil. All of the girls are in the room with me, helping me with hair and makeup and keeping my nerves at bay. Charly offered me a cocktail, but I want to be one hundred percent sober when I walk down the aisle.

Maybe that wasn't such a good idea, because I sure could use that drink now.

"You're a stunning bride," Mama says and pats my hand. "You chose the perfect dress."

I smile and look into the mirror, surveying the simple style. It falls to my ankles. There is no train. I figured that with an outdoor wedding, it would just get mucked up, so I went with a simple, mermaid style dress, but it's all lace, and rather than white, it's a light, barely-there shade of pink. The neckline is heart shaped around my breasts, and lacy straps hold it all up.

"The shoes are the best part," Charly says with a grin and passes me the black lacy Louboutin shoes that the girls all gave me as a wedding shower gift. The heels are high, and thankfully the aisle is the brick path in front of the house, between the massive oaks, so I won't sink when I walk to my groom.

"I think the whole package is pretty great," Adam says from the doorway. None of us heard him come in.

I grin and turn around and hold my arms out at my sides. "What do you think?"

"I think Declan's going to faint dead away when he sees you," Adam says as he walks to me, wearing khakis and a white button-down.

"You look very dignified," I say and play with a button on his chest.

"I'm just relieved you didn't make me wear a tux," he replies and glances around the room. "Do y'all mind if I have a few minutes with her?"

"It's about time for you to walk down the aisle anyway," Gabby says. "So just come on down when you're ready and we'll get this show on the road!"

The girls all file out and close the door behind them, and Adam sighs as he takes me in, from my hair to my shoes.

"Nice shoes."

"This is why we're friends," I say, trying to keep it light. "Because you understand the importance of shoes."

He smirks and nods his head. "Okay, before I walk you down the aisle, I want you to tell me. Why Declan?"

"What do you mean?"

"Why, out of the billions of men in the world, did you choose to marry him?"

I frown and blink at Adam. "Are you saying I shouldn't?"

"Not at all. I just want to know, before I hand you over to him, what it is about Declan that makes you ready to commit to him for the rest of your life. That's all."

"Well, aside from the whole I love him thing…" I reply and chew my lip, thinking.

"You're eating your lipstick off," Adam says with a smile.

"Damn it. Don't let me forget to put it back on before we go down."

He nods and waits. "It's really pretty simple, Adam. I can't imagine my life without him. He fits. Every part of him fits into my life, as if he was a puzzle piece that was missing. He's the only piece that will ever fit." I shrug. "He's just… *mine.*"

"Okay." He smiles.

"I want you to feel this someday," I murmur quietly and Adam immediately shakes his head. "I know, you don't think you want to settle down with one woman, but I hope that someday you meet a girl that just fits you, and you know that you'll never be the same."

"It's a romantic thought."

"It's much more than romance," I reply. "And I think I get now why Daddy never really got over losing Mom. She was his piece, and when he lost her, he just couldn't deal with it."

Adam frowns and looks down, then back up at me. "You're in such a better place now, Cal. When I think of where you were when you moved back home more than a year ago, to now, it's like you're a new person. You're you, but you're…"

"Better," I reply for him and he nods.

"You are. You were always great, but you're

better."

"And Declan is the piece that makes me better, Adam."

Adam grins and pulls me in for a big hug, clinging to me. "I'm so happy for you, Cal. Really happy for you. I like him, and I couldn't love you more if you were my sister by blood. So, thank you for letting me have the honor of walking you down the aisle."

"There's no one else I'd rather have do it," I reply. "And speaking of, we'd better get down there."

"Put your lipstick on," he says and steps aside to watch me primp.

"Okay, I'm ready." I grab the bouquet of pink roses and cala lilies that were my mother's favorite and lead Adam out of the room and down the stairs.

It's evening. The sun is just beginning the set, sending a riot of color through the sky. The trees are adorned with white lights, and pink fabric that matches my dress is draped among the limbs. Tables are set up for eating later, and for now, enough white chairs are gathered in a semi-circle for just Declan's immediate family, my Uncle Bernie, and Adam to witness the ceremony.

I wanted a very small wedding, and that's what Declan and his family are giving me.

Adam takes my hand, loops it through his arm, and escorts me down the steps of the porch and down the brick path as a simple piano version of When A Man Loves a Woman that Declan recorded plays on the sound system.

I can see his family, all smiling, some wiping at tears, watching me make the journey to my man, but all I can see is *him*.

He's in black slacks and a white button-down, tucked in, with a blue tie that belonged to his father. But it's his eyes, holding mine, that I can't look away from. He's saying everything with those eyes: *I love you. I can't wait to spend the rest of my life with you. Thank you for being mine.*

I can't wait to marry him.

Finally, we approach, and Adam passes my hand to Declan's, kisses my cheek, and takes a seat.

"Dearly beloved," the justice of the peace begins. "We are gathered here, on this beautiful spring day, to join Declan and Callie in matrimony. It was their wish that only those who are closest to them be here to witness this sacred day, and it's also their wish that they take over from here, reciting their vows and exchanging rings. So I'm going to let them get to it." He winks at Declan and takes a step back.

"Calliope," Declan begins, earning a mock-glare from me, but he simply smiles and squeezes my hand. "I love you. Nothing, not even time, will ever change that. You don't complete me, because we're both complete on our own, but you compliment me in ways that I didn't even know I needed.

"Your love is like a song, and our song is an easy melody that plays, over and over, in my heart. Some days it's slow and sweet, and other days it's fast and loud, but it's always love. It's my favorite song."

And, cue the tears, damn him.

"I promise you today to always be your partner. To never forsake you, or be unfaithful. I will respect you and I promise to do my best to listen and have your best interests at heart, even in times of anger. I'm going to screw up, Callie, but I will always be here, ready to fight for us." He swallows and squeezes my hands, three times. "Our family will always be my only priority, for as long as I live."

He kisses my forehead, then steps back and gives me a moment to catch my breath and wipe the tears from my cheek, not even caring that I've already ruined my makeup.

"I wasn't expecting you, Declan Boudreaux," I begin and grin at him. "You were not a part of any of my plans, but you were the best surprise I've ever been given, the piece of my puzzle that I didn't know was missing." I sniff and nod a thank you at Beau as he passes me a handkerchief. "I thought that I'd walk through life taking care of myself, and I'd done a pretty good job of it. But, then I met you and you taught me a few things.

"First, I learned that it's okay to lean on someone who loves you. You are my greatest supporter, my fiercest advocate, and I know that when I can't speak for myself, you are there to help me." He nods, his beautiful hazel eyes smiling down at me.

"Second, I learned what true unconditional love is. It's saying, I don't care what happened yesterday, I'm going to love you today, and every day. No matter what.

"You've shown me patience, and loyalty, and you've shown me what it means to be truly safe with another person. Loving me isn't always easy, but then, I guess the best loves aren't. And ours is the best love I've ever been in."

Declan's eyes fill as he watches me, listening intently to every word.

"I promise to always value our love, and hold it in the highest regard. I promise to respect you, be faithful to you, and support you in every endeavor, at your side, for as long as we both live."

He smiles, wipes a tear off his cheek, and pulls my rings, the engagement ring and a matching wedding band that he had made for me, out of his pocket, slipping them on my finger. "These rings represent my love for you."

I've been wearing his band on my thumb, and I

slide it onto his finger, repeating the same words back to him.

"I now pronounce you man and wife. And now, ladies and gentlemen," the justice of the peace says happily, "it is my pleasure to introduce Mr. and Mrs. Declan Boudreaux."

***

"It was such a pretty wedding," Gabby says with a wistful sigh and leans on the table, resting her chin in her palm.

"Did you write your vows ahead of time?" Charly asks. The sisters and I are all sitting at a table, enjoying some girl talk, while the boys are standing nearby, laughing and giving each other shit about something.

"No, they were spur of the moment," I reply. "That's one of the reasons that I didn't want a lot of people here. I knew I'd get stage fright."

"Well, they were perfect," Van says. "You and Dec had us all blubbering."

"Are you leaving on your honeymoon right away?" Kate asks, taking a bite of cake.

"No, we leave in a couple of weeks," I reply. "We have some work to do on the house still, and it just worked with our schedules that way. But don't you leave tomorrow, Charly?"

She rolls her eyes and nods. "Yes. Van talked me into going to this retreat."

"All I'm saying is, Simon is one hot man. There are worse things than having to look at him all day for two weeks."

"*Two* weeks?" Kate asks. "That's quite a retreat."

"It's in Montana," Charly agrees with a nod. "I've never been up there, so it should be interesting."

"I'm sorry, ladies," Declan says, reaching over my shoulder from behind me to grab my hand. "I'd like to dance with my bride."

"Take her," Gabby says with a wide smile.

"I plan to," Dec says, a mischievous grin on his handsome face as he guides me onto the brick path so my heels don't sink into the ground.

"We don't have dancing at this wedding," I remind him.

"Is there music?" he asks, cocking a brow and leading me into a simple slow dance.

"You know there is," I reply.

"Then, my lovely wife, there is dancing." He pulls me against him and tips his forehead down to rest on mine. "How are you, Mrs. Boudreaux?"

"I'm great," I reply with a laugh. "How are you?"

"Couldn't be better. This dress is a work of art. Of course, so are you."

"A work of art?" I reply with a smile.

"Yes. You never just look good, you look like art, and just like a piece of art, you make me feel things, Callie."

I sigh. The words that come out of this man's mouth never fail to surprise me.

"That's a lovely thing to say."

He spins me around and dips me deep, kissing me soundly as our family claps and laughs around us.

"When are we going to start filling that nursery we finished last month?" he asks.

"As soon as possible."

"How do you feel about getting out of here and getting a head start on it?" He leans in to whisper in my ear. "I need to get you out of this dress, and my hands on you."

"I think that's the best idea you've ever had."

"Oh no, darlin', my best idea was telling you to go to dinner with me."

"I'm so glad you're bossy."

He grins. "I know."

EPILOGUE

~Simon Danbury~

"This is going to be an amazing two weeks," I tell my staff, getting us pumped up for the first day of the *Know Your Worth Women's Retreat*. I only put one of these in-depth retreats on each year, fitting it in between weeks of touring all over the UK and the United States, speaking to women about how to make themselves a priority, and to get what they want out of life.

I can hear the roar of the one hundred women filling the ballroom of the host resort here in Montana, along with the music we have pumping through the room, getting the women ready for a fast-paced day.

"Let's make a difference in these women's lives, friends."

"Let's do this!" my best friend and business partner Todd exclaims as my staff of ten hurry out of the room and into the ballroom to mingle with the girls.

I stay behind and take a few deep breaths, preparing my body for being on my feet all day, speaking to a room full of women of all ages and ethnicities, all here for their own very personal reasons. It's going to be a fun, and sometimes difficult, journey for all of us.

I jump in place, shake my hands, and join the others, walking out on stage. The room breaks out in applause, and I smile and wave, checking to make sure the mic attached to my ear is securely in place.

"Hello, ladies!" More applause. "Are you ready for the best experience of your life?"

Applause.

"I can't hear you! Stand up and tell me that you're ready for your life to change!"

I watch a sea of women all stand, clap, whoop and holler, and smile.

"I'm so ready for this week with you! We are going to laugh and cry, and I'm going to give you the tools to make your life everything you've ever wanted. Are you ready, you beautiful women?"

I crank the music, and to their surprise, I begin to dance. I want the energy in this room to be electric. I want the women to be excited to make changes in their lives.

And, just as they always do, most of them start to dance with me. My staff, out in the audience, engage each of the women, dancing and laughing, and as I watch, one woman in particular catches my eye.

I glance at the name on her seat. Charly.

Charly is a beautiful woman, with her long dark hair, and almost golden hazel eyes. She's thin, and her lips are full.

And she's standing, but not dancing. And her eyes are saying, *I don't buy it.*

Challenge accepted, darling.

THE END

Don't miss Simon and Charly's story in EASY KISSES, releasing in the Spring of 2016!

ABOUT KRISTEN PROBY

New York Times and USA Today Bestselling Author Kristen Proby is the author of the popular With Me in Seattle series. She has a passion for a good love story and strong characters who love humor and have a strong sense of loyalty and family. Her men are the alpha type—fiercely protective and a bit bossy—and her ladies are fun, strong, and not afraid to stand up for themselves. Kristen spends her days with her muse in the Pacific Northwest. She enjoys coffee, chocolate, and sunshine. And naps. Visit her at KristenProby.com.

OTHER BOOKS BY KRISTEN PROBY:

The Boudreaux Series:
Easy Love
Easy Charm

The With Me In Seattle Series:

Come Away With Me and on audio
Under the Mistletoe With Me and on audio
Fight With Me and on audio
Play With Me and on audio
Rock With Me and on audio
Safe With Me and on audio
Tied With Me and on audio
Breathe With Me and on audio
Forever With Me and on audio
Easy With You

The Love Under the Big Sky Series, available
through Pocket Books:
Loving Cara
Seducing Lauren
Falling for Jillian

Baby, It's Cold Outside
An Anthology with Jennifer Probst, Emma Chase,
Kristen Proby, Melody Anne and Kate Meader

CPSIA information can be obtained
at www.ICGtesting.com
Printed in the USA
LVOW13s1756140318
569840LV00011B/383/P